Sign up for our newsletter to hear
about new and upcoming releases.

www.ylva-publishing.com

In FaSHion

JODY KLAIRE

"I praise you because I am fearfully and wonderfully made;
Your works are wonderful, I know that full well."

Psalm 139:14

FOREWORD

Writing has taught me so much and this book is no different. Darcy is one of those characters who strutted onto the page and connected to me. It was an absolute joy to write her story which I filled with every chuckle and smile I could, but somehow, Darcy brought something far deeper to the surface that I pray resonates with you. I hope that when you have seen her embracing her design, you will feel stirred to do the same.

Thank you for giving me the chance to tell you a story, to make you smile and uplift you. May Darcy's story touch you, move you, and remind you how very special you are.

Be you, be proud to be you, you are truly unique. Embrace your truth, your core, you are beautiful. You are designer. #EmbraceDesigner

Big Smiles,
Jody

DEDICATION

CHAPTER 1

DARCY McGREGOR WAS A BITCH. A big one. She knew it as she snuck into the cab before the elderly woman on crutches, but cabs were like gold dust in London. Surely an internationally acclaimed supermodel, celebrity mum, and star of *The Style Surgeon*—the best live-makeover TV show in existence, thank you very much—had more important places to be.

The cabbie turned, a scowl on his drawn ruddy face, but then his eyes twinkled and he gave her a half-smirk. "Guess I'd better not argue, or you'll try dressing me."

She flashed him a smile. "And you wouldn't enjoy that?"

He coughed, turned back around, and roared the cab into life. He even closed the Perspex screen, muttering something about privacy for ladies. Good to see someone with manners.

She flicked out her mobile and tapped out a quick tweet about hackney carriages needing a redesign. What was with the bland grey anyway? So they needed to be black outside, yes, but where was the sparkle? She glanced through the screen... Better to add something about banning silly ornaments dangling from rear-view mirrors. Hawaiian Flower Chains were so last year. Frankly, it surprised her that such an apparently avid fan of her show would have such dated tastes. Was he not learning anything from watching?

London rolled on outside: The sparkle of Harrods in Christmas lights, the ice rink full of skaters in purple glow overlooked by the Gothic architecture of the Natural History Museum, the city awash with Christmas trees and snowy air. Shoppers laden with items they couldn't afford ducked out of the way as businessmen dashed across from offices to cabs. Odd people shuffled or slunk their way along, muttering at teenagers with rucksacks and oversized headphones peering over at the ice rink. Cyclists with tinsel on diced with danger as they whipped through the stream of traffic chased by couriers on mopeds. Fluorescent-clothed workmen in Santa hats, wide-eyed tourists rosy cheeked with cold. London in a festive rush hour. But not a touch of the cheer made any impact on her. She had parties to attend.

Her phone jingled, and she swiped to answer. "If you tell me you've broken something or are sick, I'm sending you to that hovel your father lives in."

"Hi, Mum," Susannah muttered. Sounded like she was eating something, again. "You think Barcelona is a hovel?"

"Yes." She glared out of the window at a man with a camera in hand. But when he lifted it to his face, she turned on her media-ready smile. Idiot. "It doesn't matter *where* he lives. He wouldn't know what domesticated was if it took his football away."

"You have a cleaner *and* a maid." Susannah chomped even louder. She knew full well how much it irked. "But, seeming as you love me so much, *why* am I coming to the stupid party?"

"Because you have left school, and you are not becoming a bum." Oh fantastic. The tourist was using his zoom. She hammered on the Perspex screen. "What is the hold-up?"

The cabbie half turned, then motioned to the queue of traffic trying to get around some van.

"Just take a side street," she snapped. Why wait at traffic? "Don't you sit some exam on London or something?"

He laughed, coughed up half his lungs, and tapped the wheel. "Yeah, but we have Sat Nav now." He fiddled with his radio. Was he turning it up?

"A hundred-pound if you use your brain instead. I'm in a hurry." She raised her eyebrows and thumbed to the guy with a camera. "Two hundred if you get me there in fifteen minutes."

The cabbie sucked in his chin and roared them into a side street. Some red sign said *access for residents only.*

"Don't worry 'bout that," he called over his shoulder, darting around a cyclist. "Chelsea pensioners just don't want a load of traffic."

"You know I'm still here, Mum?" Susannah muttered. "Seriously, two hundred quid?"

"What's the issue? I give you that as pocket money." She pulled her fake-fur coat around her—a bitch, yes, but animals were cute—and leaned back into the seat. The tip of an enormous Christmas tree glowed through the arched windows of the Chelsea Hospital. "Why do they need such a large building for a bunch of old people? Surely there are better uses."

"Why are you in such a bad mood?" Susannah chomped louder. Probably with her mouth open and as dense-looking as her father. "You're old too."

"You would say that, you don't know what a real woman is yet." She flicked her cellulite-free legs crossed—the wonder of Pilates. Maybe she was in a mood? She shouldn't be. Was she?

"Do you?" Susannah's solemnity echoed.

She laughed. Silly child. "Just be ready when I come in." She scowled out at the snow falling. Ice was not good for heels. "Pluck your bush-like brows, and when I say wax, I mean wax."

The phone cut out. Hmm. Screen was flashing red as if Susannah had put the phone down. Oh well, must have gotten cut off.

"Kids, huh?" the cabbie said with a smile as he pulled the Perspex screen back. "My daughter is all stripy tights and black lipstick."

She pocketed her phone in her handbag. "She's seeking identity, not to mention teenage rebellion. Better tights and lipstick than breaking the law." Susannah rebelled by doing her homework and spouting off nonsense about women only being looked at as trophies. "Let her grow, and be there to cheer her."

The cabbie screwed up his face like thinking about it hurt. "My wife wants her to take her cue from you."

Even in a bad mood? Even in the kind of mood where she thought Tower Bridge was drab and dull? Darcy gave him her most polite smile. Best appease him. "Perhaps she will when she's ready."

The cabbie pulled into Kensington and up to her house. White Georgian perfection in a five-storey townhouse, complete with mini-trees with lights on either side of the front door. Of course it was the most stylish on the street. Not only could she make the ugly look good, she had the touch with buildings too. Pleasing.

She pulled out her purse and flicked five fifty-pound notes at the wide-eyed cabbie. "Extra fifty if you are back here and waiting for seven."

"You got it." He snatched the notes off her with a grin. "You're wonderful, Ms McGregor."

"I know." She headed out into the bitter air and trotted up the steps. Gladys, her wonderful maid—whom she herself trained, of course—had the door open and her favourite lemon tea at the ready. "You are a trooper."

"Thank you, Ms McGregor." Gladys—what a name for a twenty-something Welsh beauty. Sounded like something out of the Chelsea Hospital. "Susannah is upstairs having a bath. I left the wax on for her. Marshall wants to know if you are arriving with him... And your outfit came from Mario."

"Marshall may greet me there but not before." Dates were rarely interesting. So he looked good on TV. In reality, he bored her. She plucked the cup from Gladys's trembling hand and threw her bag on the floor. Yes, Marshall didn't come close to what she wanted. She needed perfection. She glanced at the ship-wheel barometer on the wall: the hallway was the correct temperature, 22.5 degrees. Didn't feel like it. Somehow, seeing the ridiculous attempt at nautical fashion conjured her father's voice from inside her. She could see him, huge man that he was, huge beard, twinkling eyes, and always a joker. "Darcy," he'd say in his gritty voice, "I've sailed all around the world and not seen a girl as pretty as you."

She tapped her fingernails to her mug, the lemon-scented steam tickling her frozen nose. He'd always been jolly, and her mother intense, but then her mother had done the rearing while he sailed around on his ships. Merchant Navy. Lucrative. If only they'd seen some of it.

"Ms McGregor?" Gladys squeaked from behind her.

Silly to fixate on the past. She turned and fixed Gladys with a stare—dark-haired, chubby, sweet, but she needed to lose two stone at least. "Yes?"

"Mario is waiting to show you the outfit." Gladys motioned to the front room. "He wanted to check in case it needed adjustments."

Adjustments? She honed her body. Not a pound under or over eight-and-a-half stone. Perfect.

"I did try to explain," Gladys mumbled, scurried ahead, and pushed open the white-panelled door. "But he was set on it."

"Mario, *why* are you here?" She strode in. Gladys had done a good job of the Christmas tree, and there were stockings hanging from the mantlepiece. Good. She put her hands on her hips.

Mario, a short faux-Italian who thought camp worked with a bodybuilder's physique, turned and rubbed at his "arty" beard. "Not you, Ms McGregor, but Susannah." He let out a giggle and covered his mouth with his hand. Thumb out, of course.

"Oh, in that case, stay." She clicked her fingers, and Gladys hurried off. Good luck to her trying to help Susannah preen. No girl should have such manly legs. She'd told her several times over that running was good, Pilates was good. They both elongated, not bunched. Strength and grace. But no, no, not Susannah; she wanted to play football like her father.

She sipped at her lemon tea and let out a long sigh. One could give out half their genes, but it was always a battle to remove the inadequacies of the other. Served her right for getting drunk with a footballer seventeen years ago. Good thing neither of her parents had been around to witness that little slip-up.

"Mum?" Susannah wandered in with her dressing gown on. She was unmistakably her daughter, but her father's Portuguese influence would make Susannah breathtaking when she got through adolescence. Although, knowing Susannah, she'd tie her hair back and cover it all up with baggy clothes.

"You've eaten?" Darcy stroked a stray hair from Susannah's forehead. "You need me to make something?" She glared at Mario, who was watching. Best not to show too much emotion; he might think she was nice, and it was not wise to be nice when in unpleasant company.

"No, I'm fine." Susannah glowered at Mario, who waved at her. "Marshall called again. He told me that if you didn't call back, he'd have me fired." She scowled until her forehead wrinkled up. "He threatened to fire Gladys too, twice."

"He'd better not have." Marshall had been barely tolerable as it was, but he seemed to think he could get his feet under her table. That would have to be fixed. "Gladys is far too useful."

Susannah narrowed her eyes. "This like when he clicked his fingers, and you spent the whole day having pictures taken—on *our* holiday?"

"He had a film coming out." Susannah had enjoyed the day at the hotel pool while she'd had to pretend she wanted to be drooled over. The things one had to do to be "caught" by hired paparazzi.

"But he didn't have a clue who I was." Susannah put her hands on her hips. "Bit like you."

Didn't she understand they had the gaze of gossip on them? "Of course he did." Marshall better know who Susannah was. "He was just teasing." If he knew what was good for him. She fussed with Susannah's hair again, dark like her father's, with a touch of a wave through it. "He will have the two most beautiful ladies with him. How could he forget who you were?"

"You look wonderful," Mario said, fiddling with his stubby fingers. "I know the dress will dazzle on you."

"Yes, it will." She smiled around her cup. Yes, she was a bitch, but at least she was a beautiful one.

CHAPTER 2

KATE BONVILSTON CLAPPED HER FROZEN hands together and let out a shuddering breath as she stood at the school gates. Always reminded her of a prison with the high walls and spiky rails on top. Wasn't much more welcoming inside. Then again, when were schools meant to be friendly places?

"Kate?"

Ah. Laura—her cheating, lying scumbag of an ex. Even the sound of the voice grated. Flipping fantastic.

She took a breath as Laura plodded over with a smirk on her face. What was her deal? "Yes?"

"You look rough. Did you catch another cold?" She laughed. Why was that funny? And when had she decided to get her nose pierced…three times? Ouch. "Bennie always uses that wash stuff. She never looks rough."

"I know." But why would she care? Why should she give a shit about her ex-friend? The ex-friend she'd been a sucker for until she'd decided on a fresh start with Laura… Yeah, that had worked out great, hadn't it? She rubbed at her aching forehead, frowning again.

Mum had issues with her frowning, some weird advice from a TV show saying it would turn men off. Hopefully men were a lot less shallow than that. The men she knew were. The Style Surgeon? She shook her head, hoping that Laura would take the hint and find someone else to natter at. Who called themselves a Style Surgeon?

"You here for Mikey?" Laura wasn't going anywhere, by the daft grin and lack of personal boundary. It had been bad enough when they *were* together. Who wanted to cuddle with an ex?

"Yes." Why else would she be there freezing her ass off if she wasn't waiting for her brother? If Mikey's teachers hurried up, she might not get hypothermia...or need therapy.

"How is he?" Gone was the smugness and the Laura she'd known. Kind, quirky, compassionate peeked through. Nice to know Bennie hadn't completely squashed that side.

"You know Mikey. He's good." She shrugged. Mikey had a lot more resilience than her. He smiled more too. Considering he was the one with a traumatic brain injury and he didn't look like he understood and couldn't always speak, he was the wisest person she knew. Maybe having more shit on his plate made the small stuff more heartening?

"Is he getting any better?" Now Laura had threaded a hand around her arm. She peered up, a soft look in her eyes.

"No, it's permanent." She pulled away. A sudden urge of irritation flushed through her. "What do you care anyway?"

Laura sighed. "Yes. I messed up." She shoved her hands in her pockets. "You never let me explain. You never let me close to you...not really."

Three mums bustled by, waved, and called out "Merry Christmas." Kate glared up at the school. What were the teachers doing? Why did they have to wait so long to let the kids out? So they had a "disco," but it was five o'clock. "Mikey needs dinner."

"I want to explain... Bennie wants to." Laura reached for her arm again. "I love her, I really love her. She loves me. I didn't want to come between you. Can't you see that?"

She snapped her arm away. Stepped away. "He'll get a bad stomach if he doesn't eat. It'll bring on a fit."

"I miss you, but Bennie... She's heartbroken." Laura stepped closer again, glancing around as if only now she got the whole being in public, school gates thing. Yeah, best the parents didn't know too much. Don't show, don't get stressed. "She talks about you all the time. You don't want to give up on so many years together, right?"

"You make it sound like I was married to her." She shut her eyes. Great. There was the opening. Laura never missed an opening.

"Weren't you? Even though you were with me, you spent more time with her... You were inseparable." Laura stood shoulder to shoulder and snaked a hand down to clasp hers. "Thought it would be you and her."

"You made sure it would never be." She pulled her hand away. What were they doing in the school, having a sit-in?

"She said it had been." Laura's tone filled with the edge that had become so familiar. Yeah, the nice side never lasted long. "Friends with benefits?"

"Before you came along." She slapped her hands together again. A fresh start with Laura to forget Bennie? Yeah, that had worked out. Stupid, but she didn't even feel cold now; she just wanted to smack something. "But, then, a lot of things were better before you."

Laura winced. "Ouch."

"Not half of what you laid on me." Great, now she was pitying herself? What would Mikey think of that? She was better than that. "Anyway. Enjoy the holidays."

Laura laughed. "Ah, there's the polite side. Always count on you to buckle. Shame you weren't so polite with my kids."

"Your kids throw bricks through windows and think it's funny." She glared at her. Yeah, the three brats only visited Laura on the weekends, but she thought filling them with sugar and sticking them in front of a computer was good for them. Kate hadn't. But then, they'd never agreed on anything. Why had it taken so long for her to see that?

"They're just being kids. It was an accident." Laura strode up to the gates as her three brats ambled out, coats hanging around their waists. They looked the spit of her; they *were* the spit of her. One even stuck their middle finger up while the other started a dirty version of some pop song. Laura just laughed and ushered them to her pimped-up Subaru. How did Bennie cope? She hated kids. Guess that's why she wasn't doing the school run.

"Kate-oh!" Mikey's jolly soprano rippled over the buzz of over-sugared kids. There he was, reindeer hat on, a snowman Christmas jumper with half his lunch over it, and the biggest beaming smile any nine-year-old could muster.

Her mood vanished, and she held open her arms. "Alright, babe?"

He broke into a stuttered run, his left side not quite catching up with his right, and flung himself into her arms. "I made snoooowballs."

His American accent always sounded a bit Scottish, but it was better than hers.

"To eat?" Dumb question as there was no snow.

"Yup." He pulled something out of his pocket and handed it up to her. "Made this…you."

She gave him a squeeze and tried not to pull out tissues and mop his face. Laura had always said she was more like his mother than his sister, but wasn't that what a big sister really was anyway? She pulled open the card, which told her she was the coolest sister ever complete with igloo and some kind of penguin, if the flippers on black blob were anything to go by.

"Thanks, babe." She scooped him up and wriggled him about. He giggled, carefree and joy-filled. "You're the coooolest brother."

He pulled back and gazed up at her with awe. "I am?"

Yeah, who cared about exes when Mikey was around? "Yep, who else would I sing carols with?"

He burst into "Silent Night" amid fits of giggles.

She held his freezing hand and led him across the busy road. Would take ages to warm up, even walking. Ah well. It was Christmas. They'd warm up with song.

CHAPTER 3

IT WAS A LITTLE-KNOWN FACT to the millions of followers on social media that Darcy McGregor, in possession of an award, was more smug than most. She enjoyed the victory over her fellow celebrities, the victory over other shows, the victory over those in the media who tried blackening her good name, and that her name looked good on expensive chunks of gold.

"Darcy, you're wonderful," Marshall oozed, swanning over and kissing her on the cheek. They both turned to the camera, beamed, and snuggled close.

"I know." She shoved him away and headed to the side. Had he really threatened to fire Susannah? Could one fire a family member? Be forced to resign as a daughter? She held up the award for Susannah to see. "What do you think?"

"That a load of money went into that, and all it'll do is sit on the shelf." Susannah shrugged, her sleek brown hair around her slender shoulders, dress tight at the waist and flowing over her hips. She looked delightful when dressed correctly. "Probably enough to pay for someone's retirement."

"They can pay for their *own* retirement." She pursed her lips. Marshall was approaching again.

"Darcy, you're a busy thing, aren't you?" He smiled at her and tapped her on the buttock. He was good stock. Well-known, well-established acting dynasty. His frame was elegant, his jaw broad, and he did look right on camera. "You haven't had time for me."

Susannah glared up at him. "She's a woman, not a piece of meat. Hands off."

Darcy laughed. She shouldn't encourage her, but it was endearing.

Marshall looked Susannah up and down. "Why don't you run off and get me a glass of champagne?"

"Get your own champagne," Susannah snapped back. "You could do with the exercise."

Marshall narrowed his eyes at her. "If you don't want to lose your job, girl, get me a champagne." He clicked his fingers. "Now."

"Stay where you are," Darcy said, her tone icy to her ears as she moved in front of Susannah. He must know Susannah was her daughter. Who didn't know how wonderful she was as a mother? *Shimmer Magazine* had voted her Best Mother five years on the roll. "Marshall, she has more column space than you, darling. At least be a good sport about it?"

Marshall sucked in his chin. "Column space? Who would want to write about a nobody like her?"

"Susannah is my baby girl." She yanked Susannah to her, giving her the best motherly squeeze she could. Another camera—she placed a kiss on her forehead and beamed at the lens—trying not to let the odd curl of anger in her stomach show.

"And a photo opportunity," Susannah muttered and folded her arms. "Whoever *you* are, you're a sleaze."

Marshall narrowed his eyes. "I'm an award-winning actor, girl."

"So? Why does that make you clever?" Susannah's eyes glinted like his tone hurt. "Why does that give you the right to talk to people that way?"

The anger bubbled. Susannah was right. But the key was to keep cool. Cameras were watching.

"The fact I have more money," Marshall hissed, towering over her. Something odd rumbled up at his tone, icy and fiery all at once. "And I'm worth more than a little dy—"

Darcy slammed her fist into his jaw.

He dropped to the floor with a yelp.

Susannah stared at her with complete awe. "Nice shot, Mum."

Her hand was swelling. She would have puffy fingers for days. What would the skin care sponsor say? They didn't pay her to advertise puffy fingers, did they?

"Bitch." Marshall clambered to his feet and brushed himself off, his chin sporting a gash. "We'll talk about this through my agent."

"Not unless you want me to accuse you of…" Think. What would an ignoramus like him worry about?

"Assault, harassment, discrimination…" Susannah stood beside her and lifted her swelling hand into the air. "My mum knows what to do with jerks."

The snapping press cheered—no doubt they hated Marshall because he was richer, handsomer than them, *and* he had dated her. Perfect reason to dislike him.

Susannah kept hold of her hand and dragged her out of the doors to the limo, then shoved her inside. "I can't believe you just stuck up for me," she said once the door was closed behind them.

"I'm your mother. It's my job." She placed the award on the seat. Good thing she hadn't clocked him with the award, or she'd have needed to sell it for the bail.

"You don't normally let that bother you." Susannah took her hand and pulled off the rings. She shoved her hand into the ice bucket, yanked the cloth off the champagne bottle, and put the ice in it. "I mean, you belted him one."

"What do you mean I don't let it bother me?" She took the ice wrap and placed it on her knuckles. "Do men talk to you like that normally?"

"Everyone talks to me like that." Her frown was deep like the bad-tempered child who whined about wearing dresses and gave the dolls man-cuts just to irritate her. "*You* talk to me like that."

"When have I ever talked to you like that?" She tied the ice wrap tight, grabbed for the champagne bottle, and popped it open. Forget the glass. Pain management needed.

"When you tell me I have to straighten my hair to go out with you, or wear a dress, or wax." Susannah snatched the bottle off her. "Or you tell me no one will look at me if I don't wear make-up."

"I heckle. I'm your mother, it's my job." She took the bottle back. "Heckling is allowed."

"Yet you just belted the bloke who talked to me the same way?" Susannah splayed her fingers over her chest. "Double standards from the star herself."

Darcy downed a fair few gulps, not sure if she was wobbling or if they were in motion. "Why are you angry with me when I just hit him?"

"I'm not angry. I'm shocked. I'd be in awe if I thought you actually meant it." She shook her head and stared out of the window. "Nothing you do is genuine."

That stung. Stung more than her throbbing knuckles. Must be the champers. More needed. "I am completely genuine."

"No, you're more of a fake than the rip-offs on the stalls." Susannah sighed and tucked her hair behind her oversized ears—from her father's side, of course. "But I can hope."

The stinging seeped into her chest and knotted her stomach. It was the same thing she'd told her father before he left. He was a fake. In fairness to her, he'd had another family, and her mother had never known. "I stick around. I don't abandon you."

"Don't you?" Susannah met her eyes, tear filled, and her mascara was definitely not waterproof. "I'm only around when I'm needed for promo."

Swigging more champers didn't help. The pain was squeezing her stomach in two. "You don't even like me." There, there it was. *Why* would Susannah want to be around her? She hated clothes, she hated fashion, she never shut up about equality and all that angsty teenage rubbish. But she didn't have to put money in the bank now, did she?

"No, but I'd like to. I only wish you'd bother to like me." Mascara lines blotted her now-ruddy cheeks, and she looked a fright. Hopefully there were no cameras outside the house.

"Fine. You can come to the set. I'll even get you a job. But don't whine when I am talking about important matters." She nodded and poked herself in the eye with the bottle. Ow. "Body shape is the cause of so many fashion crimes."

Susannah rolled her eyes but then let through the sweetest smile. "You know, I'd actually like that."

"Good." She leaned over and rubbed the mascara off Susannah's cheeks, then held up the bottle, still squinting. Ow, ow. "Marshall had to go. Skinny trousers are not flattering. I don't care what the designers say."

"We agree on something, then," Susannah said with a sniff, and that smile grew.

"You don't find skinny trousers flattering?" Could this be a breakthrough?

"Not that. I don't care what the designers say." Susannah chuckled and tapped her on her good hand, then swiped the bottle from her. "And champagne gives you a hangover."

Darcy sighed. So close.

CHAPTER 4

KATE PULLED THE BOTTOM PANEL off the photocopier and wriggled her shoulders inside, wielding her torch. She could hear the machines in the workshop on ground level grinding out pencils, the chatter from the canteen through the open window sending a draft up her shirt—or was the chatter from the cupboard-like breakroom? Then again, it could be everyone in the open-plan office: bosses and admin staff all buzzing with catch-ups from the holidays while *she* worked.

She'd changed three lights, Rog from promotion's chair twice; replaced the lead to Rita from accounting's keyboard; and taken all the decorations down single-handed already, and it was only half past nine. Place always looked bigger without all the decorations, but it felt bare too somehow.

Christmas highlights had seen Mikey full of song and laughter, her mother and stepdad attempting karaoke like always, her dad trying to get her drunk and take her go-karting. There'd been a load of lowlights too, but she was shoving them out of her head. Christmas always filled her with cheer, but somehow it felt lonely. It *always* felt lonely. Ah, ignore it. She scrunched up her face and focused on fishing out the paper jammed in the printer-photocopier.

"You rescued it yet, Kate?" Frank asked somewhere outside the printer. The CEO was busy as always, then.

"Nearly. Why did Rog need to print off a thousand pages of the report again?" She wasn't technically IT support, but then no one in the office was remotely IT gifted, so she spent most of her day rescuing them. One small factory plus no IT department equalled her being the go-to IT guru. Good thing they didn't actually need security. Why a family-run factory making pencils needed security guards, she didn't know, but she wasn't arguing.

"There's a new mechanical pencil coming out on the market that has more lead, better action, and holds the page better." He let out a yawn. "I told him our pencils are the cheapest and do the job. Who pays fifteen quid for a pencil?"

"Someone with more money than me," she mumbled, leaning in… further…nearly…got it. "Who knew pencils were so…technical." She extracted herself and held up the shred of paper. "Congratulations, it's A4. You must be very proud."

He snorted, flicked his long ginger hair out of his face, and took the page with stubby fingers. "Pencils are highly technical. If you tried them, you might like them."

Was he hitting on her? She could never tell. "I prefer pens, mate. Big ink-spreading pens."

He pursed his lips. He looked camp when he did it. Best not to tell him. "Traitor."

"Eh, what can I say?" She switched the printer on and hit the button for it to continue. It churned into life, and paper spat out Rog's tome on pencil competitors. Job done.

"So, did you meet anyone at a Christmas party?" He grinned at her and stroked his chin beard. That was the best way to describe it; he had no other facial hair apart from two inches on the rim of his jaw all the way from one side to the other. Why? "A lovely lady?"

"My parties involved a nine-year-old throwing cake at my stepdad for giving him the wrong colour vegetables, my mum whining that she never gets help from my dad and she shouldn't have to put up with Mikey alone, and me consoling him when he overheard." She let out a shuddering breath. It had been a relief when Mikey went back to school and she could hide in work. "Oh, and shitloads of that crazy woman telling people that their clothes are the most important thing about them."

Her mum was way too into *The Style Surgeon*. Who watched back-to-back episodes of it? Plus, the surgeon was a bitch. A bitch who loved herself and made her poor victims stand around in their underwear. Sad sacks, that's what they were.

"You don't think Darcy is hot?" He grinned, and his beady eyes twinkled. "I'd stand in my underwear for her."

Hmm. Not sure that would be good TV. "Have at it. Hot comes from the inside."

"Are you seriously saying that if she turned up on your doorstep and said she wanted a coffee, you'd send her away?" He snorted and tidied Rog's piling papers.

"Yes. Imagine the nagging when you got to the bedroom?" She shook her head. Imagine the nagging full stop. "Not to mention most of her is probably fake, and she isn't going to dig your pencil."

"Bet she'd go for a fifteen-quid one." He pulled his mouth to the side. "But in my head, she loves Y-fronts."

She patted him on the shoulder. "Dream away."

He let out a wistful sigh, then flashed a cheeky grin. Oh, here came the teasing. "You'd look good in the stuff she puts on people, though." He smiled and scanned over her—like he could be a letch if he tried. He'd blushed and stumbled off when Rita in accounting had been talking about periods. "Bet you'd be hot in a dress."

"I'd be freezing in a dress." She shook her head and patted his shoulder again. He'd had three girlfriends at the age of fifty, and she was sure two of those had been when he was still in school. "And I've got knobbly knees." Or so her mum told her. Knees were bone—what else would they be?

"I could work with that." He chuckled, then heaved the mountain of sheets into his arms. "I should enforce dresses as a dress code."

"Only if you wear them. And should anyone steal your pencils, *you* can chase them." She gave him her best scowl. Frank wouldn't dream of enforcing anything. He'd tried making the staff clock out for breaks once, an idea which had lasted five minutes until Rita told him it was discrimination against smokers. "You want to see Rog in a dress?"

They both glanced back at Rog, shuffling up the floor plate. He was at least a hundred; she didn't care if her boss said he was fifty-five. His clothes hung off his withered frame, he'd lost his hair decades ago, his eyesight not long after that, and she wasn't sure if he'd ever been able to hear.

"Your report," Frank said to Rog. "Happy reading."

Rog stared at him. "Eh?"

"Report!" Frank yelled. What was the point in shouting? Rog hadn't heard the fire alarm go off when everyone else had needed ear defenders.

"Eh?" Rog looked down at the sheets. "How many people are in the meeting? I haven't even read the minutes."

"Haven't you sent him for a hearing test?" she whispered, covering her mouth with her hand. Mikey had hearing aids. Amazingly, they helped him hear. Who knew?

"I tried. He said he has perfect hearing." Frank handed the papers to Rog, who strained to hold them. "All yours."

Rog squinted down at the sheets. "Ah, my report." He turned and shuffled off.

"What do you do with that?" she asked, then frowned. Why was Frank blushing? Why couldn't he look at her? What was on the ceiling that was so fascinating? Oh, right. She'd popped a button in the printer. "It's a bra, Frank. It won't hurt you."

"Didn't want you to think I was staring," he mumbled, staring at the printer like he wanted to hide in it. "Guess you don't like all that lacy rubbish, huh?"

"Do you want me to put your head in the printer?" She did up her button. Her ex had always complained that she wore sports bras. That there wasn't anything sexy about them. But then, Laura had never been near a gym. They didn't let you smoke in a gym.

"Hey, Darcy said that a bra gives you the key to a woman. She says that we need to break the divide between us and be able to talk about each other with respect," he said like it had been a training seminar. "She says, women should be celebrated, and if you get her in lace she will feel like the lady you love." He nodded with utter seriousness. "Not sure she said that at the same time…" He pulled his mouth to the side. "I got lost at 'bra.'"

"Darcy is an idiot." What was he doing watching her—apart from the blonde hair and full lips? She just pranced about, talking clothes. "Are you going to wear a bra to test it out?"

He cocked his head to the side. "Would it show I respected you? I could do that." His eyes flickered with some cheeky thought. Best not pry into that one.

"Well…anyway, I'd better go make sure the drinks' machine is secure." She scurried off and ducked through the doorway into the cupboard with a TV monitor she called an office. But at least no one ever entered without knocking. Keeping pencils safe was a serious business. She slumped into her chair and flicked her boots up on her desk. Car park was full. Gates were open. Canteen staff were having a sneaky cigarette outside the back door. Lacy bras? Darcy the Style Surgeon? How could anyone take her seriously? She smiled and closed her eyes. Hmm... Darcy in a lacy bra wasn't a bad picture at all.

CHAPTER 5

DARCY COVERED HER MOUTH AND stifled her yawn. It had been a long day. They'd—she and Susannah—been discussing new prospects for some style surgery with Marge. Susannah was going to shadow Marge, doing whatever producers did all day. Darcy had three interviews with top magazines, one radio interview with a delightful ex-pop star, a meeting with her agent about hosting an after-dinner talk about successful women in media, and they'd even fitted in lunch with the latest date prospect.

Oh, and Marshall had called to beg for her forgiveness, because he'd been turned down for three roles since she'd punched him. Oddly, she'd not returned his call. Funny that.

"Darcy," Marge said in a low tone. Why did she think bass was a good sound for a woman? Scruffy jeans, wild-grey hair, so much better off behind the cameras. "We need to pin down the next guest. The channel wants something with more…spark."

"They don't think that changing a fifty-five-year-old mother of five into a style icon is spark?" How could they? Whoever had told Marge that needed to be fired or, better yet, made to wear skinny jeans. Hmm. They probably did already.

"Not enough. Yes, we own that evening slot. We have the whole country watching, but they want to make it more…reality TV. So we'll do some live segments this time." Marge tapped her phone to her chapped lips. "They loved the interactive tweet sessions. We'll keep those." She leaned onto her paper-piled chaos of a desk. "I've narrowed down a list. Guests you don't go for. A challenge." She said it like Darcy would balk at such a thing. Didn't she know she'd hosted fashion shows? She knew a challenge when she saw one.

"Fine, get Susannah to pick. It'll give her something fun to do." She waved it off and tweeted about challenges: *Undressing a woman and uncovering her inner beauty*—No, no…that sounded a bit…diverse. She deleted it—*Undress the woman, uncover her beauty, then dress to make her shine for all to see.*

Yes, that was poetry. Why hadn't she won literary prizes? She tweeted about that too. Yes, someone needed to add that award to her collection. She had a good feeling her upcoming book, and she tweeted to hint at that fact—would secure those awards with ease. Yes.

"Maybe Susannah could read the tweets out. Get her involved a bit more?" She said but Marge was studying her with a sly smile. "She has wonderful enunciation." Private education was useful for some things, even if the house was empty, too empty, without her. She looked up. "What?"

She didn't like that look. Marge hadn't looked at her like that since she'd conned her into doing two extra shows using celebrity guests. Seriously, if celebrities with dressers couldn't get it right, why bother?

"Nothing. You almost looked proud when you said that…" Marge eyed her with caution. "Like you actually have a heart."

"Don't be stupid." She put her phone in her stunning clutch-bag—the bag pulled out the colour on her heels to perfection. She sighed. It was so hard being so fantastic all the time. "She's my daughter. I expect her to do my genes justice. She's merely doing as nature granted."

Marge shook her head, hair like twisted pipe cleaners. "That was almost nice…almost." She tucked her hands in the back pocket of her jeans and shifted on her feet. No bra was not acceptable. Not on any woman whose breasts had dropped to waist level.

"You need more support…or any support." Had Marge not watched the show? She needed to be a lacy lady—sexy and showy—not sporting sagging potato sacks.

"And you think a seventeen-year-old does that?" Marge's unshapely wire-caterpillar eyebrows flicked about. Looked like they'd crawl off and make an escape.

What was she on about? Why would Susannah know what to do with women's breasts? Hers had been lazy and decided not to grow, but then her growing had needed improvement too, because five foot three needed some tall heels to get that elegance, and Susannah was not blessed with balance.

"I'll take that as a vote of confidence, then?" Marge waved her hand about. "Darcy, are you in there, or did the batteries run out?"

"How amusing." She stared at her nails. Manicurist was almost as good as her. Not quite, but acceptable. "Well, is there anything else? I have a facial to go to."

Marge's sly grin returned. "No, nothing else. You go to your facial. How about I drop Susannah home when we've picked you a sparky challenge?"

Darcy looked her up and down. "Only if you speak to her nicely. She doesn't like it when people are less than glowing. It's jealousy, if you ask me."

Marge laughed. "That was almost sweet in a condescending way." She shook her head and turned. "How is that kid yours?"

She glared after her. Must have meant the lack of dress sense. Yes, that's what it was. She strode out of the poky office and to the waiting driver. "If you miss another pickup, I'll find a new chauffeur. I had to take a cab to the awards."

"But, Ms Darcy, my wife was in labour." He scurried to open the door for her and tipped his hat to her.

"Are you an obstetrician?" She peered at him when he got in and started the car. She'd gone through it alone, like her mother. Only reason she'd informed the father at all was because she wanted it clear he was below her and it was not happening again. Champers was to blame.

"No, Ms Darcy, but I love her. I'd take getting fired for her." He met her gaze in the mirror. "And our baby girl."

She smiled. She couldn't help it. He was clearly insane. But it was a charming sort of insane. She dug in her clutch and pulled out an envelope. "If you tell a soul what I have done, I'll flatten your tyres."

He reached out and took the envelope with a smile. "You didn't have to."

"Yes, I did. The cab cost more than you, and he was slow." She turned to the window. London was grey with rain. "I don't like slow."

The chauffeur chuckled and eased his foot down. At least someone knew what she wanted.

⎯⎯⎯⎯⎯∙◦❦◦∙⎯⎯⎯⎯⎯

Susannah folded her arms as she read her mum's latest tweet. Like she could ever write a book. The nearest to the classics she'd ever read was *Hello!* magazine.

"So, we need someone special for this show," Marge said, her smile lines wrinkling up with her chuckle. "We need to get the public seeing the real Darcy McGregor."

Susannah rolled her eyes and threw her phone onto the desk. "Not sure there is one." She scowled. Her mum confused her. It was like she cared, but she didn't. She punched Marshall, then flipped when Susannah had mentioned that she wanted to volunteer at a project raising awareness of the battle for intersex people to have their inaccurate birth certificates changed. She'd been as touchy when Zoë got married. Susannah leaned onto her fist. She missed Zoë. Her mum never bothered with many people, but Zoë…

She sighed. Zoë had always managed to get her mum being more… human.

"Anyone that will get under her skin?" Marge asked in a conspiratorial tone.

Zoë did. Weirdly in a good way, though. How was arguing good? "Gay women."

Marge stared at her.

"Seriously," Susannah mumbled. What was with the shocked look? "Should have seen her when Zoë got married. Not impressed." At least when no one was looking. To the guests, to Zoë, she'd been perfectly poised. Then she'd been in über PMT mode for months like she was ashamed of Zoë.

Marge's brows dipped, and she flicked her finger across her tablet. Some dark-haired woman, tall, sunglasses on, dark wavy hair, denim shirt, jeans with holes in the knees, trainers, and a super cool scuffed-up denim jacket with patches on. "How 'bout her? She's just broken up with another woman?"

Susannah picked up her phone. Her mum was tweeting about how important supporting the inner woman was. Hah. How genuine was that load of rubbish? "Yeah, yeah… She's perfect."

CHAPTER 6

KATE TRUDGED UP THE CONGESTED Cardiff high street. Cars were parked half on the pavements; buses coughed black soot into the air. The school run was in progress, and she was running late. It didn't matter that Mikey was always straggling behind. He liked her to be there, and Mum was cooking dinner. Hopefully, Mum didn't ask her to stay again. She'd like to get in an hour at the gym, take a long shower, and curl up on the sofa. Mum called her boring, and Kate always laughed. Anyone who watched Darcy the flipping fake surgeon needed their heads checked. Didn't help that someone had decided Darcy needed to be on huge billboards. One of which was outside the school gates, proclaiming that beauty came in stylish packages. Great message for junior-school kids: they were only worth their clothes?

"Kate," Bennie, ex-friend and complete bitch, called from behind her.

Oh no, keep walking. Selective deafness. Her stepdad had it off to a T, which was why he was probably still married to Mum instead of living in a rented flat in Splott. Although, maybe Dad had the right idea. Saved him from eating Mum's "Darcy delights." Why did dressing people make her a cook too? Mum wasn't a cook. Mum murdered toast for fun. Even Mikey could manage toast.

"Kate, come on." Bennie huffed loud enough that she had to be close.

Shit. Just walk faster. She picked up her pace, only for a thick hand to grip her arm.

"Kate. Stop being a baby." Bennie yanked her around. Her enticing dark-brown eyes twinkled, and those long eyelashes fluttered.

Wow, she'd decided a grade two shave—a buzz cut—was her. Made those eyes look huge. Had to be Laura's influence. Bennie had always had long, flowing brown hair to her shoulders. "Stare all you like. You need to talk to me."

"I don't need to do anything." Kate pulled her arm free. Yup, the shaved head definitely removed all attraction. What a relief. "Later."

She turned back around and smiled to herself.

"We're getting married," Bennie said. Her tone was as if she wasn't too pleased about it either. "Soon."

That familiar pain prickled through her stomach, and she stopped. A bus puffed out a cloud of thick, black smoke, and she spluttered. She hurried on, tears stinging her eyes. Married. Nice. Bennie wouldn't even commit to a relationship with her. She'd never done relationships.

"Kate-oh!" Mikey yelled it through the February crisp, damp air. Yelled it in a way that filled her with some kind of strength. Just keep walking. Don't give Bennie the satisfaction.

"I want you to be there," Bennie called out, but Kate fixed her eyes on Mikey breaking into a run. Focus on Mikey. "I want you to be part of it."

"Hey, babe," she said, throwing her arms out to catch him, one eye on Bennie. "How was your day?"

"I sent the invitation to your mother's." Bennie leaned against the wall, close enough to watch her. She'd always been able to read her.

"I fell." He held up his hands, grazes on them. "Mrs Jones said I got my feet in a twist."

She studied his scratched-up palms.

Why would Bennie do that? Why would she send it to Mum's house? Why inflict *more* pain? "Did she bathe them?" she asked Mikey.

He nodded, then grinned. When he turned and spotted Bennie, his smile faded. He'd get stressed. It made all his problems worse when he was stressed, his speech especially. He scowled and blew a raspberry, a big one that made three kids strolling by snigger.

Bennie waved like she didn't care. Kids were not her strong point. "Hey, Mikey."

"No hi." He scowled at her. "You…naughty." He flopped forward into Kate's arms and clung on. "You hurt."

She pulled him back. He sounded really upset about it. How had he noticed? He'd noticed?

Bennie sucked in her chin. "Nah, Kate's tough."

Mikey turned and stomped over. "You make cry." He booted her in the shin and narrowed his eyes, wagging his finger at her. "You... Mum say..." He blew another raspberry. "Mum say...you...slapper."

Kate clamped her lips shut and hurried to him, scooping him into her arms.

Bennie just stared at him, wincing.

"You think I should be at her wedding, babe?"

Mikey narrowed his little eyes. "No."

Kate nodded and glared at Bennie. "Me neither."

She turned, and he wriggled around to piggyback as she hurried across the racetrack of a road. "Did Mum really say that about Bennie?"

"No." Mikey blew another raspberry into her ear, and she chuckled. "She says...she says...ladies... box..." He took deep breaths and sighed. It would take him hours to get the flow of his speech back now. "Lady box slapper."

"You mean the TV?" She skipped past the kids congregated around the local corner shop. Mum needed to watch her language. She knew Mikey picked stuff up; when had she let that slip?

"Yup. Dad-step watch..." He took more breaths as they headed up the steps through the large park. His speech must drive him nuts, but he never grumbled. "Mum say lady box slapper." He giggled, then blew another raspberry.

Hmm. Maybe best not to think too much on what her stepdad was watching, but Mum was rich when she drooled over the men on her programmes. "You can't really call people slappers."

"Dad-step say." Mikey squeezed as she puffed her way up a steep hill. Two joggers ran towards them in Lycra-patterned trousers. They were too busy chatting to each other, so she had to deviate onto the squelching grass. Mikey cheered. "But Ben slapper. She not...true. She mess... She hurt you. Slapper."

She was. How come it took hearing Mikey to say it for her to get it? The joggers carried on, ignorant to everything aside their gossip session. Yeah, she'd been ignorant too. How had she missed so much? "I need a change."

"Why, you pee?" Mikey let out a sigh. "You too old to pee."

She chuckled, and they headed out onto the grassy tree-lined street occupied by tall Georgian houses and luxury cars. "No, I meant..." How did she explain?

Mikey cuddled in. "You need find smile."

Mikey-speak always seemed to capture a wisdom.

"Yeah. I do. Any ideas?" She jogged up the road to her stepdad's house, passing the homes of doctors, lawyers, and financial gurus. Her stepdad was none of those things. He owned a building firm. He was as rough and ready as Mum. Dad was a tradesman like him, but her stepdad had a business head and less of a love for beer.

"Darcy says style new." Mikey giggled. He knew how much Darcy bugged her. "She say no to black and yes to colour." He flopped into her shoulder. "Weird."

"She is, yeah." Darcy wouldn't like her in her work uniform, then—black men's trousers, a navy jumper, and a white shirt, complete with boots and a keychain. "You think some posh clothes will make me happy?"

"No?" Mikey shrugged, and she placed him on the front step. "Think love. But..." He sighed and took long, slow breaths, then set his jaw. "New clothes make love follow?"

"Doubt it." She kissed him on the cheek and rang the doorbell. It hurt watching him struggle. "If you see a letter from Bennie, you ditch it before Mum sees, right?"

He nodded. "Ben slapper."

"Yes. She is." She could hear movement behind the door and gave Mikey another squeeze. She ducked behind her stepdad's van as the front door opened.

"Where's Kate?" Mum muttered. "I have some things to say to her."

"No yell. Kate sad. Ben slapper." He muttered it back like he was the adult. "You make her leave. No."

"I..." Mum stopped, then sighed. "Where do you pick this stuff up from?" She glanced out the door, and Kate ducked further behind the van. "Never mind. I have smiley faces for you."

"Cool!" Mikey and Mum headed inside, and Kate shuddered out a breath. Maybe a change should involve leaving the country?

CHAPTER 7

DARCY STUDIED HER NAILS, THE shimmer on them quite pleasant in the romantic glow of the restaurant. The clientele cast glances her way and smiled when she met their eyes. She offered the correct level of smile in return: long enough to appear genuine but never long enough to invite conversation. Nerves swirled in her stomach, but she knew she'd made the right decision. Susannah needed her to make a good decision.

"Sorry, traffic was a pain in the ass." Zoë grinned as she leaned in, planted a smacker on her cheek, and plonked down into the chair opposite Darcy. "What happened? Another one get ditched?"

Darcy leaned onto her elbows, then stopped. Manners—where were her manners? She dropped her hands to her lap. "Gerrard was very nice."

Zoë pulled a face, her shaggy flicked-out hair perfectly highlighted, her eyes glinting with irritation. "Not good. I know most think he's hot but… eh." She wagged her hands around, her diamond-encrusted ring sparkled in the light. "He looked…dull, but at least he wasn't a jerk like Marshall."

Zoë was right. She'd always been right. It infuriated her at the best of times. Now she half wanted to stomp off, but then Zoë would stomp right after and cuddle it out of her.

"He was." She tapped her nails to her wine glass. "He was dull, Marshall was dull. Why are they so dull?"

"Um, asking the wrong lady here." Zoë flashed a cheeky smile at her. "Or did you forget the babe at home?"

Darcy waved it off. "She just has a huge glittering light over her label."

Zoë pursed her lips. "She wears tracksuit pants around the house and eats Jell-O by the bucketload." She picked up the menu, scanning down it. "I find her onesie hot."

Laughter burst out before Darcy could clamp her lips together. "Yes, well…she models underwear in such a way that…I imagine *anything* would look good on her." Bitch.

Zoë studied her, then flicked her gaze back to the menu. "I'm starting to think you believe that shit you spout on TV. If I didn't *know* you, then I might think that and wonder if you're hiding something."

"It's not shit," she whispered, hiding her mouth with her hand. This was why meeting Zoë in public was treacherous. She wasn't shy of saying how she felt in public places, out loud, at high volume. "It's about helping women reconnect to themselves."

"It's about making you look good and pretending that a label fixes everything." Zoë leaned in, her dazzling wedding ring glinting again. "And it's based on flawed research, honey, and you know it."

"Then why are you using my guides to design your shows?" Darcy sat back with a grin. Oh yes, she knew those lines. She knew that Zoë loved a sharp look.

"Oh, the design part is perfection." Zoë tapped her hand and waved her menu in the air. "How long does it take to get a drink around here?" She threw both hands in the air and clanged a fork to Gerrard's empty glass. "It's the odd psychology you have going on that confuses me."

"Women need to change, and they don't want to make the effort to do so. I help them find something more exciting in their lives." She was doing a good job. Countless women had emailed and tweeted and written to say so. "They feel good when I dress them."

"Uh-huh." Zoë's eyes twinkled with a twinkle she didn't like. What was she thinking? When she had that look, it meant being humiliated. As if yelling for the waiter wasn't humiliating enough. "You feel good when you give women something exciting?"

Now she made it sound seedy. "Clothes."

"Right." Zoë let out a huge burst of laughter and slammed the table with the empty plate. "I read your book, honey." She rolled her eyes. "And we both know you're hiding a whole lot more."

Darcy scowled at her. "You keep that silent."

Zoë laughed even louder. Now the staff were glaring. "Now why would I do that…?" She tapped her finger to her lip. "How would I think you could be hiding something?"

"Fine." She had to give Zoë something, or she'd just raise the volume. "It was the buzz of the show."

"Or the buzz of androgynous style." Zoë wagged her ring-laden finger through the air. "I kept your confidence."

"Yes, but you have held me hostage with it ever since." She picked up her menu and slapped Zoë's hand. "And will you desist with the waving. Everyone knows you have the ring on. We know. Let it drop."

"Spoilsport." But Zoë did put her hand down. "I wear men's jeans." She frowned. "I look good, and the boyfriend look is hot right now."

"Hot? To whom? You're different. You know how to accessorize." Zoë had always been unique. It worked for her. Designers did as they pleased anyway.

"Yes, but I am offended." Zoë grabbed her by the scruff and planted a smacker on her lips. "So if you mention butch and manly as a threat one more time, I'll dig out some photos."

"It isn't a good look." She held up her hand. Let's hope no one inside had a camera. If they did, she was suing. She was. She would sue Zoë too. Was she flushed? "I don't care what you say. Who finds androgynous attractive?" Oh, now the manager was coming over. That was it. They'd be done for lewd conduct. "I don't care if it's men or women looking… It's not."

Zoë raised her eyebrows.

"Get over yourself." She flapped the napkin around.

Zoë leaned back and grinned up at the manager who stopped next to their table. "You taking my order, honey?"

He straightened his tie, and Darcy put her head in her hands. Every time. Did Zoë know how many restaurants they'd been banned from? Darcy could go there alone, but not with Zoë. At this rate, they'd have to meet at a café, and then what would the press say?

"Ladies, please could you keep your behaviour to yourselves?" the manager said in a stuffy English accent. "We run a distinguished establishment."

"Nope." Zoë flicked her menu around. "If I'm thirsty, I just get louder."

He glanced around, then looked Zoë up and down. "I've called your chauffeur, Ms McGregor."

And there it was. Ejected. Every flipping time.

"Why? You don't do lesbians?" Zoë scowled up at him and said it at high volume until every face was watching. Oh wonderful. Make a scene. That would help.

The manager eyed her. No, he clearly didn't like lesbians or loud people or maybe women. He'd been delightful until Gerrard left but then ignored her. Nothing like some prejudice to keep a girl humble.

She pulled out her phone. She could deal with that. "I am tweeting about our treatment. Think it's only fair that people know who serves them food." She winked at Zoë. "I think your treatment of my dear *friend* is deplorable."

The manager held up his hands. "Now, Ms McGregor…"

"And…posted." She stood up and held out her hand to Zoë. "Hashtag discrimination."

Zoë stared at her but followed as she led them out to her chauffeur. London was full of Valentine's Day couples all trying not to get in trouble for forgetting.

"No bawling at me for getting us thrown out?" Zoë whispered as they got into the back. "No, 'why do you have to flaunt yourself' again?"

"I'm your…friend. It's my job to stick up for you." She met her chauffeur's gaze in the rear-view mirror. "Home."

He nodded and screeched them out into the building traffic. Why was Zoë still staring?

"What?" She concentrated on the statues and crazed drivers navigating Hyde Park Corner.

"You've never stuck up for me before." Zoë shifted in her seat to stare. She knew how much that grated. Why did she need to do it? "You'd have socked me one for kissing you in public before."

Her chauffeur looked focused on the road as if he were deaf. Good man. "You didn't kiss me, you merely smacked me on the lips. Kissing is gentle, loving, not an assault."

Zoë bellowed out a laugh. "Then you've forgotten how to do it right." She winked at the chauffeur, whose lips twitched in a smile in the mirror. "Anyway, it worked. You're taking me home."

"Susannah misses you for some reason. Can't imagine why." But she could feel a smile tickling at her lips. Zoë had something not many people had. "And it's about time you paid a visit to your daughter."

Zoë grinned. "Oh, I get that title back now?"

"You always had it. Stop being a baby." As if that would have ever changed. Yes, it was a problematic issue publicly when Zoë had married another woman. Personally, she hated the idea, but…Zoë needed stability. Her wife, as suitable as she was aesthetically, balanced her. Was that the right word? Yes. Before, Zoë would have thrown things, ranted, got violent. Balanced, yes, that was the perfect word.

"Either way…thanks." Zoë whispered it and cuddled into her arm, much like the homesick child who'd huddled with her in their photoshoots.

She tensed, then sighed and relaxed. "You're welcome."

CHAPTER 8

KATE TOOK A DEEP BREATH and rang the doorbell. Mum had sent her a simple text telling her to get her backside round there and explain before she tracked her down and tanned it.

Weirdly, it worked just as well as it had when she'd been a kid. Her backside had been tanned…a lot. She told Mum it was abuse, and Mum had told her that the law isn't retrospective and to get over it. Too clever for her own good, that's what she was.

"In?" Mikey flung open the door in a pea costume with some kind of toolbelt. Cartoon? She loved him, but she drew the line at kids' TV.

"Yeah, until she kicks me out," she mumbled, hoisting him into her arms. "What mood she in?"

He poked out his tongue and groaned.

Great. Tanned backside it was.

"Kate, sit down." Mum's stern tone made her freeze in the hallway. She'd been through this already. Why did they need to do it again?

"I'll stand. It'll be easier to get to the door." She put down Mikey, who stood in front of her in the kitchen doorway, hands on hips. "Thanks, babe."

"Not babe, Sproutman." Mikey smiled up at her. Something in his eyes flickered, and he blinked, a vacant expression on his face, then wandered off into the living room. "Where's Dad-step?"

"Decided you want to watch the race, huh?" her stepdad said, sounding delighted. "We're on lap twenty-five."

There went her bodyguard. She turned to Mum, who had a cigarette pooling smoke upward in one hand, a cup of tea in the other, and Bennie's letter in front of her.

"Hit me with it, then." She folded her arms. Wouldn't hurt less, but she felt better doing it.

"Bennie is marrying Laura?" Her mother touched up her curly blonde hair—used to be grey before Darcy "grey hair equals ancient" McGregor. What was she on?

"Looks like it." The big letters declaring "getting married" made it pretty flipping obvious. What did she want, a fanfare?

"Laura is gay too?" Her mother rolled her eyes. "Do you know anyone normal?"

"No." Family included. Was anyone normal anyway?

"She was hanging around you a lot." There were the narrowed eyes. Here came the pasting. "Bennie never left you alone, even after I told you to stop talking to her."

"You kicked me out at twenty. You lost the right to tell me anything." Only reason she stuck close now was for Mikey. If Mum had bothered paying attention or doing something other than running off with another bloke, then Mikey might have been fine. Someone had to look out for him.

"Don't be like that. Bennie is a slapper, and even Mikey knows it." She dragged on her cigarette. "Laura cheat on you?"

"Yes." She shoved her hands in her pockets. The sound of race cars whizzing around a track like a heartbeat, *zoom, zoom; zoom, zoom.*

"You didn't know?" She tapped the ash off the tip and sat back.

"I suspected. Just didn't think Bennie would do that to me." And she'd been blind. It was always a competition with Bennie. Didn't matter that only Bennie saw it like that, she always had to win. She was probably marrying Laura just to prove something.

"Which is why you've been so quiet." Mum sighed and leaned further into her seat. "I made it impossible for you to talk to me."

Duh.

Mum pursed her lips. "I know that look. Fine. I reacted badly about things…but I had good reason. I had hopes for you." She rolled her eyes to herself. "Stupid, because my mother said exactly the same to me when I married your father."

"Yeah, guess she did." Okay, how quickly could she leave this conversation? Maybe she could pretend some competitor had broken into work to steal their lead?

"You're not happy. I don't like it." Mum dragged on her cigarette again. "You never dress up. How do you expect any decent woman to look at you?"

Cue double blink. Huh? "Excuse me?"

"You're not butch. You're not a girly girl, but you're not one of those..." She waved her hand around like that would make it any less offensive. "You're not either...so what are you?"

"Me." She'd had that lecture off Laura and Bennie at various points. She wasn't butch enough—Laura; she wasn't girly enough—Bennie. She was sick of it. What did it matter?

Mum laughed. "Yes...but you have no...definition. No style."

"If you tell me to read Darcy, I'm going to tan *your* backside." She scowled. Mikey didn't shut up about the program. Every time she picked him up, there was a new saying of Darcy's.

"I want you to meet her." Mum held up a card. "I want you to let her help you." She held up her cigarette-wielding hand. "Don't say no. You can't. I signed the form saying I was you." She sighed. "She really does help people. I went and read up on the people on her first series. Every one of them is doing great. Being on the show got them respect. People knew them... They even got better jobs."

Kate turned around. Mum had lost it. Nicotine had finally smoked out her brain.

"Kate, they'll be here next week. You want to get me in trouble?" Oh, Mum knew how to work her, didn't she? What could she do, tell them that her mother had committed fraud? Was it fraud? "Bennie is getting married just after the reveal airs..."

"So?" Kate folded her arms.

Mum had a shifty grin on her face. "Would be a nice way to send the message that you're over her."

And double whammy. Shit. Her heart lurched with her stomach. "Next week they'll be here?"

"Yes. Laura likes the show, if the photo is anything to go by." Mum's tone said she knew she'd won. "Be nice to stick it to her too, right?"

She glanced in the living room. Mikey the Sproutman was roaring around the living room. He loved Darcy. He said he didn't, but he didn't shut up about her. She wanted a change, right?

"Yeah, it would." She nodded without turning around and headed out the door. Only then did she let the tears spill over with a smile. What a change. Mum hadn't kicked her out for once. Hadn't spouted off about being abnormal. In fact, she was sticking up for her. Now, there was a first. Stick it to Bennie and Laura? She could do that? Yeah, Mum and Mikey would love it.

She smiled. Yeah, it was well worth suffering Darcy the flipping Wonder-Surgeon just for that.

CHAPTER 9

DARCY WATCHED THE CITY OF Cardiff tootle by outside the minibus window. It was tipping down to the extent cars ploughed through deep pools of water, and plumes gushed into the air and soaked the wide pavement complete with fenced-in trees. The sun had been warm and pleasant, the sky clear until they'd flown over the Severn and thick clouds enveloped them. She hadn't been to Wales before but was noting not to bring suntan cream. Yes, if in Wales, bring raincoat.

"Mum, aren't you going to watch the video?" Susannah sounded delighted. She'd been beaming and chattering on the whole journey into Cardiff from the airport. Mostly with Marge, but it was pleasing to hear her appreciating good television.

"Yes. I like to do it outside the residence. It gives me a nice feel before I head in and pick up the patient." She smiled. Her routine was perfectly timed. She pulled a pencil from her bag and twirled it between thumb and forefinger. It would be one of the live snippets. Every evening, seven p.m., primetime, one hour of fashion dreams would be made.

"What's that?" Susannah leaned in and frowned at the pencil. "Did you seriously buy something cheap?"

"This is a quality product. The lead is far less prone to breakage, and it has a pleasant red and orange." She smiled. They'd been the pencils she always used. Her first pack that her mother bought her. The feel of the ridged angles was pleasant to the fingertip.

"It's cheap." Susannah sniggered and tucked her hair behind her ears. "They hand those out in school. How do I not know this about you?"

"Because they are more than adequate." She tapped Susannah on the nose and put her headphones on. "Now go have some make-up applied, and do not chew your lip." She sighed. Chapped lips on high definition television? Not a good mix. She turned to her tablet, flicked it on, pulled up the video Marge had uploaded, and hit *play*.

"Kate is cool," a boy dressed as a sprout yelled, then jumped up and down. Why a sprout? At least it was healthy. "Needs a smile."

"Mikey," a woman with very badly dyed hair muttered. She ushered the boy to the side and peered up at the camera. "Oh, it's on?"

Mikey jumped up and down. "Tell Doctor Darcy Kate smile."

Oh, he was cute, and he'd had peas for lunch. Should sprouts eat other vegetables? A touch on the violent side.

"Right. Hi, Ms McGregor. My name is Mildred Bonvilston." The woman now had an odd attempt at a posh accent. Sounded more like she had a cold. "I'm Kate's mum, and I—"

"We!" Mikey jumped up and down.

"We," Mildred said with a sigh. "We need your help with Kate. She's a good girl. A really good kid who has been heartbroken…twice."

Twice? She frowned. Once was unfortunate, but twice was just careless.

"She was in love with Bennie, her best friend, for a very long time, but Bennie isn't very nice." Mildred lit a cigarette.

"Ben slapper," Mikey said with utter seriousness.

"Mikey!" Mildred covered his mouth. "Sorry, children… Anyway. Then her partner ran off with Bennie, and, well…" She puffed on her cigarette. Hmm, she had crows' feet and needed a more mature skin care regime. "Kate's been very quiet since."

Darcy twirled her pencil. Bennie? If he'd run off with her partner, then Kate fell in love with gay men? How were clothes going to help that? She glanced at Marge, who was studying her as if waiting for a reaction.

"You did say you'd decided on a challenge, but don't you think Kate is beyond our remit?" Just a gentle suggestion. She could change the clothes and rejuvenate the woman, but she wasn't going to be able to change who she loved, was she?

"What do you mean?" Susannah snapped from the back of the bus. She tussled with the poor make-up artist, Harold or George or whatever his name was. Marcus? No, no that was the hair stylist.

"I mean that Kate's case is hopeless. How can I change her…tastes?" Not quite the correct term. Love focus? No that sounded like something Zoë would say.

"See, told you," Susannah muttered to Marge.

Marge scowled enough that her wild eyebrows covered her sunken eyes and her overly large nostrils flared. "You try, like you do with everybody else."

Did Marge fall in love with gay men too? Darcy turned back to the screen to ignore the glare. Kate walked into a room, some family function with girls in white tights giggling as boys in waistcoats slid across a dance floor on their knees.

Kate was tall, slim, had a graceful way of walking, yet was not quite feminine. Her body shape was more athletic. Yes. No real shape, or at least none in that disgusting excuse for a dress. Who put a bridesmaid in floral and straight leg to the knee? She looked like she should be in the Women's Institute, not a function. Then she turned to the camera, strolled over, and beamed. Green eyes, long eyelashes, glossy lips, and a handsome smile—charming, sure, sexy.

Darcy swallowed. "Definitely hopeless." She clutched her pencil. Had she squeaked? Did Susannah notice? "Can't do a thing with her."

"You'll have to." Marge nodded to the guys at the back, who rolled open the doors. "We're here."

"No..." She flicked her pencil through the air. She couldn't. No, no, no.

Marge motioned to the doorway. "You can sit and sweat or have a touch up... Or would you prefer Susannah took the lead?"

Susannah scowled at her from the back. "Yeah, I could tell her there's nothing wrong with her dress sense and to be happy with who she is?"

The video rolled on. Kate was in work as a security guard. Somehow, she looked more feminine, but in that stage-like way when a voluptuous screen siren strolled out in a tux. She snapped her pencil. Oh dear. Oh dear. Shit.

"That a yes?" Susannah went for the door.

"No." Darcy stood up. Her tablet dropped onto the floor, the headphones yanking at her earlobes. "No, you stay." She rubbed at her throat. She'd need champers for this...a lot of it. "I'll—" She rubbed harder, then stopped. Best not to leave marks. "Touch-up." She stumbled off the bus and straightened out her jacket, only to see lead on her hands. "Wet wipe."

The make-up artist hurried over—Joe, no, Lionel...no—and dabbed at her neck.

"And rolling…" Marge nodded to her and motioned to the house where the crew were lurking.

Darcy turned on the smile. "Good evening. Self-confidence is all about knowing who you are." Go with it; the opening spiel was always drivel. "It's a balance of what you want and what you need. Kate Bonvilston is a young woman who wants the unobtainable…yet needs to love herself first." She strolled forward, stumbling over the wire. Never did that. Idiot. "Many women are forced to wear a uniform, whether that is physical or emotional, but it's easy to lose oneself in that corporate battlefield. So in this style surgery, we secure the security guard some style and help her find her inner smile."

"And roll the opening credits." Marge barked into her radio, then rolled her eyes and stomped over to the front door. "I want a picture of the door before Darcy treads all over the wires again."

Darcy wheezed out a breath and looked to Susannah, who studied her.

"Inner smile? So you listen only to super-vegetables, or all of them?" Susannah picked up the discarded tablet with a daft grin. "Do you give peas a chance too?" The screen showed a frozen picture of Kate with that sure, sexy smile on her face. "Maybe I need to dress up as a carrot—no, an onion—so you pay more attention to me?" She motioned around her. "Or, as we're in Wales, how 'bout a leek?"

"He wasn't a pea, and he was right." She narrowed her eyes. She could Google the national emblems of Wales too. "You'd have to be a daffodil, not a leek. Less pungent." She smiled and touched her thumb to Susannah's cheek, wiping a splodge of foundation. "But one must always listen to sprouts. They often make sense…a bit like daughters."

She held Susannah's gaze, the twinkle of a smile in her brown eyes. She hadn't seen that look for so long, too long. A swell of love bubbled up, and she kissed her on the forehead.

Susannah stared at her.

"Darcy, in position," Marge snapped. Clearly the hormone replacement needed a higher dose. "Credits are nearly finished!"

"Of course," she chimed, and strolled over on shaky legs. Now to meet Kate…live on camera.

Shit.

CHAPTER 10

KATE CHECKED HER HAIR IN the mirror again and took a slow breath. Mum was polishing the living room for the fifteenth time, Mikey was running through the living room, kitchen, hall on some imaginary racetrack, and her stepdad had decided to work late. He always got out of things. Why couldn't Darcy make him over? He had cement-dusted skin and a bald head. That'd be a challenge.

The doorbell rang.

Mum shrieked, threw the polish like it bit her, and sprinted toward the front door.

Kate caught her in the doorway. "Mum, calm...calm down. You're not supposed to know they're out there." She dragged her to the sofa and plonked her down, picked up the polish and duster and shoved it into the side cabinet, picked up Mikey mid-zoom and shoved him under her arm, and pulled open the door. "Alright?"

Darcy stared at her, then her gaze dropped to Mikey, then back up to her. Darcy was tall in heels. Really tall. What did they feed her? "Kate," she said in a clogged-up voice. "The Surgeon is paying a house visit."

Yeah, that line wasn't cheesy, was it?

"Okay, I'll get Mum," she said, like Darcy flipping McGregor *always* knocked on the door. Her hands were shaking. She turned and headed to the living room. "Mum, Darcy McGregor is here to see you."

"No, dear," Darcy said in her patronising tone. "I'm here to see you." She breezed into the living room. Wow, was it weird seeing the woman on TV standing next to the picture of her and Mikey eating ice cream in Western-Super-Mare and Mum and Stepdad's wedding day. "Your mother called..." She beamed at Mum. "Hello, Mildred."

Mum just nodded, dumbstruck.

"And your brother, Mikey...or as he was then...Sproutman?" Darcy stooped to smile at Mikey, who'd ceased wriggling and stared up at her.

"You know?" He dropped down to his feet and peered up at her with awe. "I love you."

Darcy "ahh'd" to the camera and then tapped him with a manicured finger on the nose. "I always love a superhero."

Mikey wobbled. He was going to faint.

Kate picked him up and plonked him next to Mum. Two gibbering family members on national TV. Dad must be laughing his ass off. "So, why are you helping me?"

Darcy cleared her throat. "Kate, it's clear that you have a condition. Inside you're heartbroken, and outside it's showing. But don't worry. You have the Style Surgeon at your service, and I'm going to give you back that smile."

Mikey cheered and clapped.

Wow, it was so much cheesier in reality. Kate clamped her lips shut. How did so many people watch this shit? "What if I'm happy and I like my clothes?"

Darcy laughed, patronising. Yeah, she was hot, but what was with the laugh? "I know it's hard to accept help." She motioned to the camera. "But give it a shot. You'll be surprised how good I am."

And that sounded so much like a line. Darcy's eyes flickered like she realized. Yeah, not awkward at all.

"At clothes," Darcy managed, her voice clogged up again. "Now, we have a process—"

"I'm still not sure." Okay, it was fun baiting the woman. Why was she teasing her? She should be gibbering on the sofa too. "I mean, I have to go to work. I don't have time to shop."

Darcy's eyes glinted. "You have time off."

"I need the overtime." She nodded. When did she ever do overtime?

"You need some help." Darcy narrowed her gorgeous blue—but not really blue—eyes. Yeah, she was hot when she was fired up. "And I'm *going* to help you."

"No thanks." Kate turned and headed toward the camera. Some woman with grey hair that fired out at all angles clamped her hand over her mouth, eyes watering. A young girl beside her, or Susannah McGregor—

unmistakable. She looked like her mum in every detail but the brown hair and brown eyes—sniggered as she kept one eye on her phone and one on Kate.

"Kate, don't you think you should listen to the professional?" Darcy hurried around to stand in front of her. Her cheeks were flushed, her neck was flushed, and her chest rose and fell, up and down, up and down.

"I didn't see your credentials," came out as she smiled at the necklace dangling down below Darcy's top button.

Darcy cleared her throat. "I'm Darcy McGregor. That should be enough." Said through gritted teeth.

Kate smiled and lifted her gaze. "You got a smudge on your shirt." She nodded to it. "I'm not sure you're qualified."

"Fine." Darcy held out her hand, and one of the crew handed her a tablet. "Fashion shows in Milan, New York, London, Paris…more awards than you could fit in this room." She shoved the screen up. A slinky model strutted along a catwalk. "I make women look good."

And that sounded like another line.

"You don't think I do?" Kate asked and held Darcy's fiery gaze. Something flickered there again.

"No." Darcy lowered the tablet and put her hands on her hips. "Which is why I'm here. Now, move it, we have a process to follow."

"Are you always this pushy?" she fired back.

"Only when dealing with awkward people." Darcy's brow dipped. Brown eyebrows. So she wasn't a natural blonde?

"Maybe I wouldn't be awkward if you stopped muttering at me." She put her hands on her hips. Was it her, or did they look like they'd have a punch-up?

"I'm *not* muttering at you." Darcy slammed her tablet to her thigh.

"Yes, you are." She couldn't help the smile creeping up.

"Am not." Darcy threw her hands in the air and growled. "I *will* style you, so get in the minibus." She glared at the camera. "Cut." She wagged her finger at Kate, then stormed out the front door.

"Switch to adverts. Run the sponsor segment," the woman with grey hair said into a radio. "We'll shoot Darcy's next section on the bus."

Kate stared through the open door as the cameras lowered. Wow, what a woman. She grinned at the crew and gave Mikey a thumbs up. "I think she likes me."

CHAPTER 11

Darcy put her tablet on the table at the back of the minibus. She supposed it was much like a large camper van: eight seated in front facing forward, and the table area at the back with a booth-style feel. The crew travelled everywhere, and a van with cameras followed on behind, but she hopped in for just the short stretches. She'd completed her analysis of Kate in transit and, thankfully, that was the live section out of the way, for now.

The live segments hadn't bothered her with her previous case. The routine was simple: The recorded clips gave a round-up—a build-up, in essence—then a half-hour live segment went out with some interaction from the viewers. Easy. In theory. Usually she offered her "patients" a flight with her, but maybe Kate would be better off with the crew, seeming as they liked her so much. What was so funny about being irritating? She scribbled *irritating* in big letters on her notes.

"Oh, we're trending!" Marge was another irritating awkward pain in her backside. Yes. If Marge wasn't careful, she'd send her to Marcus the hair stylist. "They love it."

"Of course they do." Her tone was pleasing. Calm, professional, and no hint of anger.

"No, Mum, it's like crazy trending. People want Kate to give you a run for your money." Susannah snorted, then grinned at Kate beside her—and irritatingly opposite Darcy.

"I think that I get like that when I'm nervous," Kate mumbled and rubbed the back of her elegant neck. She'd suit a showpiece necklace. It would draw attention to her... Darcy caught herself trailing the seam with Kate's shirt and cleared her throat. Maybe not.

Kate cocked her head, green eyes twinkling. She'd never plucked her eyebrows, that much was clear, and they didn't look too bad. Naturally shaped—even more irritating.

"Then feel free to stay nervous," Marge said with a grin, spiralled hair bouncing about. "You're a hit."

"Doubt that," Kate said. Her accent held a hint of Welsh and some neutral-sounding tone. "They just want to see how I'm tackled."

Darcy raised her eyebrow. Of course that's what the viewers wanted—irritating and stated the obvious. She noted that one too.

"So, what's the...um..." Kate shrugged and flapped hands. Oddly camp. She'd note that. "The process...thing?"

Susannah snorted with laughter. "You don't know?"

"Mum's the fan." Kate glanced down at the table. Was that quite the truth? Her eyelashes fluttered—she didn't wear mascara. Her brown hair flopped into her face—would suit a good chop to it and some feathering. "Mikey too, of course."

She smiled. Ah, yes, her little sprout. "He feels you need to find your smile."

Kate met her eyes—hers were intense, passionate, then cheeky. "I found that already, thanks."

Darcy scowled. Defensive. She added that to the list. She'd pin it somewhere and memorise it. Yes, many negative issues. Many.

Marge cleared her throat. "There are several segments, as you can expect from a month-long live show. Some bits are prerecorded. Some of it is live."

"It's seriously that long?" Kate stared at her. "You don't just tape it and play it?"

"No," Susannah said with a grunt. "Which is why I get palmed off to boarding school."

"You demanded to go," Darcy muttered. She'd rather have not paid the huge bill.

"I was ten. You upset me." Susannah folded her arms, scowling inner child on show. "I wanted to come home after a week."

Kate sucked in a breath "Yowch. Maybe your mum wanted the best education?"

Susannah laughed—sounded very familiar—too familiar, like her own, and she used it out of annoyance. "Not Mum. It's just easier when she's shopping."

Darcy twirled her pencil. Good thing she kept spares: 2B, 4B, technical. "You hate clothes."

"I hate being sent away." Susannah got up and stomped off down the bus.

Kate watched her go. "My boss will be bouncing."

"Why, does he have difficult teenagers?" she muttered. She'd never backchatted her own mother, but then, her mother had passed on not long after her father had left, and she'd lived with the neighbour.

"No, he makes your pencils," Kate said with a sweet smile—a smile that oozed sensuality and showed off her stunning dental work—natural, no veneers.

Darcy twirled said pencil. "They're the best."

Kate fished in her pocket and pulled one out. "Yeah, they are. Just don't tell him, or you'll need a restraining order."

She laughed. Shouldn't have. The woman was irritatingly humorous too. "Show consists of this: diagnostic—that bit we've done; consultation, examination, surgery—various sorts, rehabilitation, follow-up, the discharge reveal." She reined in a smile. No smiling even if Kate was cute—cute? No, oh no. Shit. "Each segment takes a few days to film, longer if you're problematic." She noted *problematic* down and underlined it. "Then we rehab. You go away for a month, and we discharge you." She met amused eyes. "And you can go back to your pencils."

Kate smiled. That sensual smile. Whether Bennie was gay or not, no wonder the poor man couldn't resist her. "I just protect them."

Marge looked from Kate to her, and some smug smile crossed her face.

"You protective of pencils, dear?" she snapped. She knew that look—never trust her smug smile.

"Might take to them," Marge said, smile wider. "We'll take Kate on the plane back." She smiled over her glasses at Kate, who winked at her.

Charmer—she noted that down too. Then frowned. Her notes didn't say: irritating, awkward, stated the obvious, defensive, oddly camp, problematic, and charmer. No, her notes said: lovely voice, gorgeous neck, long eyelashes, good taste in pencils, sensual, stunning smile, cute, irresistible, oh, and yes, a charmer. Darcy rubbed the frown line forming.

Oh dear.

She pulled out her phone and texted Zoë. She needed backup.

CHAPTER 12

Kate stared around at the spacious apartment. Marge said it belonged to Darcy and she allowed clients to stay during the show. The full one-wall-window overlooked the Thames, the London Eye—which was lit up—Westminster Abbey, and Big Ben. Every inch was chic; the kitchen was shiny and slick and looked too expensive to touch; the squishy leather sofas oozed money; the opaque glass doors had a switch next to them. Kate knew them well; her stepdad installed them. Flick the switch, and the door was a solid wall of colour. Flick it again, the door was see-through to let light in. The rosy oak floor was so rich and warm and exquisite that Kate swore the Queen would love it. Then there were slick pictures of Darcy on the catwalk in black and white with a black frame, and one of her and Susannah. Darcy was gorgeous in photos, but so much more potent in reality.

"I don't charge for using the furniture," Darcy said, rounded her, and started flitting about in the kitchen. "Sit."

Kate followed Marge to the sofas, then wandered over to the window seat instead. Passers-by hurried through the misty London night.

"Are you always this unwilling to follow requests?" Darcy muttered and strolled over with three cups. She gave a cup to Marge, placed one next to Marge with a biscuit, and held one out to her. "Tea, one sugar, and more milk than necessary."

Kate stared down at it. "How did you know?"

"I study." Darcy's fingertips brushed hers as she handed over the mug. Nails tickled Kate's knuckles, and her breath caught. Best she keep that reaction to herself.

"Me?" Sounded clogged.

"You." Darcy held her gaze with intensity, passion, and something close to uncertainty.

"Maybe I need to make notes too?" Kate glanced at Marge, who watched with amusement in her eyes. "Any goss on her?"

"More than is worth the legal bill," Marge said with a chuckle as Susannah strolled in and plonked down beside her.

"Ooh, biscuit." Susannah chomped on the biscuit with delight. Ah, so Mum did know her daughter.

Darcy glanced a brief loving smile at Susannah, but when Susannah looked up, she turned, and walked back to the kitchen. Why? Why wouldn't she want Susannah to see she doted on her?

"So, Kate, why don't you tell me how you shop?" Darcy said as Marge pulled out a small camera and pointed it at her. "This part is recorded, do not get nervous."

Kate looked back out to the misty London night. "I buy what I fancy."

"And you fancy playing football?" Darcy's tone held that smug arrogance girly girls loved to put on.

"Why not?" She smiled at Susannah. "Fancy a kick-about?"

Susannah grinned.

Darcy's perfect eyebrows dipped. She cracked open a bottle of water and poured it into a glass. So she didn't like her daughter having fun? Or only fun she approved of?

"Kate, what do you think when you look at me?" Darcy asked, strolling back over. Her purple jacket swished, some kind of sage-green top with a flashy necklace and jeans that slid over her long legs to heels that made her well over Kate's height, and she was six foot one. Best she didn't say "incredibly hot."

"You look girly," she said instead. Not the wittiest response. Ah well.

"Do I look drab and dull?" Darcy flicked open her eyes in some potent way. Wow, did she want to be a photographer right now. "Do you miss my eyes?"

Only when she looked away. "No."

"Do you know why?" Darcy patted the couch and took up the chair beside it. "Sit."

Kate wandered over, but she didn't want to—Darcy's eyes had some weird stun-thing going on. Real women didn't do that. It was only meant to happen to people in fanfiction stories where the writer pulled her in, made her feel like she was falling in love just with a look. They so needed

Darcy McGregor fanfiction, if some didn't exist already. If she could write, she'd do it.

"Kate, I know my colours. I wear midtones because I have aqua eyes." She sat back and undid the button on her jacket, her lips glossy with a smile.

Aqua eyes. Yeah, definitely aqua.

"This jacket is plum, this top is sage, and a pair of well-fitted jeans for my shape work wonders, yes?" Darcy's tone was sure but gentler this time—like older women used sometimes, which just made her feel sexy and subservient all at once.

"Yeah." Now she was grunting. Great. Drooling on national TV. That would give the boss a laugh.

"I'd like to make you look so good, Kate, that no one will be able to resist you." Darcy winked. Her lips flicked up into a sexy smile.

And her brain was going to dribble out of her ears. "Why...?" Bit of a squeak. Try again. "Why, are you trying to pimp me out?" Yeah, there was the defensive humour. Bennie had always laughed at her when she did it. Nasty laugh.

"Perhaps." Darcy's lips twitched in a smile again. "However, it would be to a catwalk, not a brothel."

How did that sound better? When had she ever wanted to prance up and down a catwalk? "Not sure you'll pull it off...but have at it."

Darcy turned to the camera and smiled, that full, dazzling smile. "So let's find out just where Kate's smile lies."

"And cut." Marge smiled at them both as she lowered the camera.

Susannah grinned. "It's dynamite. Seriously. You're like...wow together... You're...wow." She shook her head, eyes drifting as she read something. "Mum, you are so cool right now."

Kate nodded. Could someone be beauty-beaten? Stunned by sexiness, floored by charm? Whatever it was called, Darcy wielded it like...like...like she really needed fanfiction.

"I'm not going to dress you in some hideous frilled balloon." Darcy's gaze flicked from confident to gentle. "It's about making you feel incredible."

"Thought it was about viewing figures." She gripped hold of her mug, hoping no one could see her hands trembling. She'd laughed at her boss drooling, and now she was at it. She sipped at her tea and groaned. "Perfect."

Darcy nodded like she knew it would be. "It's not."

"What? The viewers or the tea?" She cradled her mug and sipped at it again. "Because this tea is really good."

Darcy laughed. It was the second time she'd done it. Like a Julia Roberts-style blurt that filled her eyes with shocked amusement. But just that touch more sensual, lower tones, breathy.

"Viewers, Kate. If it was just about figures, then Marge would have me dressing celebrities."

Marge nodded and cleaned her glasses with her sleeve. "Would help. Celebrities are always gold to viewing figures."

"But changing women's lives by bringing them out of their shells means more," Darcy said with some pulse of passion, her eyes intense. Then she frowned like she hadn't meant to let it out.

Susannah stared at her, eyes wide and a daft smile on her face. "It does?"

Darcy pursed her lips, then sipped at her water, leaving lipstick on the rim. "It does."

CHAPTER 13

DARCY ALWAYS FELT UNEASY DURING the examination where the patient would stand in front of a full-length mirror on some horrid platform. Any TV fashion show included it, even when she'd fought against it, but even as the face, there were some things she couldn't control. The ethos was to discuss the aspects the viewers at home would want to know. So the camera crew would be at every angle, and the screen to the left of the mirror showed every side to the patient standing in nothing but underwear. The foundation of the woman was her shape. To dress her well, you had to know her body.

Still, it brought back memories of being a self-conscious adolescent under the care of an elite designer, forced to stand on a table in the middle, in underwear, surrounded by scouring eyes. Every imperfection was detailed—not to be harsh but because those eyes watching saw a mannequin to dress, not a girl. The idea was to dress her shape, her assets, and cover the problem areas.

To her, there were never imperfections, as hard as that was to explain. A woman was a work of art, a shaky one at times…but all the more beautiful because of it.

She had steered away from design because of that, because of her need to create for real women, full-bodied women, stick-thin straight and boobless to pear-gone-wild or little-shape-among-the-folds women.

Kate gazed at her with a cockiness that was unsteadying. Defensive? Perhaps alluring? Better to ignore that. Difficult and exposing? Without doubt.

Darcy cleared her throat and turned to the main camera, the red light flicked on, and Marge gave her a thumbs up. "This is where we find your lines. Every body has its form, its uniqueness, its beauty." She flashed a smile, hoping her lip wasn't wobbling as much as it felt. "Stripping Kate to the bare skin shows where our surgery is needed."

Susannah held up her phone—Marge always did it to signal a viewer question or comment.

"Read it out," Darcy said, sounding like a doting mother. Odd.

Susannah blushed then swallowed. "Elaine from Barnstable would like to know how Kate has the guts to strip on TV." She shrugged. "Sounded like a good question."

"It is." Darcy beamed at her. Nice to see more confidence. "It is exposing. How do you feel about it, Kate?"

Kate's eyes twinkled with another surge of cockiness. "Fine."

She did look fine. Infuriating. In fact, she looked like she was quite used to being asked to undress. "We shall see." She narrowed her eyes. "Strip."

Kate's eyebrow twitched.

Do not react. "Keep your underwear on. We're a family show."

Kate flashed the kind of smile that rolled up and down Darcy's spine with a strong, slow, *thump, thump, thump*. "Yes, Doctor."

Intolerable. That's what she was. She folded her arms. "Get on with it."

Which just made Kate cock her head and stick her shoulders back. "Are you always so demanding?"

"Are you always so slow to respond?" Didn't sound like a good retort. Sounded…flirty. Shit.

Kate yanked her football top over her head—the male way—and grinned. Sports bra—there was a surprise—although it did go with the washboard stomach. A touch of definition there. Just enough to see she worked out, but not so much that all she did was sculpt herself. Good lines in at the waist, elegant, broad shoulders with no sun damage, toned arms, should really be a pear, but she wasn't. Olive complexion, midtones. Well, she knew exactly how to work those. Her breasts were neither too big nor too small. C cup? Maybe D…

"So?" Kate eased her shoulders back and her breasts rose.

Move gaze away. "You need a bra that fits." She reached out and hoisted Kate's breasts up further, then she eased them together and pointed to Kate's reflection. "Can you see how that automatically enhances your shape?"

Kate's long neck flexed.

Why was she quiet now? She caught Kate's gaze—and her own—in the mirror. Desire filled her own eyes, deepening the colour, enlarging the pupils. And hands off the breasts. She cleared her throat. "It defines your figure, accentuating your waist, which creates a smooth curve to your hips."

Kate looked down. "Didn't think I had any hips. Mum thinks I should have been a bloke."

"You are a fashion designer's dream." She lifted Kate's chin. "There is nothing wrong with you at all. You are perfectly created. Clothes, however, aren't...which is why we need the right shapes to show you off."

Kate smiled a half-smile, eyes softened, catching extra flecks of light, which brought out blue rims. Gorgeous.

Marge coughed. "New tweet... Susannah?"

Darcy stepped away. What was she doing? "Yes?"

Susannah stared at her like she'd never seen her before. "Er...right." She looked down at her phone. "Um..." She looked from Darcy to Kate and back to her phone. "Jan from Essex wants to know how to find the right shapes, because Kate looks like she could be a model."

"Modelling needs confidence." Darcy smiled at the camera. "But any woman would look good through the right lens...and Photoshop."

Kate snorted. "Ta, Jan, but you need an eye test."

Darcy raised an eyebrow. Heckling the viewers as well as her?

"What?" Kate flashed a cheeky smile. "I don't have the knockers for that."

"More like you don't have enough plastic..." She stopped. Closed her eyes. Lovely. Make that little statement on live TV, that's it. Cue battering from semi-nude models.

Kate and the others chuckled. The cameramen even managed a few murmured objections. Lovely. Descended from high-fashion to pub gossip.

"Yes, well..." It was Kate's fault. Kate and her smile. "Drop your jeans."

Kate wiggled her eyebrows.

Do not have a flush on camera. She set her jaw. It was an innocent statement. She put her hands on her hips. Breathe through the blush. Breathe. "Well?"

Kate flicked her buttons open and yanked down her jeans—with no grace at all. She stepped out of them in tight designer boxers, which drew the eye down to her toned thighs, toned carves, slim ankles…and then back up to the button at the front.

"At least they aren't bikini briefs," she muttered, averting all eye contact.

"Oh no, you can't touch these." Kate wagged her finger through the air. "I will put up with you getting your hands on anything else." And cheeky eyebrow flick as she tapped the waistband. "But these stay."

"And you don't think I'll just wrestle them off you?" She held up her hand, blood draining from her face as Kate's mouth crinkled up. "Do not answer that."

The cameramen were sniggering, Marge was sniggering, Susannah was staring at her like she'd commit her, and…there may have been a slight flush. She rubbed at her neck.

"You can try," Kate managed, her voice cracking with a laugh. "But they make me feel good… and they are so much comfier than lace."

Darcy flicked her gaze back to the button. How did she counter that? She turned back to the camera. "Kate's shape creates beautiful angular lines. Her strong shoulders lead into ample breasts and a long waist and hips that are as wide as her breasts." She motioned in their direction, keeping her gaze riveted to the camera. "And her legs are as long as her body."

Susannah held up her phone. "James from Leeds wants to know what her shape is, because his friends can't decide."

"Kate is a mix. She has triangular characteristics, but she pulls in a touch of hourglass, and adds in leggy model." In other words, Zoë would drool over the clothing possibilities…or just drool in general. Yes, unlike her who didn't drool. No. Completely professional.

Susannah held up her phone again. "Bill from Glasgow says he's never seen a woman in boxers before. He wants to get his wife some, because she doesn't like the lacy stuff." She snorted at her phone in the manner a teenage boy would be proud of. "And he wants to know if there are ones made for women."

"Bill, they are called boy shorts," Darcy muttered, still managing a smile. "And you can get them in most underwear sections."

"Boys don't look *that* good," Marge mumbled.

Clearly she wasn't the only one flustered. "And Kate's pert bottom is always a plus."

Kate peered over her shoulder. "It's pert? Mum says it wobbles."

What was Kate's mother looking at? "Yes, you don't have to lift it." She grabbed a cheek and hoisted.

Kate shut her eyes, and her neck flexed again.

"There's no cellulite either." Clearly knew how to tone and drain the lymphatics. "So we'll have no issue emphasising those alluring lines and attracting that perfect man."

Kate ran her hand over her abdomen with an odd look in her eyes, almost amused, but part-confused, part-embarrassed. "Er…right?"

"Tweet question," Susannah blurted, and waved her phone around.

"Yes?" So nice to see her excited.

"Michelle from Barnsley says you look great in a sports bra." Susannah peered under her eyebrows. If they weren't careful, she'd launch into a speech about equality. "She says Kate looks beautiful as she is, and she's comfortable. That's what counts."

Kate laughed a cocky laugh, low, breathy. "Even without being styled?"

Michelle clearly didn't get the concept of fashion makeover shows. "So…" She wasn't being drawn into it, concentrate on wrapping it up. "We'll call in someone extra special for this one." She flashed a smug smile at Marge. Oh yes. She could launch a surprise too. "Zoë Windermere."

Zoë slunk in on cue, her shape almost as perfect as Kate's but with a touch more curve around the hips. She flashed her "no one can resist" smile and smirked at Kate's bottom. "Nice shorts, honey."

"Cut! Move to the earlier recording on body shape." Marge peered over her glasses, brows dipping. "Darcy, we *have* sponsors. You can't have a designer. They want us to use their clothes."

"We will use them." Maybe a touch. Hopefully Zoë would allow the odd garment or two. She was such a snob. "But Kate deserves a special touch, yes?" And a woman who could handle her without dribbling. John wasn't going to enjoy paying Zoë's fee, but he was going to whether he liked it or not.

Kate pulled her clothes on. "Felt a bit underdressed."

Zoë flicked her gaze along the band of Kate's boxers that peeked over her jeans. "If I wasn't married, I'd say something witty right now."

"You married a woman who covers most billboards in New York in her underwear," she snapped. Why did that sound like a protest? "Maybe she can model some boxers for you?"

Zoë smirked.

"Mum!" Susannah stared at her and put her hand over her mouth. Was she smiling?

"What?" She shrugged. "It's not on camera." She stepped further away from Kate and her fruity perfume… Or was that Zoë's? No, she'd always worn a deeper scent when… Move on. "I need to design," she squeaked. "Zoë, pictures?"

"More than enough." She winked at Kate, who blushed enough her ears went red. Starstruck? Zoë studied her, then cocked her head and smiled a dangerous smile.

"Zoë!" Darcy put her hands on her hips. They had work to do. Kate did not need to be ogled. She wasn't ogling her, was she? No. She was the ultimate professional, yes. Zoë was being… Zoë. Wasn't one modelesque wife enough? She stomped into the living room.

"Yeah," Zoë purred and flashed a dashing grin at Kate. She turned to follow only to stop next to Marge and shake her finger. "Naughty. She hasn't got a clue, and you know it. Perfect *man*?"

Marge blushed.

Zoë narrowed her eyes at Susannah who clutched her phone. "You knew too, didn't you?"

Susannah bit her bottom lip like she'd done something naughty too.

"Know what?" Darcy put her hands on her hips. What was Zoë doing now?

"That I need a good coffee." Zoë stuck her tongue out and poked Susannah in the side. Susannah giggled, blushed, and focused on her phone.

"You need a warning label," Darcy muttered and pointed to the bedroom. "Move."

"Ah, she's bossy with you too, huh?" Kate said with a smirk.

"Oh yeah," Zoë shot back, her tone far beyond decent. She clamped her hands over Susannah's ears. "Just how I like her."

Kate's neck flexed again, and she wandered over to one of the cameramen trying, and failing, to ignore the conversation if the smirks were anything to go by.

Zoë strolled over and slid an arm around Darcy's shoulders, guiding her toward the room. "*Now* I know why you called."

Darcy blew out a long, slow breath. She shoved open the door with a whimper. "I need champers."

"No, champers got you pregnant." Zoë grinned and shut the door behind her. "Better you stay sober with this one."

She met her eyes and understanding oozed back at her. She slumped into a leather chair at the side. "Yes, yes. That's probably a really good idea."

CHAPTER 14

KATE ATE HER DINNER, STARING out at the foggy, now-rainy London night. Lights along the river were in misted halos; the sand-coloured stone balcony along the river seeped with patches of rainwater, and the trees lining the street below twinkled in the bluish white light.

Darcy and Zoë had been locked away in the room for hours. Susannah was huddled close to Marge, pouring over her tablet and whispering. The cameramen had headed out, trailing muddy boots over the floor, and Kate had mopped it just for something to do.

It was just so weird being in an apartment with Susannah and Darcy McGregor *and* Zoë Windermere. These were the people in magazines, the people who millions knew by face alone. The kind of people who went to glitzy parties and won awards, the kind of women who weren't real...not really. She half expected to wake up or be sectioned. Seeing them as people was...confusing.

Susannah was the spit of her mother. Not as tall and less composed, but unmistakably related, from the eyes to the mouth to the frown. The only things that were different were their eyes and hair. Darcy had blonde hair—well, at least dyed—whereas Susannah's was black. Not that unusual black when people dyed it, but the shiny black Italian, Spanish, or Portuguese women had. Must be from her dad. Was he Italian? He was short and dark-haired, anyway. Susannah was a bit geeky, a bit nervous, like she hated being in front of a camera and being pictured everywhere.

Zoë...well... She was...Zoë. She swayed when she walked, true model gait, and she was styled to perfection. It was hard not to be in awe. When Zoë had stepped out to get Darcy and her a drink, she'd only had to wink, and Kate had dropped her mop. Shaggy blonde hair, deep-tanned skin, brown eyes, lips fuller than anyone else could pull off, and a figure that just hypnotised. Kate pulled up her knees and leaned on them. She knew everyone in the LGBTQIA, or really, any community would be clawing at her for getting to stand in the same room as the woman. Zoë had that fairy tale marriage, the great career, the looks. She just made that dream seem… possible.

And Darcy… Kate picked at her knees. She didn't know what it was about Darcy McGregor that fired up something in her, but she was either trying to tease her or reassure her, get reassurance, or just make her laugh that wonderful laugh. Emotions raged, and she *never* did that; she never got flushed because a woman was staring at her breasts, or her legs, or her boxers. She didn't get so worked up when anyone else hoisted her breasts or her bum…and on camera. She wasn't someone to be bashful, but how could she not be near Darcy and her aqua eyes? She put her head in her hands. Hopefully no one noticed.

"You handled yourself spectacularly," Marge said, leaning back in her chair and throwing her glasses onto the table. "Kate, I don't think I've ever seen her thaw like that before."

"What do you mean?" She sat upright. Must have looked upset. Darcy had been sexy, patronising, knowledgeable, bitchy, and…just Darcy.

"She's hard to wind up," Susannah said, a grin on her face. "As in, she'll be calm and then punch a guy, but she doesn't snap."

Kate leaned against the wall. "Like that actor…Marshall something?"

Susannah beamed, her eyes twinkling. "Yeah. Like that."

Kate looked out at the rainy London night. Maybe she was a lot like Darcy herself? She was always calm until she flipped. "Best I keep my guard up, then?"

Marge chuckled, then eyed the door Zoë and Darcy were locked behind. "I don't know what they are concocting in there." Her phone rang, and she picked it up. "John…yes…I know the sponsors will want full advertising, but, John, think of the figures. Who has seen Darcy working with Zoë before? You have any idea the opportunity this is?" She met Susannah's guarded gaze and rolled her eyes. "Who doesn't want to see them together on screen? They haven't been in the limelight together since *that* fashion show."

Kate smiled. Yeah. She didn't do fashion, but it was played on most programs or recreated. Zoë and Darcy had been, what, in their early twenties at most? They'd burst down the catwalk to some thudding pop tune in floor-length trench coats, then ripped them off to reveal see-through, ripped-up jeans, slashed tops, and attitude that pulsed when they turned and posed as a pair. Then they'd turned and strutted back up the catwalk to a standing ovation. Sounded simple, but wow, it was the sheer power of the looks in their eyes, the stances the, "I own this," that made the designer who he was.

Susannah studied her, then narrowed her eyes, frowned, and went back to her phone.

Kate wandered over and eased into the curvy wooden seat beside her. "Must be hard sharing your mum, huh?"

Susannah met her eyes: she seemed guarded, lonely, looking for support, worried. Click, click, click, like a camera shutter capturing raw emotion. "I don't know any different."

"I always felt like I had to share my mum too." Kate studied her short nails—Darcy would mutter about those, no doubt. She'd once tried false nails for Bennie, who wanted her to be more "feminine" for a friend's wedding. All it had done was make it hard to grab anything, make a lot of things more…awkward, and she'd lost one in the photocopier on the Monday morning. Frank had been fuming for days about that false nail; not once did he figure out it was her, though.

"But did you ever think she was…false?" Susannah glanced at Marge, then tapped at her phone.

"Oh yeah, really fake. She had an affair when I was a kid. She kept having an affair, even when Mikey was born." She pulled over the tissue box, ripped off a corner of it, and cleaned her nails. Maybe she was being a bit deep, but it still got to her. "Mikey was a toddler when I was in my mid-twenties. Everyone thought he was mine."

"They did?" Susannah tapped at her hand and fished something out of a designer handbag. "Mum's. Just don't let her catch you."

Kate grinned and pulled out the nail scissors—had Darcy's name engraved, huh. "Yeah. Even when Mum said he wasn't, they still thought she was covering me." She picked at her thumb, which always got grubbier for some reason. "She never paid attention to either of us…not really." She cleaned off the scissors and stashed them away. "We fell out, big style, and I moved out." She sighed. It still gnawed at her. "I came home to see Mikey try sliding down the bannister and fall from ceiling height onto his head." She pushed the case toward Susannah. "Mum was too busy with her bloke."

Susannah put her hands over her mouth. "No…like that?"

"Oh yeah." She leaned back in her chair as Marge nattered away to the guy on the phone. "I took Mikey to hospital and flipped. I smacked the bloke so hard I broke my knuckle and his front tooth."

"I would have too." Susannah nodded, that frown deep, her eyes full of compassion.

"Yeah, anyway. It's why Mikey is…and he'll always be…" She tapped at the edge of the table. "Just a kid on the surface."

"He seems happy, though?" Susannah patted her hand, leaning in. "He likes seeing you smile. I saw the video."

"Yeah." She shrugged and picked at the edge of the table again. "I haven't forgiven Mum, even though she married the guy. Dad got really messed up over it." She leaned onto the table. "I did the same thing."

"Sometimes it's hard to forgive." Susannah leaned onto her fist. "I don't know my dad, not really. Zoë was around…" She shrugged. "But then she got married." She glared at the door. "And the only thing Mum has an affair with is a camera."

"But, unlike my mum, she does pay attention." She nodded at the door. What were they doing in there, anyway? How hard was it to dress a person? "She notices."

Susannah let out a full teenage snort. "Yeah, right."

Kate turned and winked at her. "Yeah, right." Full teenage impression right there, yeah.

Susannah giggled.

"Look, John. Zoë is a designer." Marge tapped her finger to the table. "What do you mean a family show?"

Kate winced. "I guess John doesn't rate my boxers, huh?"

Susannah giggled again. "He's the head of the channel. He always yells."

"John, choose your words carefully. There is no need for that kind of talk." Marge gripped the table, fingertips white. "I will not have a male designer."

"Because a male designer is family-friendly?" Kate motioned to the door. Yeah, Zoë had punched a few photographers, been drunk and pictured drunk, but she was a celebrity.

Susannah smiled. "More than Zoë, probably."

"John, I'm hanging up now." Marge scowled at the table. "Why do I need to check the Twitter feed?" She shook her head. "I'm running with Zoë." She cut the call and pinched the bridge of her nose.

"Did Zoë make his clothes too tight or something?" Kate bumped Susannah's shoulder. Hopefully Marge would calm from purple-faced. It did not look healthy.

"Zoë is a lesbian. That's the only thing I can think of." Marge flicked through her phone. "He's not like that. He's never been like that."

Susannah's face dropped as she stared at her phone. "Um…there might be a good reason."

Marge leaned over, and her face dropped into the same ashen grimace. "Oh dear."

Kate folded her arms. She'd give them space. This was their thing, their lives.

Susannah met her eyes. "There's a picture of Mum leaving the restaurant…and in a restaurant on Valentine's Day." She flipped the phone around. A picture of Zoë planting a smacker on Darcy's lips. "Kissing married women on Valentine's Day isn't really family-friendly."

Kate chuckled. "It's hardly steamy." She shook her head. "Zoe's kissed her before like that." And she so did not have that picture on her phone.

Susannah exchanged a look with Marge.

"She wasn't married then. It was for show," Marge mumbled.

Kate flicked down the screen. "Yeah, but look, she's talking about the restaurant. It's support." She tapped Susannah on the hand. "Don't worry about it."

Susannah smiled, but it was more guarded than before. Marge was much the same.

"Come on, your mum is not like mine. She's not going to have an affair with a married woman." She held up her hand. "Okay, that sounded like my mum is a lesbian. But you get the idea."

Marge tapped Susannah on the shoulder, her brow wrinkled. "Of course. Kate is right."

Susannah nodded but went back to her phone, her frown line deep. "Sure."

Kate picked up the case with the nail scissors in and grinned. "If she is, we'll cut her nails short. That'll teach her."

Susannah chuckled, and whatever worry was in her eyes faded. Yeah, it was crazy to think Darcy and Zoë were an item. She glanced at the door… And she was not pulling that picture and saving it to her phone. Nope.

CHAPTER 15

DARCY LAY HER HEAD BACK against the wall, feeling the softness of the leather seat against her thighs, the dimples against her back, forcing herself to be grounded, calm, and serene.

"Babe, that shrink shit is not going to get Kate dressed." Zoë tapped the draftsman's table. "You want me to work on the whole wardrobe?"

Darcy nodded. Focus on the leather. "I want to create something she'll actually wear. She likes pockets."

"So, let's redesign these cargos; pull out some sharp lines over the hips to accentuate curves, and twist it over the thighs to show off her tone?" Zoë scribbled away.

"Side pockets might work, but I want front pockets, nothing on the hip." She let out a slow breath. "We want to pull that material forward when she fills the pocket and accentuate her"—she tried not to visualise the toned, pert bum asking to be squeezed—"assets."

Zoë laughed. "Haven't seen you that flustered in a while." She scribbled away, her tone laced with irritation. "You want flared. I think that's too much."

"You're right. Let's go for a wider than standard, but only slight." She swiped her finger through the air. "I was not flustered."

"Honey, you squeezed her breasts on TV." She laughed, but it sounded more irritable than jolly. "Then you freaked out…as always."

"I squeeze a lot of women's breasts." She scowled. Who was Zoë to talk? "It's my job."

"Uh-huh." Zoë scribbled faster—either she was inspired or angry. "I know the look. I used to see that look."

Darcy glanced at the door. "Quiet." She glared at Zoë's back. "Susannah could hear you."

"You really think she doesn't know we had sex?" Zoë rolled her eyes. "No matter if you shoved her in boarding school for a few years, she was around enough to know."

"You say it like I abandoned her." She frowned and gave up on meditating, slumping down next to Zoë at the draftsman's table. "It's the best education."

"And you didn't want her growing up to be you." Zoë smiled at her and stroked her cheek. "Don't forget, I *know* you."

"Too well." She glanced back at the door. "I'd like an angular shape on the jacket. Let's celebrate her shoulders."

Zoë pencilled in her idea.

What was that? She pulled a pencil from behind Zoë's ear and corrected the mess. "I said celebrate, not neon-sign them."

Zoë attacked the pencil, thwacking it with her own and causing a wonky line. "Who is the designer?"

"Me. I taught you everything you know." She swatted Zoë's pencil back.

"Most things." Zoë tapped her on the nose. "Some you needed to be taught."

And there was a blush. She frowned and turned back to the design board. Every piece of clothing Kate could need. Still, she liked Zoë's touch on an outfit. They worked together…on paper.

"Try not to act like it was torture to sleep with me, will you?" Zoë muttered and threw her pencil down. "You need to get past this."

Something Zoë had always wanted to say? Seemed like it by the frustration, the intensity in her eyes.

"I don't need to do anything." She focused on the few skirts and dresses and hoped Kate would try wearing them.

"Yes, you do. You're not going to be happy if you keep dating the wrong gender." Zoë pulled her chin up to stare into her eyes. "And *this* gender is not going to put up with lying through their teeth."

"You didn't lie." She pulled her chin free and flicked through the colours she'd picked. Kate would look incredible in hot pink, but would she wear it?

"Yes, I did, which is why Susannah can't figure you out." Zoë scribbled a new line on the shirt, making it almost flamingo. Perfect.

"She doesn't need to. She just needs to understand that I'm capable of doing my job and I can be happy by myself." She drew Kate's figure, her abdomen, her smile.

Zoë drew an arrow to it. "Because sketching a woman is 'happy on your own?'" She stretched out an exaggerated yawn. "Whatever, honey, that chick has you hot, and it's about time you let someone close."

"I did. She ran off with an underwear model." She thwacked Zoë across the knuckle.

Zoë thwacked her back. "I ran off with an underwear model *because* I was living with you, sleeping with you, because we taught Susannah to walk together, taught her to talk, and I wasn't even allowed to use my own front door."

"Yes. I'm a bitch. You knew that when we met." She rubbed out the arrow.

"You were a sweet kid who mothered me then cried when the other girls insulted you." Zoë drew another arrow. "You spent one hot night with me and slept with a football player to prove you were straight."

She rubbed out the arrow. "I am aware I'm a bitch."

"Just a bitch?" Zoë thwacked her across the nose. "You freaked out because you felt something, then crawled back to me pregnant. I was there. I saw her being born."

"I didn't crawl anywhere." She'd expected Zoë to hate her. Why hadn't she? Why had she put up with so much?

"I agreed to be quiet because it was different then: our careers needed it, Susannah was the main concern, and because I stupidly thought I could live that way." Zoë kissed her on the lips. "Fourteen years and you told me if I didn't like it, I could leave."

"Again, I'm a big bitch." And she wanted to say she was a scared one, one who'd regretted saying it ever since Zoë had left and never got the chance to tell her otherwise; instead, she drew boxers on the silhouette. "What do you want?"

"To know you give a shit." Zoë pulled her around by the shoulders. "You smiled, supported, and didn't even look bothered that I got married."

For Susannah. "You have every right to be happy." She turned back to the sketch.

"Where *are* you?" Zoë yanked her back around. "Where's the babe I snuck into bed with, who begged me to touch her, who begged me to do it again?"

She glanced at the door. "Keep it down."

"If you don't show me, I swear I'll go out there and holler it." Zoë narrowed her eyes. Hurt flickered across the gentle brown irises. She was sick of seeing that pain. It had been why she didn't run after her. She was a bitch, but she loved Zoë.

"I sing with a hairbrush in my underwear, happy?" She pursed her lips. Why had she come out with that? How did that help?

Zoë rolled her eyes. "I *know*. I used to do it with you." She glanced at the door, her eyes seemed to fill with pain. Was she going to leave again? No, she couldn't do without her being around anymore. Not as a lover, but her presence, her friendship, her care.

"I miss you so much," she whispered, hearing the crack in her voice. Hopefully anyone near enough to the door was listening to headphones or learning to play the drums. "I miss picking up the phone to call you. I do it…then remember I can't call in the middle of the night anymore. Your wife wouldn't like it."

"She knows. I didn't tell her, but she goes crazy at the mention of you." Zoë scrunched up her mouth. "She went nuts at the picture of us on Valentine's Day."

"I was defending you." She folded her arms. That was no reason to have a hissy fit.

"Yes, but I *kissed* you." Zoë held her gaze like she was dense. "And you looked beyond relieved."

Of course she was. It had taken every ounce of self-control to keep it at that single kiss. She couldn't have cared if the manager threw them out or not. "It doesn't matter how I felt. You're married." She turned back to the sketch.

"And you don't sound happy about it." Zoë ducked her head down to meet Darcy's gaze.

"I hate her. I hate you for marrying her, and I hate that it's permanent. Happy?" She cleared her throat. They hadn't been alone, not since Zoë walked out. Just felt inappropriate. Zoë wasn't hers to hold anymore.

"Why?" Zoë leaned in. Oh, she'd forget all about her wife in an instant and they both knew it. If she told herself that, it made her feel better anyway. "Why wouldn't you just be proud of me, not ashamed?"

"She gives you what I could never give you. You're happy with her." She was not ever going to be that woman. Never. "I won't ever not feel...not want..." She flicked her gaze away. "She's better for you."

"Yes, she is." Zoë whispered it, but it rang out through the room like she'd bellowed. Hollow-sounding, hurt filled. "I love you too." Full of pain, of longing. "That's not going anywhere." She smiled and stroked her cheek. "I miss Susannah."

"She misses you too." She went back to her drawing and drew a lacy bra on Kate's figure. Ooh, nice shape. That would work.

"Do you have any idea how much it hurts that she doesn't know she's my kid too?" Zoë stilled her hand. "She *is* mine too. You promised me."

"Yes, I meant it. Legally, emotionally, she's our daughter." She drew a slash-necked top over the bra. "You left, and it broke her heart even more than mine. She cried more than I did."

Zoë shuddered out her breath. "You *cried*?"

"Are you devoid of all sense?" She glared at Zoë. How could she think she wouldn't cry? She breathed like her, smiled like her. How could she not know how devastating leaving them had been? "The woman I loved ran off and married some twig within three months...three." She smacked Zoë across the nose with her pencil. "And you were happy until you started working with her a few months before you ran out on your family."

"I never cheated on you." Zoë thwacked her back.

"Yes, you are... You'll always be." She thwacked her back harder.

"If that's the case, you are shamelessly flirting with a security guard." Zoë poked her in the shoulder. "And publicly."

"It's not my fault she's the most gorgeous women I've ever set eyes on." She poked Zoë right back.

Zoë scowled.

Yes, even more attractive than her.

"Is that it? Because I've never heard you laugh like that." Zoë kissed her on the cheek.

"I haven't, that's why. She's irritatingly funny." She kissed Zoë back.

"She is not going to put up with your shit." Zoë smiled, her eyes misting.

"She's not available." She shrugged. Why was she even thinking about it? "She is attracted to gay men."

Zoë howled with laughter.

"She is." She folded her arms. "She was in love with a man called Bennie."

"In that case, she's as crazy as you." Zoë drew a heart next to the sketch of Kate. "Which means you're in a load of trouble."

She rubbed out the heart. Not having that. "I know. Why do you think I called you?"

"I don't know." Zoë smirked. "To torture me with the fact you're moving on?"

"That would only make us even." She sighed and threw her pencil down. "I've only ever been in love with you. I don't know what I'm doing." She scowled. "It's the least you could do for leaving me and *our* child."

Zoë sucked in a breath. "Yes, guilt-trip me even more. That feels real good."

"You deserve it, but it's up to you to make it up to her." She shrugged. "So, are you going to stop me making a fool of myself on TV or not?"

"No. That chick is going to spring you from your shell." Zoë grinned. "And I want to see you free, so I'll hold your hand the whole way." She pulled her in and planted a kiss on her lips, then yanked her into a hug. "Thank you for letting me back in. I miss you both."

"You're welcome." She squeezed back.

"Mum?" Susannah mumbled from the doorway.

Darcy groaned. Perfect timing.

CHAPTER 16

KATE YAWNED AND WANDERED TO the kitchen. She'd left Susannah and Marge to it and spent hours trying to video-call Mikey and Mum. Mum was not good with anything technological, and Mikey had needed to explain, slowly. So funny. When they did talk, Mum and Mikey were so excited that Susannah and Marge thought it would be fun to bring them up on weekends to watch filming. It was a relief. As nice as it was being in an apartment with Darcy and company. It wasn't like she knew them...or was allowed to.

"You're not a morning person, I take it?" Darcy's head stayed down as she stood at the counter, munching something in a bowl—brown sticks? Yummy.

"Not really." She stretched out her back. "Is there somewhere I can pick up breakfast?"

Darcy raised an eyebrow. "I think I can afford to feed you."

Patronising. How nice.

"Maybe I don't *need* you to feed me," she snapped. Okay, so she was grumpy first thing.

Darcy smiled. "Not what I meant."

"I know." She folded her arms. Didn't matter; she'd pick up something on the way. "You still made it sound snobby."

"Unlike you, I grew up on one of the most crime-riddled council estates in the UK," Darcy said, crunching away. "Chip on your shoulder better?"

"I do not have a chip," she growled. Why was Darcy so irritating? "I grew up in one of the richest areas in Wales. I went to public school and never worried about money."

Darcy smiled around her spoon. "I know."

"So then I don't have a chip, and I should buy *you* breakfast." She nodded. Yeah, take that, McGregor.

"I have my own, thank you." She slid a box of cereal at her. "Help yourself."

How did that feel like Darcy had won a battle? She yanked the packet over. "Oh, I can't have these, sorry."

"Yes, you can. Susannah is a celiac too." She tapped the packet. "Gluten-free cornflakes."

"She is?" Kate poured a bowl. She'd never tried rice milk before, but… ah well. "So, what's the plan for today?"

Darcy flicked a page over. Looked like a clothes catalogue. "Thousands of people apply every week for me to dress them."

"Yeah, but I didn't." She tucked into her bowl, then winced. Gross. Maybe just needed sugar…

Darcy slid a bowl of it over, smile on her glossy lips. "You signed the form."

"I didn't. But if you take me to court, I'll swear I did." She spooned a load of sugar on. Yes, lots of sugar.

"Ah, mothers know best." Darcy flicked her elegant eyebrow. The light bathed her face. She looked so gorgeous…achingly gorgeous. How? "You're staring."

"Yes." She cleared her throat. "I have a thing for…" Her—No, don't say that. "Lighting."

Darcy finished her bowl of twigs—or whatever they were—and picked up a glass of orange juice. "That your story?"

Kate cocked her head. Was that the hint of a smile? "Yes. Light is diffused by whatever your glass windows are made of. It balances it out and softens your features." Like they needed a soft focus; Darcy looked untouchable. Like a moving picture or sculpture that she didn't dare get too close to.

Darcy leaned back against the counter and sipped on her orange juice. "Photography?"

"No, not really." How did she explain? "Dad makes…or used to…lights for studios and public places." She forced down another mouthful of the disgusting milk. "I used to like hearing him talk about it."

"Why *are* you a security guard?" Darcy studied her. The aqua eyes popped with colour against the high-key white background. If only she could pull a camera. What a shot.

"I like pencils." She chomped more cardboard flakes and milk that wasn't close to milk.

Darcy laughed. There it was. Full, warm, breathy, sexy laugh. "You don't like rice milk though, do you?"

She shook her head. "This has to be the foulest breakfast I've ever had."

Darcy smiled around her orange juice. "It stops you getting cramps, so it's worth it, yes?"

"That what you tell Susannah?" She wagged her spoon, which bounced light onto the ceiling. "Because I'm calling in social services."

Darcy laughed again, eyes pulsing with that shocked, sexy laugh. "Took her a while to like it." She smiled a maternal smile, then it turned to sensual until the light played on her lips. "Are you going to be a good patient today?"

"No." She downed the dregs of her bowl. Still gross. "Are you going to be any less..." What word wouldn't get her slapped?

"Of a bitch?" Darcy sipped at her orange juice, just studying her like she might eat her.

"You said it...but yeah." She cocked her head. "What is it with that, anyway?"

"I like being one?" Darcy finished her glass and poured one for her. "Drink."

"Why? You're..." She held up her hand. "Actually...sometimes..." It was sexy—correction: beyond flipping sexy.

Darcy raised an eyebrow like she could read her.

"Sometimes it's alright?" Oh great. Now she sounded like Dad. He was never the master of overstatement.

Darcy slid the glass to her. "*Just* alright, Kate?"

Ooh, challenging tone that dipped into husky and did all kinds of things to her stomach until she had to rub it. She caught the glass, and Darcy's hand. "Why, are you hoping to hear something else, Darcy?"

Was she using the same tone? The mood seemed to switch. Darcy's eyes deepened and her lips twitched. "Now, what makes you think such a thing?"

"Don't know." She trailed her finger over Darcy's, over the dazzling diamond—or whatever it was—ring. "Feels like you do."

Darcy threaded long, elegant fingers through hers. "And how do you know what I feel?" Guarded tone, edgy, confused?

Yes, how would she know? Darcy was a woman who millions thought they knew, a woman who had some kind of attraction to other women, yes, but seemed to date a lot of men too. Darcy was a woman she could never know. What would Darcy McGregor want with a normal person like her? A real person. A person who put out the recycling in her pyjamas?

She pulled her hand free. "I'll read your tweet on it."

Darcy grabbed her hand, squeezed it, then let it go. "And there is the chip."

She frowned. "Is this some kind of shrink crap?" She folded her arms. "Like, I'm insecure so I wear rugby shirts?"

"That's not *my* take on it." Darcy placed the dishes in the sink. "Rugby shirts are tribalism, just like any team shirt."

"And you dislike them?" Why had Darcy's tone been so noncommittal?

"I have no opinion either way." Darcy went back to her catalogue.

"Why? Don't you tell women they look like bin bags because they wear a tidy coat to walk the dog?" She knocked back the orange juice, then winced at the bitterness and the bits. Yuck.

"Professionally, yes." Darcy smiled and took the glass. "Let me guess, you don't like orange juice either?"

"Only if it doesn't have bits." She shuddered, then winced. "You don't think it personally?"

Darcy rolled her eyes. "If you want to walk the dog looking like a sack of coal, enjoy." She washed up the glass. "Just don't expect a man to appreciate you looking like it."

She laughed. "Why—?"

"You did *not* finish before me," Susannah shot as she waltzed in, Zoë in tow.

"Yeah, I did." Zoë wrapped an arm around her shoulder. "You cannot deny that I inhale donuts."

Darcy tutted. "I'll send you the bill for the doctor."

Zoë poked out her tongue, kissed Darcy on the cheek, and lifted the box. "Hers were gluten-free, honey." She placed a second box on the counter. "Mine is full of the stuff. So much tastier."

Susannah nodded. "It is." She sighed at the milk. "Rice milk is so gross."

Kate smiled. "Definitely."

Darcy shook her head at Zoë and tapped her on the cheek. "Healthy."

"Eh." Zoë kissed her cheek again and stole another gluten-filled donut. "I get enough of that at home, thanks." She pushed the gluten-free box toward Kate. "So fattening."

Kate took a pink-covered one.

Darcy raised her eyebrow.

"Thought you'd appreciate the girly colour." She winked. Hopefully, Zoë wouldn't get irritated. It was clear something was going on between them. They were so easy together. "Compromise?" She chomped into it. Now *that* was how to do gluten-free.

Darcy tutted, but her mouth twitched into a smile. "And you were saying you'd be difficult."

CHAPTER 17

DARCY MADE SURE THAT SUSANNAH, Marge, and Zoë were between her and Kate as they drove to Oxford Street. She wasn't sure what had happened at breakfast, but linking fingers with Kate? Stroking hands, squeezing. Flirting. She didn't even know this woman. Yes, she'd studied her and could pick psychological assumptions about her, but Kate wasn't gay. She wasn't interested, so why did it feel like they were straying over lines?

Kate was someone whom she would dress and send on her way. Easy. Kate knew nothing about the spotlight.

She pulled out her phone and sent out a tweet about how to pull things together, with the help of the right underwear. #FoundationDressing.

"Mum, I have so many tweet questions, I don't know where to start." Susannah chewed her lip as she studied her tablet.

"Honey, just pick a selection," Zoë said, leaning in like she used to when helping Susannah with reading or homework. Nice to see that again. She leaned back in the seat. Bittersweet. "They all have a theme. You see?"

Susannah beamed up at her like the awestruck child she'd been. She'd always been so different with Zoë. No scowling, no doll-shaving when Zoë was around… And someone was watching her. She looked over, expecting to see Marge gloat, only it was Kate and her big green eyes studying her, almost as if she wanted to send reassurance.

Darcy snapped her gaze to her phone. Tweet: *eyes show our deepest expressions and our inner self. Dressing with mascara enhances the effect. And don't forget a good eyelash curler.*

Although Kate didn't need any of it. Not really. Should they skip that? How was she going to cope with dressed-up eyes undressing her so easily? Was she doing that? Why did it feel that way?

"Ms McGregor, we have a lot of press outside," the driver muttered. She marvelled how he could roar a minibus around as easily as a prized luxury car.

"Marge?" She wasn't risking Susannah's safety.

"We have a security guard," Marge said with a wink at Kate. "And the crew will step in if we need."

"But pencils are not really as dynamic as you lot," Kate muttered, scowling out at the swarm of paparazzi. "What if Darcy punches someone again?"

Everyone but her roared with laughter.

"Yes, funny. It may well be you." Darcy fixed Kate with a glare.

Kate bumped Susannah's shoulder. "Told you I need to keep my guard up."

Susannah snorted. "Hopefully it's not the one with the ring on." She winced. "You'll have an imprint like Marshall."

"Marshall insulted *you*." Darcy folded her arms. "Kate is not that much of a buffoon."

"Should hope not." Zoë scowled, then hugged Susannah. "Marshall is a jerk."

Kate held up her hand. "Backward compliment aside..." She pointed out of the window. "How do we get through that?"

Darcy nodded to Marge, who drew back the door. "Like this."

Marge bounced out. Zoë and Darcy sandwiched in Susannah, and Kate scurried to walk in front, blocking the charging cameras' view. The usual insults fired off, camera lights blinked red, flashes popped, calls, grunts, jostling as the paparazzi fought for that perfect picture. Kate puffed herself up and strode at them, shoving them aside and clearing the doorway. Susannah hurried in.

One guy grinned up at Kate. "How does it feel hanging out with—" The deafening glare of sirens screamed out, covering the insult as an ambulance screeched down the road.

Kate seemed to hear it in full as her eyes hardened.

"In." Darcy grabbed her by the elbow and threw her into the shop.

Marge hurried in behind and the doors shut, cutting the calls, the fading siren, and the clicking shutters. Staff scurried to lock up, and she let out a weary sigh and exchanged a glance with Zoë. Yes, this was *exactly* why she'd kept quiet. Susannah did not need to be barged at.

"Do you have any idea what that..." Kate glanced at Susannah and took a breath. "Idiot...called you...?"

"Nothing we haven't heard before." Zoë checked over Susannah, fussing over her until she giggled.

"Are you kidding me?" Kate glared out at the doors. Then pulled out her phone and tapped away. "Hashtag bully...idiot."

"Susannah, go have a drink with Zoë, okay?" She sounded tired to her own ears. Susannah looked shocked but nodded, and Marge led them away. She turned to Kate and slid her hand to the small of her back, easing her from the doors. "There is little use in getting annoyed." She led them through islands of clothing racks, shiny floors interjected with carpet. "You can be angry at a wasp for stinging, but you can't change its nature."

"Wasps are tiny creatures. Those lot...are definitely not tiny." Kate glared over her shoulder. "He called you a load of things."

She nodded. "He wants a picture. Any picture." Kate's green eyes were so full of intensity. She was so incensed, so fired up, so beautiful. So easy to just lean in and—she caught herself. What was she doing? "Now you have experienced paparazzi. Well done."

Kate flicked her gaze over her face—had she noticed the leaning?—then sighed. "You make it sound like an insult."

"Not what I meant." She tapped Kate on the nose. Cold nose? Better she didn't hold it or rub it with her own.

Had she just thought that?

Kate took her fingertip and held it. "They don't see this side."

"Who?" She stroked her thumb over Kate's hand. She shouldn't let her hold on, shouldn't walk so close.

"Susannah and Zoë." Kate dropped her gaze to Darcy's lips. "You're different when other people are around."

She pulled her finger free. "Let's fix your underwear." She turned in the direction of Marge and the waiting camera crew. "Enhance your breasts. We'll work around the boxers for now."

Kate laughed. She was still walking too close, tantalisingly close. "I'd say that's a battle won for me."

Zoë and Susannah ambled over. Good, Susannah was chatting and laughing again. Zoë could always reach her.

"We shall see." She headed to the camera. "Ready?"

Marge nodded. Marcus and whatever the makeup guy was called fixed her up; Zoë sprayed spritz over her, and she pulled back her shoulders.

"Rolling," Marge mouthed.

"Women spend too much time in the wrong cup." Nice start. Direct. She turned to Kate. "Why spend hundreds on clothes when your bras look like something from a museum or a desert island?"

Zoë nodded—like she'd ever owned anything for more than a season.

"Strings hanging off, lace lost, the white now a beige grey, and it gives you three cups in one." Darcy sighed and fixed on the camera. "My dear, dear ladies, and those across the spectrum, please...love your breasts."

Zoë murmured her agreement—a touch too heartily. Kate raised her eyebrow, and Darcy cleared her throat. She was ignoring that smutty look. "So how do we find the right size?"

Zoë set on Kate and wrestled her out of her coat. Kate blushed but gave in, then blushed enough that her entire face and both ears went red as Zoë pulled off her top.

"This is an A cup," Zoë muttered, shaking her head.

Zoë had always possessed the ability to fluster most women, but it was a step further to fluster a woman who was interested in gay men. Typical. "Kate, you either have an inability to see your own body as it is...or your bra is older than Susannah."

Susannah chuckled behind Marge.

Kate shrugged. "It does the job. What's the issue?"

What to do with her? "Point proven." She nodded to Zoë. Her measuring tape came out accompanied by a dangerous smile.

Kate cleared her throat. "Why am I always half-naked around you?"

Zoë winked. "Because you're very, very lucky."

Kate snorted with laughter and relaxed. She looked like she was quite enjoying Zoë's attention.

Darcy put her hands on her hips. "Just measure her up."

Susannah held up her tablet. "Um...how do you measure?"

Why was *she* blushing? "Who sent it in?"

"Um…Susannah from Kensington?" She shrugged. "Thought it might be useful, and some of these questions are…" She cleared her throat. "They need age restrictions."

Darcy glared at Marge, who handed the small camera to one of the crew and took the tablet off Susannah.

"It is *essential*. Zoë is measuring the band size, which sits underneath the breast"—she scowled at Zoë—"far too slowly for anyone so highly trained."

Zoë chuckled. "I'm demonstrating."

"Yes, of course you were." She turned back to the camera. "The cup size is the fullest part of the breast."

Zoë winked up at Kate, who suddenly found the ceiling fascinating. "Going in."

Yes, that would help the show's image, wouldn't it? Fondle the patients. It could be a Zoë Windermere offshoot. "You take the band size from the bust size." Kate flashed an awkward smile back at her.

"We have a thirty-four and a thirty-seven." She grinned up at Kate. "Thirty-four C. Definitely not an A."

"How did you get that?" Susannah frowned. Was she really interested?

"The difference is your cup size." She really was interested. In fact, she looked like she had when Zoë taught her maths or how to say three-syllable words. "Less than one is a double-A, one is an A, two is a B, three is a C, and so on." She pulled a bra from the rack. "However, many bras are not accurate, so you need to make sure they fit well." She smiled to the camera. "Support helps promote a good posture and helps your back and shoulder muscles. So let's get Kate in something that fits."

"Cut." Marge cocked her head. "I never thought I'd learn something useful." She looked down at her potato-sack breasts.

"Zoë is more than happy to measure any woman who strays close enough." She motioned to Zoë, who grinned and brandished her tape measure once more.

"Want my tape, honey?" Zoë flashed a brilliant smile at Marge's laughter.

"I'm not sure my wife would approve." Marge winked back. "And you're measuring a thirty-something there… You'd have to lift mine with a hoist to find any band."

Darcy nodded to Zoë. "Enjoy."

Zoë yanked Marge off to the changing rooms as the crew, once again, feigned deafness.

"Maybe your mum can show you while I figure out how to remove underwire from my ribcage." Kate held up the bra Darcy had handed over—oh dear. It was a touch on the raunchy side. Extreme Freudian slip?

Susannah chewed on her lip. "That looks painful."

Kate sighed. "Anything related to being female usually is." She trudged off toward the changing rooms.

Darcy pulled a tape measure from her pocket. "Not if you have expert help." She held up a finger. "And you are *never* wearing anything like that." She ushered Susannah over to the everyday bras. "As your mother, I vote for these."

Susannah smiled up at her the way she often gazed at Zoë. "Me too."

Who knew lingerie would crack the ice? She led Susannah to the changing rooms with a selection. Considering she was in the middle of a shoot—that Zoë, Kate, Marge, and a blushing contingent of men were watching, not to mention the staff—she actually felt like a real mum for the first time in a very long time. #Heartwarming.

CHAPTER 18

KATE WORE THE BRA. IT felt like it was going to shove her breasts into her face, but if Darcy felt better with her in something from a strip club, she'd go with it. She was not going to show anyone, though. Marge and Susannah had both been kitted out, but in comfortable bras. Yeah, Darcy was just trying to torture her.

"We want to emphasize the legs," Zoë muttered, camera rolling as she and Darcy yanked clothes off racks. This was where the cameras got to watch Zoë and Darcy work—terrifying, but whatever; she'd just go with it.

"Yes. Watch the shape." Darcy tapped her finger to her lip as Zoë held up a pair of charcoal trousers. "And the size."

"Why? She *is* a size twelve." Zoë gave Darcy a *duh* look. "I think I can pick out a pair of cigarette pants."

Kate frowned. Pants? "Are we back on underwear, because I am keeping my boxers."

Zoë raised an eyebrow. "I didn't say panties."

"*Pants* in normal English"—Darcy peered under her eyebrows at Zoë—"mean trousers." She motioned to the pair Zoë was holding. "And they are nowhere near a size ten, let alone twelve."

Zoë held them up. "Then who labelled them?"

"A machine, probably." Darcy rolled her eyes and headed over. Zoë glared at the trousers with suspicion. "High-street shops make their own rules. You can be a size ten in one and a fourteen in another." Darcy looked to the camera and thwacked Zoë across the head with the trousers. "Designers let loose right there."

Zoë scowled and threw the pile of clothes on the floor. "How am I supposed to work with this?"

"The way all other women do: ignore the size and learn how to measure it against yourself." Darcy handed them to Kate. "And keep the receipt." She smiled a gentle smile. "By that size, we will need a sixteen."

At least. "Medium men's always fits, if that helps?"

Darcy scowled at her.

Right. Well, there went being helpful. She looked to the camera. "Style Surgeons let loose right there."

Zoë howled with laughter.

Darcy narrowed her eyes, intensity rippling through them. "Would you like me to force you to wear floral embroidered jeggings?"

Mean.

Zoë winced. "I may need therapy just for that image." She shuddered and turned to the camera. "FYI, fashion crime. Big, big crime." She flicked her hands out like flashlights.

Darcy handed her another size in the same cigarette…whatever they were. "Try them on, and this shirt."

Zoë nodded. "Worst tailoring ever on those sleeves, but you have me to rescue you." She winked at Kate.

Marge cleared her throat. "Made by our sponsors," she mouthed.

Zoë looked at her in disgust. "How low you stoop."

Darcy shoved Kate into the changing room, muttered something under her breath, and closed the door behind them.

Kate stared at the tiny space. Wasn't much space to fit her in, let alone change. She turned enough to be smack up against Darcy's back. "Are they funny sizes with the changing rooms too? Because I think I need a large."

"No." Darcy turned and narrowed her eyes. Then passion, sheer intense passion, sparked from them.

Kate brushed her lips over Darcy's, alarm bells dinging in her head, her brain saying, "Not a good idea." She pulled back. Oh shit. Had she just kissed Darcy McGregor? Oh shit. Something rattled. She looked at her shaking hand still holding a load of hangers.

Darcy raised an eyebrow. "You're not meant to pick up tips from her," she whispered and tapped her on the nose with a long fingernail. Her glossy lips slid into a smile, and she wiped over Kate's tingling lips with the pad of her thumb. "Change."

No assault charge? No "get out of the shop?" Nope, Darcy looked amused. She'd take it. She yanked down her jeans, trying not to headbutt Darcy's chest, and tried to ignore Darcy's gaze on her boxers. Fruity perfume tickled her nostrils. The heat from Darcy's breath tickled her neck as she exhaled.

"You're not making this easy," she managed, her voice hoarse. She stooped to pull off her shoes—that'd help—then glanced back up. "It's like a cupboard in here."

Darcy raised her eyebrow, peering down at her with the kind of look that just made Kate want to rip at Darcy's very plush jacket and shirt.

"You need a referee in there?" Zoë yelled and hammered on the door. "Or do you want me to continue to go through the serious design flaws in these clothes?"

Darcy scowled over her shoulder at the door. "If the sponsors pull out, *you* can sponsor the show."

"Fine. At least we'd have sense." Zoë sounded like she was grinning.

"Sense?" Darcy glared harder at the door. Kate wrestled on her trousers—weird shape, weird fit. "Sense? You dress skeletons for a living."

Kate sniggered. "Or very short people." She motioned to her trousers. Her ankles were on show. Looked crazy with stripy socks.

Surprisingly, she got a smile from Darcy. "Wonderful. Try the top."

Wonderful? Darcy liked stripy socks? She rolled her finger around in a circular motion. "Only if you look the other way."

Darcy put her hands on her hips. How could she pull off a catwalk pose in a cupboard? "I've seen you in a bra already, what is the issue?"

Kate leaned in and planted her lips to Darcy's, again. Lingered. Kissed each lip in turn. Fruity. Okay, kissing her once had been cheeky, but twice and lingering was... It had to be assault. Could she still be on the show with a restraining order?

Darcy eased back. "Is this another defensive tactic?" Her tone was husky, eyes twinkling as she wiped her lipstick from Kate's lips again.

"I think it might be." It had to be. Who went and kissed someone they didn't know, twice, in a changing room? "Turn."

Darcy sighed and turned around.

"Are you beating her in there?" Zoë's tone was full of a laugh.

"No, Kate is shy about her underwear suddenly," Darcy muttered and turned, just as Kate slid off her shirt. Great. Darcy's gaze dropped to the bra, and her neck flexed several times.

"Defensive thing is going to trip again," she whispered. The intense gaze wasn't helping either.

Darcy snapped her eyes up. "Definitely a masterpiece."

Kate smirked. "The bra or the breasts?"

"Both." Darcy helped her wrestle on her shirt and buttoned it up, wheezing out a breath. "You look good in purple."

"The shirt is blue, though." She cocked her head. Was Darcy blushing? Nah, must be warm.

"The bra isn't." Darcy ripped open the door. Cameras fixed on them, and she dragged Kate out. "Now this is how to define shape."

"If I want cold ankles," Kate mumbled, then grinned as Mikey and Mum wandered over to Susannah in the background. "Mikey will think I look crazy."

Darcy wagged her finger. "My dear Sproutman." She strode over to Mikey. He gazed up at her. "Can you help us?"

He puffed out his chest. "Kay."

Darcy took him by the hand and led him over. Zoë high-fived him as Darcy placed him in front of Kate. "What do you think? Kate feels she looks silly."

Mikey beamed up at her. "You look like a lady." He burst into laughter. "Kate-oh!"

Was that a "yes, she looked crazy?" She hugged him. Stupid how much she missed him. "I lost half my trouser leg."

Mikey pursed his lips. "They're ciggie pant." He nodded to Zoë. "Kate likes pockets."

Zoë nodded. "So I've heard. These have them."

Mikey turned back to her. "You don't wear socks with them, Darcy says." He blushed and wandered off back to Susannah and the drink she had for him.

"Darcy does, does she?" Kate put her hands on her hips. A flash went off, and she blinked away the blue blocks in her vision. "Ow?"

Marge smiled. "Sorry, kid. Light in here is tough on the camera." She hit the shutter again. Just a blink of a red light flashed. "Better."

"Is that to bribe me?" She could only imagine what Bennie would think. She would laugh at her and say she looked like a bloke.

"You haven't seen yourself." Darcy nodded to Zoë. "Workable?"

Zoë grinned and gave Kate a wink. "Workable."

CHAPTER 19

THE MORNING WAS SPENT HACKING through the department store for decent clothes. Zoë would play with them to pull out the right cuts and lines, but it should appease the sponsors.

Kate had been a good patient. She'd tried everything on—whether or not she was comfortable—mostly for Mikey. He had become Zoë's style apprentice because, like always, Zoë came into her own when children were around. Being Italian-American and one of eight would do that. It was nice to see it captured on TV, and even nicer when Susannah was acting like a big sister to Mikey, firing off questions with growing confidence—once Marge had vetted them—and smiling. Yes, put Zoë in the mix, and people shone.

Darcy leaned against the wall outside the changing rooms at lunchtime. Mikey, Kate, and their mother sat with Susannah and Zoë on a bedsheet from the linen section, eating a picnic. The crew had done the same—hopefully the shop staff didn't mind—and Mikey was entertaining everyone by marching up and down in some slippers he'd found.

She flicked out her phone and typed a tweet, after snapping a picture of the moment: *Lunch amongst bedlinen and granny slippers, as Mikey calls them. #Glamorous.*

Susannah looked down at her phone and snorted, then showed it to the others before shooting a goofy smile her way. Darcy winked and wandered into the changing rooms, where Marge was arguing with someone on her phone.

"John, Zoë is a hit." Marge leaned against one of the doors and fed her hand through the head-spaced gap at the top as if to check anyone was spying. She looked far better with a well-sized bra. Who knew she had such shape? They just needed to pin her down, cut her hair, and pluck her eyebrows and she might look presentable. "John, they are not an item. Zoë has been talking about her wife." Marge turned, saw her, and jumped. "Just ignore it. You know it's rubbish."

Darcy took the phone from her. "John, is there an issue with Zoë?"

John had been soft on her for a while. He'd even asked her if she'd consider a date a few times. He sighed, a sad sigh. "Darcy, I don't care that she married Blanche Friedman. I don't blame her. *I'd* marry Blanche Friedman for the underwear alone." He tapped something in the background. Probably a cigarette. He liked to tap the pack to slide one out. "Thing is… she is married. Complaints are firing in from all angles. I'm under pressure here."

She laughed. "Why would her being married be an issue?"

"Marge didn't tell you?" He groaned. Then muttered something under his breath. "There are pictures of you and Zoë on Valentine's Day and now, in the papers, there's pictures of you both from years ago, old photos. They look…intimate." He sounded like he'd put the cigarette in the corner of his mouth. "I know you're just being supportive and you're friends, but the blow-up with Zoë and her wife didn't help."

She looked to Marge. "What blow-up?"

"Check your emails. I sent you what I have. Zoë's wife on camera, screaming at her." He let through another sigh. "I've got a lot of pressure. I just need a statement from you both, something…just to clear up that there is no affair going on."

She handed the phone to Marge and pulled out her own with a shaking hand. Zoë had been at the house all Valentine's Day and then dragged Susannah to the cinema. They always went to the cinema, because Susannah had said there was nothing like a chick flick to celebrate love. She clicked onto her emails and followed the link.

"Again?" Blanche threw a heel at Zoë. Hot sunny street. Her LA house. "She calls, and you just go running."

Zoë glared at her. "Of course I do."

"Then why are you here at all?" Blanche screamed it out and kicked at the metal rubbish bin. Gate was next to it. Why was she heckling outside on the street? "Why buy me flowers when you're going to get on a plane to her?"

"I always take her to the cinema. I miss taking her to the cinema." She picked up the heel and sighed.

Yes, Darcy had texted her just after punching Marshall. Zoë had been happy to be let in from the cold, but hearing Susannah say how badly people treated her had spurred her on. Zoë was better at people, always had been.

"You miss her?" Blanche threw her hands in the air. "You miss her?"
"Oh, get over yourself." Zoë glared again.

She knew the face. Protective. Susannah was her girl, her baby as much as Darcy's.

"Get over...?" Blanche hurled her other heel. It pinged off the Ferrari roof. "I married you. Me. I didn't see her even holding your hand in public!"

Blanche must mean Darcy. Why? Surely Zoë would have explained who Susannah was, wouldn't she?

Zoë looked at the roof of her car, her brown eyes fired up.

Yup, here came the Latin temper.

"Get over yourself. If you don't like what I give you, find someone else." She threw the heels back at Blanche, got in her car, and screamed off.

Darcy closed her eyes. Zoë always put Susannah first, even if it meant protecting Susannah from the truth and risking Blanche's love to guarantee that. What a mess.

Darcy took the phone back from Marge. "John, Blanche is on about Susannah."

"That really doesn't help." He groaned a long groan and thunked something. "That's... I'm sure that's not legal."

"Susannah is like family to her." Publicly, that was all she could say. She wasn't sure if she could quite face how...exposing calling her anything else would be. She scowled. She was not going to follow his deranged thought path. "They always go to the cinema on Valentine's Day."

"But she met you in a restaurant. She kissed you," he muttered away under his breath. He sounded slightly awed by it.

"Yes. Italian roots and a gregarious nature. You would be hard pushed to find a woman she hasn't kissed." She smiled at Marge, who looked ready to kiss her herself. "Zoë does not like her car being hurt. She loves that car. She was not going to explain anything in that mood."

He sighed. "It still doesn't help us… Maybe if Susannah said—"

"No." She tapped her finger to her lip. "However, I know something that will." She handed the phone back to Marge and dialled Blanche's number.

"Great. It's you," Blanche spat down the phone. "I'm in Knightsbridge, so if she is leaving me, the least she could do is tell me herself."

Brat.

"If I wanted her, I'd have her." Yes, she was a far bigger bitch than this green rookie. "You're needed. Get your bony excuse for a body here and erase the damage your pathetic tantrum caused."

"Who do you think you are to talk to me?" Blanche growled.

"I'm Darcy McGregor, dear." Turn up the bitch. She smiled at Marge, who raised her eyebrows. What? She'd spent years in fashion—she could out-bitch anyone. "If you don't play nice, I'll have her back in my bed before you can flash that expensive smile." She tutted and checked her nails. Still perfect. "Wouldn't do well for that career of yours, would it?"

"I don't give a shit about my career," Blanche snapped, but her voice wobbled. "I love her, don't you get that?" Plaintive was so boring.

"Yes, sob, sob." She yawned down the line as Marge continued to stare. "She has a daughter, dear. She's going to see her regularly from now on, so here's a touch of advice: fit the label or the scissors will come out." She cut the line. Marge blinked a few times, shock in her eyes. "Oh, as if you didn't know already."

Marge blinked again. "I really didn't."

"Then your gaydar needs retuning." She turned and strolled back to the picnicking brigade. Zoë must have been desperate to talk to her, desperately torn to choose between Susannah and Blanche. She couldn't let that happen. Zoë shouldn't have to choose, and that meant taking a step back. She rubbed her hand across her aching stomach. So, why did it feel like she was cutting her own heart in two?

—————◦◦⟆⟇◦◦—————

Half an hour later, Mikey, Kate, and Susannah had taken to playing imaginary cards—Zoë's idea—as the camera crew set up various sections in the store for more shopping challenges. Kate's mother was nose-deep in some steamy romance, if the delightful cover was anything to go by, and Darcy had resumed her position, watching.

"Why did you call her?" Zoë muttered as Blanche strolled in, looking fit to grace any billboard. California sunshine would do that to a girl.

"You love her, and you love your daughter. It's time she knows about Susannah." She smiled as Zoë double-checked. "Oh, and she knows I could steal you anytime I choose, so she needs to stop playing up."

"Out comes the bitch." Zoë rolled her eyes. "Explains the outfit."

"Yes, enjoy her making a point." She nodded to Susannah, who glared at Blanche like she'd throw her imaginary cards at her. "Best she learns your daughter comes first."

"You mean it, don't you?" Zoë's eyes misted. "I can tell her...tell Susannah?"

"Yes, just give me chance to explain to Susannah first." She kissed Zoë on the cheek and shoved her forward. "Now take her somewhere away from cameras, because I am *not* tolerating PDAs."

Zoë winked and strode to meet Blanche, who shot a glare at Darcy, grabbed Zoë's hand, and yanked her in the direction of the café. Susannah rolled her eyes, then that frown—that all too-familiar frown—formed, and she went back to her game.

Mikey glanced up at Darcy, then pulled his mouth to the side. "I think idea!" Yelled so loudly that even Blanche looked over her shoulder. He slammed his hand to the bedsheet. "Snap!"

"What's that?" Kate tickled him, and he squirmed.

Marge wandered over with her handheld camera. "Always good to have some extra footage, considering how the live segments keep going."

"I think..." He beckoned Darcy over, then hurried and grabbed her hand, pulling her to the bedsheet. "I think...I think Darcy... Yeah." He grinned, then took deep breaths. "I think that Kate-oh surgeon Darcy." He grinned at Susannah. "Darcy in baggy trousers."

Susannah burst into laughter as Marge's eyes lit up. "Yes...yes, that sounds like a fantastic idea. Surgeon styled by the patient. What a way to round off the series."

Darcy scowled. What? No. Wasn't it bad enough she had to suffer Miss I'm-on-Every-Billboard? No way.

Mikey jumped up and down, gripping Kate, who winced. "Darcy," he said, tone serious, brow furrowed. "You lovely." At least he had good taste. "But you sad. You need to find smile too."

Susannah nodded to the camera. "She does. She's really lonely."

Darcy folded her arms. Why had she said that? On camera. "I'm perfectly fine, thank you."

Susannah glanced over at the café. "I don't think so."

"I do." She glared at Marge, who kept filming. "Must we have this on TV?"

"Yep." Marge grinned. Wonderful.

"You scared I'll dress you in skinny jeans?" Kate asked with a wink.

"More a bin bag with pockets." She was not being dressed by Kate. That meant spending more time around her, and...it was safer if she didn't.

Mikey met her eyes with ultimate puppy dog and pouty lip combination. "We need to find you smile."

Ugh. Someone would think she had a heart. "Fine. *When* we've finished with Kate."

Marge—still filming—high-fived Susannah. "*Now* we have a program."

Susannah pulled out her tablet as Mikey danced about. "Oh, they are going to go crazy for it. Styling the Stylist will be the hottest trending hashtag." She grinned. "Eat that, happy snappers."

"Susannah." She tried for stern, only she was laughing too hard to pull it off.

"Happy snap?" Mikey looked up at her.

"Yeah," Susannah said, leaning in. "The goons with cameras outside." She thumbed in the direction of the door.

Mikey nodded. "Goon snap. Snap scum."

He did have a way of summarising.

"Cut." Marge grinned and led Susannah and a bouncing Mikey off somewhere...to plot, most likely. They were a dangerous combination.

"I...er..." Kate rubbed the back of her neck, a crooked smile on her face. "I...I should say sorry for earlier."

"'Should' generally means you won't." She glanced over at the café. Best not to think how exciting it had felt, how easy it had been to let Kate linger, how much she'd considered kissing her back. It was more potent... more...thrilling than even being with Zoë had been. Somehow... No, that couldn't be right, could it? That it was deeper somehow? How was a quick peck on the lips deep?

"Yeah. I'm really not sorry at all." Kate shrugged and shoved her hands in the pockets of her ill-fitting jeans. "But thanks...for not flipping."

"I don't get angry." Hmm. Not quite the truth, but she'd run with it. "Not much..." She laughed as Kate raised her eyebrows. "*You* get me angry." She laughed harder, and Kate smirked. "And some people...I don't...normally."

"Yeah, I see that," Kate said with a grin. "Defensive thing?"

She blurted out her laugh, full of confusion, of attraction, of exasperation. Everyone turned to stare at her, and she tapped Kate on the chin. "Yes, perhaps it is."

CHAPTER 20

THE DAY WENT BY IN a blur, but shopping was officially exhausting. Seven p.m. and the show aired; seven-thirty and it went live. All with Kate as a human mannequin. She didn't know about anyone else, but it took some stamina just whipping clothes on and off, and even more so with Darcy inches from her. By eight, shooting had wrapped, and Zoë had whisked off Blanche and Susannah somewhere, much to Susannah's irritation, if the Darcy-style scowl was anything to go by; Mikey and Mum had headed out—Marge's wife worked in a theme park just outside London, so she'd arranged for Mikey and Mum to get free run of the rides the next morning and a hotel stay for all his help during the day. Mikey had won a load of fans by himself.

Darcy had taken her on a tour of London—or the driver had—filling in little touches of places where famous people lived or details that only people who knew the city intimately could know. Fascinating and really exhausting. So much so she was ready to drop as she followed Darcy into the empty apartment. She checked her watch—nine-thirty—and she was ready to curl up in bed. Shocking.

"Are you going to wince through dinner?" Darcy asked as she flitted around the kitchen. How was she so full of energy? Must be the twig breakfast.

"Depends if it tastes nice." She slumped onto the sofa with a groan. "How do you do this all the time?"

"Practice." Darcy chuckled like she'd heard that before, a lot.

Kate focused on the black-and-white picture of Darcy, collar turned up, sensual eyes, hair falling into her face. "It's easier than a photoshoot?"

Darcy flicked her elegant eyebrow and tossed ingredients into a wok. "Or a fashion show."

Kate rolled her head to focus on her. "Why did you choose to be a model?" She held up her hand—with effort. "I mean, you were right to... but why modelling?"

"Are you looking for insight or some glamourous tale of local girl done good?" Darcy swished the pan around and shrugged off her plum-coloured jacket. Her shirt had no sleeves and some frilly bit down the middle that made her arms look all kinds of toned and showed off her slim waist.

"Insight." Kate squinted through bleary eyes. The spotlights over Darcy cut a small shadow under her deltoid, around her triceps, and pulled out the tone of the muscle. Somehow, it looked feminine yet so strong.

"I always wanted to design. I needed money to do that and contacts." She splashed something from a bottle into the wok. "I developed early, so it felt natural to model. When you're twelve, things seem like a really good idea."

"That's young to know what you want to do." Kate sighed and leaned back into the sofa. "I still don't know what I want to do."

"Ah, so we come to the security guard," Darcy dished out with a knowing smile. "Who decided to get you the job?"

"Bennie worked there for five minutes." She chuckled. Was she that see-through? "I stayed on, though. I like it there. No stress."

"But you have five A levels at A-star." Darcy tapped the small table and placed the plates and two mugs down on it. "I don't sit on sofas to eat, it's bad for the digestive system. Up."

Kate smiled, groaned to her feet, and headed to the table. Bossy was off again. "I did my A levels *after* I left school." She slumped into the chair. "You're bossy a lot."

"Yes. I'm a mother." Darcy smiled and handed her a bowl with sauce in it. "Try it before you pour it on."

"Why, is it made of rice milk?" She eyed it. It smelled okay.

"Amusing." Darcy tapped her hand. "Why did you study after leaving school?"

"I like learning things." She tucked in. Nice. She tested the sauce. Gross. No, she would stick with the nice food. "Just for the sake of learning. Sad, huh?"

"Intelligence is never sad." Darcy tucked into her own food. "Are you planning on doing anything with your qualifications?"

"No." Kate sipped at the tea. Darcy made a fantastic cup. "I love A levels. Well, used to. Degrees just bore me. I don't like studying some of the dummy modules."

Darcy smiled around her fork. "Yes, I've got one on understanding social fashion." She rolled her eyes. "Highly useful."

"Is there such a thing?" Sounded a bit vague.

"No. It's about how people follow everyone else to feel accepted." Darcy munched away, her lips shiny with the sauce. "Because I needed someone to tell me that?"

"That where you get the tribalism thing from?" She reached for the salt, but Darcy did the same and caught her hand.

"No, various other courses and experience." Darcy laced their fingers together and held her hand, going back to her dinner like they held hands all the time.

"This your way of telling me not to add salt?" She stroked her thumb over Darcy's thumb. Was she really holding her hand? Had she fallen asleep?

"No. I just don't want you to pull away," Darcy whispered, then sighed. "It feels…nice."

"It does." She grinned. Darcy didn't want her to pull away. Wow, did she wish she had a camera or something just to capture that so she could replay it…a lot.

"Stop looking so smug." Darcy squeezed her hand, lips glossy with that sauce again.

"I'm trying not to. It's really hard." She shrugged. How could she not look pleased?

"I shouldn't…we shouldn't…be doing this." Darcy slid her fingers out then back in between hers in an easy motion. "I don't do this."

Kate stared at their hands. Her stomach clenched with nerves and…so did somewhere else. "But 'should' usually means you won't, right?" She met Darcy's eyes: intense, passionate aqua bliss.

"Yes," Darcy whispered. "Yes…I think I am." She slid the half-eaten dinner away and pulled Kate close. Two warm, soft hands held her face. Darcy only inches from her. "I can't help it."

"Oh." Her heart pounded so hard. Was she going to faint? Seriously not cool to faint.

"Oh." Darcy stroked over her lips with a soft, salty-tasting thumb. Tickly, tingling. Sauce tasted so much better this way. "You kissed me."

"Yes," she whispered. Kissed Darcy's thumb, kissed the sauce from it. No, still gross, but who cared?

Darcy flashed a sensual smile and eased her thumb in, eyes locked on her lips. "Twice."

"Yes." She pulled Darcy in onto her lap, swept the hair from her neck, and brushed her lips to the warm, soft skin at the nape.

Darcy leaned to expose more skin. "In a changing room."

"Yes." She lifted Darcy up onto the table, leaned her back. "You really like me in lace."

Darcy pulled her down, slow, sure, into a fleeting kiss. "I do...far too much."

"Yes. I don't think Marshall would like it." She leaned in, kissed Darcy's neck from the nape to the ear and to her mouth.

Darcy fluttered her eyelids. "I'm... I don't care what he thinks." She leaned up, eased her into a kiss, and pulled her in, sliding around her tongue with salty sauce. Acquired taste. She'd go with it. "We shouldn't... I shouldn't... I..." Darcy sighed into her mouth and lifted her hands upwards over her stomach, easing her down further.

Kate pulled back. The buzz building too fast. "I... We..."

Darcy's eyes filled with intensity, with passion. Oh right, the lacy bra was out. Darcy ran her hands over the lace and Kate swallowed. That wasn't going to help her resist. "Kiss me."

She dropped back down.

Darcy yanked her into a kiss. "Please."

Resistance broke. She met Darcy's eyes. Yeah, and Darcy knew it. Right. She grabbed for Darcy's shirt, tore at it. Darcy smiled against her lips and helped her, pulling at her jeans.

"You did not get a strike." Susannah's voice filtered in as the door opened.

Shit.

Darcy shot back to her chair, fumbling with her shirt, and Kate thunked her head to the table with a groan.

"Kate, you okay?" Susannah asked in a sweet tone.

"No," she whimpered and dropped down into her seat, doing her buttons up and hoping it was in some way covered by her collapsed in a heap. She lifted her head up, and Darcy was chomping on her dinner. Guilty look much?

Zoë looked from her to Darcy and laughed a cheeky laugh. "You got leftovers? I'm starving." She dragged Susannah over to the kitchen and shoved plates into her hands as Blanche glared from the doorway.

"I will charge you for viewing," Darcy muttered, her focus too intent on her food.

Blanche grunted and slunk inside. Didn't miss the sour gaze at the pictures of Darcy on the walls.

"Honey, you want some?" Zoë asked, licking sauce off her finger as she dished out.

"Sure." Blanche's voice was deeper, like a whole octave deeper, and her tone was Southern? Smooth, whatever it was.

Susannah slumped into a seat next to Darcy with a piled plate of food. She pursed her lips. "Zoë cheated...again."

Zoë poked her tongue out and took the plates over to Blanche—guess she didn't eat at the table—then met Kate's eyes and wiped her finger over her lips with a wink.

Oh shit. Lipstick. Kate buried her mouth in her jumper. Was she blushing? Could Susannah tell she was blushing and sweating?

Darcy looked up and chuckled.

"What?" Susannah—head in food—looked up like she expected to get told off.

"Nothing." Darcy leaned into her palm, blush on show, and tided Susannah's hair. "Zoë *always* cheats."

"I do not." Zoë winked at Kate, then kissed Blanche on the cheek. "Do I, honey?"

"Remains to be seen," Blanche said in her deep-toned accent. Ooh, she should do audiobooks. She glared at Darcy, but she rolled her eyes.

Zoë tapped her plate with her fork. "We're in her apartment, hon. Let's remember we're polite guests."

Blanche glowered at Darcy, then tucked into her food.

Susannah looked from Zoë and Blanche, to Darcy, to Kate, and back to Darcy, her frown dipped and mouth pulled to one side. Darcy studied her nails.

"I know it's a shock, right?" Kate blurted out, plastering on her cheekiest grin.

Both Darcy and Zoë eyed her, visible tension flowing from them.

"What?" Susannah cocked her head.

"Three models eating real food." She splayed her fingers over her thudding chest. "Imagine what the press would say?"

Susannah chuckled and went back to her food. Zoë smirked as Blanche pursed her lips, and Darcy let out that beautiful breathy blurt of a laugh, relief in her eyes. Yeah, Darcy didn't need to cheat. Kate had no doubt she could get what she wanted when she wanted. She poured sauce onto her food and winked at Darcy, whose eyes flickered with that intensity once more. Yeah, she could get used to the sauce. Really used to it.

CHAPTER 21

DARCY MADE A HABIT OF having her patients stay with her at the apartment on the Thames. She made a habit of getting to know them, cooking for them, treating them, because it helped build trust. It was trust she needed to get their style reflecting the woman she'd uncovered: a true woman with all the imperfection, strength, intelligence, sexiness, and class that term embodied. She did *not* make a habit of revealing personal information; she did *not* make a habit of holding hands, allowing fleeting kisses during filming, or full make-out sessions on her dining table.

Years of carefully constructed, practiced, displayed image had buckled with a few witty comebacks from a pencil-guarding security woman.

Morning sunlight broke through rain-soaked grey clouds beyond her skylight. Darcy sat on her bed and buried her head in her hands. Thankfully, Susannah had remained at the apartment talking to Kate, Zoë, and Blanche until the early hours. Darcy had excused herself and hidden in her room. She hadn't dared come out even when she heard Zoë and Blanche leave and Susannah and Kate head to bed. Nope. If she didn't come out of the room, she wouldn't find herself in Kate's room. Where had her self-control vanished?

"Mum," Susannah whispered from the doorway. "Are you...are you alright?"

Darcy pulled her hands away and smiled. "I'm fine. Kate left already?" In other words, was it safe to come out?

"Yeah. She went with Zoë and Blanche in the minibus. Marge wants a segment with them helping Kate to walk the catwalk." She rolled her eyes. "Don't get why. Do they have runways in pencil factories?"

Darcy blurted out her laugh. Why was she laughing so much? "Then why aren't you with them?"

"Blanche is weird about you. Every time Zoë so much as mentions you, she gets moody. I don't get it." Susannah shrugged, then sighed. She looked out of the large skylight, then sighed again. "I...I need to know what is going on, Mum."

Fair question. "Zoë needs to see how Kate moves naturally to understand how the clothes will move on her."

"Not the catwalk." Susannah pulled her *duh* face. "With you...Zoë was always here. Then she left, and you...you went so quiet, and she...she got married and then..." She chewed on her lip. "You seemed happy for her, but we didn't see her anymore...until now."

"She is happy, and that's what counts." She got up and flexed her calves to fire up the lymphatics—puffy ankles would not look good—and kissed Susannah on the cheek. "I'm not sure why she finds Blanche appealing, but there you go."

Susannah frowned up at her. "Did Zoë...?" She sighed, looked up at the skylight, then sighed again. "Did she make a move on you or something?"

Darcy's breath caught, and she spluttered. "Excuse me?"

"Did she try it on with you?" Susannah furrowed her brow further. "You didn't guess she was gay or something? I mean, she was always here." She played with the silver bracelet Zoë had given her for her birthday. "She feels...like a mum and... She's not you, though. But she feels like family."

"Of course she is." She smiled and squeezed Susannah's hand. "She loves you."

"Yeah, but she loves you too, and way more than friendship." Susannah held on like she was desperate for reassurance. "Blanche knows that."

Darcy tutted. "She is very happily married."

"Because her wife loves her, but she would have married you." Susannah held on. "She would have if you were gay." She studied her like she wasn't sure what the truth was. "She... Whatever she did that upset you, I know it took a lot for you to ask her back in, and I think you did it for me."

"I'm your mother. It's my job." She shrugged. She didn't deserve the support. What had either of them done right? She'd hidden away Zoë, forcing her to lie, forcing her into that rash decision. Yes, it seemed to be working out better than expected, but it had severed any chance of them getting back together. Maybe that was the right thing? Kissing Zoë, being with Zoë had moved her, moved her and ripped at her, but it wasn't powerful enough? Perhaps. It was different. Zoë's presence and friendship anchored her, but it wasn't the mesmeric pull that tugged at her core whenever Kate smiled.

"But...if she hurt you, it hurt me that she left." Susannah tucked under her arm. "I don't know how to talk to her right now. I need to know if she messed up...how she messed up."

"She didn't do anything wrong." She gave Susannah a squeeze, then strode into the kitchen. Kate was unravelling her as it was; she didn't need Susannah probing.

"No? Then why do you look...so heartbroken?" Susannah blurted it out.

Darcy froze, then turned. Susannah's eyes flicked to and fro like an idea was forming. Always dangerous. She should lie.

"I am," came out instead. She held Susannah's shocked gaze. The words hung there, echoed. Wall smashed. "Don't blame her. I had every opportunity to marry her."

Susannah let out a long, heavy sigh that made her shoulders drop. "So why didn't you?" She shook her head, then pulled her *duh* face again. "And *why* are you dating men? Are you bisexual?"

They did not teach this conversation in parent evenings. "Because..." She took a breath. Let it out. "I don't like being gay." She shrugged. "I want to be normal."

"Mum, you're a celebrity. Nothing about you is close to normal." She threw her hands in the air. "And you're miserable."

"Yes." Nice that her seventeen-year-old was telling her so.

"So, tell her... Do you want me to tell her...? She should know." Susannah put her hands on her hips, and before Darcy was a woman. The child, her child, vanished. It sucked the air from her, hurt so much more than any heartbreak over Zoë. She gripped onto her arms, digging her nails in to stop blurting out tears.

"Mum, you look in pain."

More than she could ever show. Long, slow breath. "I don't want Zoë." Illuminating. Her brain only registered how true that was as she said it.

"Then there must be a nice woman who you can like?" Susannah tapped her finger to her lip. "Marge might know someone."

Darcy wagged her finger and fussed around with her handbag. "I don't have to look for dates... I just don't want them."

"Why?" Susannah dipped to catch her gaze.

"I'd rather be miserable." She pulled her jacket from the chair. "We don't want to be late."

Susannah pulled her own jacket on. "Mum, it's your show. You can turn up when you like." She stood in front of the door and, thankfully, the child returned, her baby. "Why do you want to be miserable?"

"I told you. I don't like being gay." She kissed her on the forehead and picked up her keys. "I'm sure I can find an appropriate man to fix me."

Susannah pulled in her chin. "Delusional much?"

"Yes, and it's worked for years. Practice makes perfect." She pulled open the door.

"What happens when you meet someone you want to marry?" Susannah mumbled as they trudged down to the car.

"I'll run the other way." She held open the car door. "No one should have to put up with me." She winked as Susannah slid in. "You can barely tolerate me, and I'm your mother."

Susannah climbed in and shifted over, high-fiving the driver as she always did. "I didn't know you before." She looked up with a gentle smile. "It helps to know why."

"Why?" Darcy nodded to the driver. He smiled. As usual, he was feigning deafness. Good man.

"Why you always shut me out. Why you sent me to boarding school... So I didn't have to cover anything?" Susannah thunked her head to Darcy's shoulder and burrowed in. "And why you have such a freakish aversion to women with short hair."

Darcy scowled, then a wave of warmth filled her. Susannah really didn't care. "Guilty as charged." She kissed her on the head again. "Thank you."

"I'm your daughter. It's my job," came back at her with exactly the right intonation and a cheeky wink.

For once, she was speechless.

CHAPTER 22

THERE WAS SOMETHING ABOUT DRESSES that just made Kate feel awkward. She was a woman inside and out, yes; she had no real issue with dresses. But standing in a changing room with a silky frock on made her feel like a bloke on a stag night—all she needed was a nurse's hat.

"Kate-oh!" Mikey called out between giggles. "Why you take long?"

"Dresses are kinda tricky," Zoë oozed out.

Kate tried to ignore the flash of Zoë and Darcy on the catwalk and them not on a catwalk… Shake it off. She picked up the twig-heeled excuse for a shoe and fanned herself with it. Over and over, her mind kept replaying Darcy under her on the kitchen table. Slow torture; she could even taste the sauce.

"Do you need any help?" Blanche asked, peeking through the gap at the top of the door. Too tall, that's what she was, and very pleasant when Darcy wasn't around. She doted on Zoë. "Honey, it goes on your foot."

Kate held up the offending shoe. "This should be on a rack in a dungeon somewhere."

"It's only three inches. That's slight assault." Blanche winked, then laughed. "You just try to remember: head up, shoulders back. Own it."

"Until I go flying into the camera and you need to pull the lens from my nose?" She sighed and bent over.

Blanche cleared her throat. "Bend your knees, or you'll look like you're on a porn shoot."

Kate snapped back upright.

Blanche laughed. Her laugh was even lower than her voice. She winked, then scowled. "Great. The bitch has arrived."

"How do you know?" She glanced around, didn't know why. What was the cupboard with a mirror going to reveal?

"Zoë just introduced her to the camera." She growled. "Suck up." She muttered something and disappeared.

"My dear Sproutman," Darcy announced like she was laughing. "How is your mission?" Her tone was so full of genuine affection.

Kate groaned and rested her head against the wall. She couldn't go crazy over Darcy McGregor. Unobtainable and then some. No, she had to… dislike her somehow, but how could she dislike the woman when she was so good with Mikey? Her heart couldn't take it. Darcy was unavailable. On another level, gorgeous level. No, no, don't think on that…

No, Darcy was mean, really mean. A mean, big, gorgeous bitch who made disgusting sauce taste sublime. Ah, shit.

Kate climbed onto the edges of the door and peeked through the gap. Yup, Darcy was fussing over Mikey and giving him some kind of toy. Then she turned and beamed at Susannah as she strode towards the changing rooms.

"Is that cellulite?" she shot at Blanche as she strode by and flicked at Blanche's very short skirt.

Blanche sucked in a breath and craned her head around to check out her own backside. Darcy strolled on, smug smile on her face.

Yeah, she was a bitch, but ugh, did it suit her. She reached Zoë and gave her a flirty wink—and cue that smug glance back at Blanche, who folded her arms. Kate leaned her chin to the top of the door. What a bitch, what a woman.

"Kate, you need to come out," Darcy said, then stopped. Her eyes glinted—panic? She glanced back at Zoë who did her best I-didn't-hear-anything-wrong-with-that face.

Blanche just rolled her eyes and clipped Zoë across the head. "Suck up."

In response, Zoë poked her in the side, and they started bickering under their breath.

Susannah smiled, a warm, sweet smile, and nodded.

It made Darcy's shoulders relax. She nodded back and turned to the door. "We're about to start filming… Kate?"

Why had Darcy looked so terrified? Kate swallowed. "Er… give me a minute."

"And rolling…" Marge grinned and motioned to the cameraman.

Darcy turned to the camera. "Helping a woman to feel good in clothes that are unfamiliar can be a difficult task." She motioned to the changing room. "Clothes that are different can pull at your insecurities, and Kate may feel this way."

Kate went to lower herself down. Her dress caught on the hooks, and she tried to tug it free. *Rip.* Oh shit.

Darcy walked over to the door and peered at it—guess she couldn't see Kate peeking over. "Kate, do you need help?"

"No?" she whispered, squeaked. Hopefully Zoë hadn't made the dress. "Just…um…hanging out."

Darcy raised an eyebrow at the door. "The camera is rolling. Please don't be worried about how you look. You'll be wonderful."

"I look like I'm in drag," she whispered down to her.

"Not in the right dress." Darcy's gaze flicked over the door, and her smile was unguarded, full of gentleness and compassion. "You'll look beautiful."

"Not sure about that." She tried to tug herself free again. Another rip. Oh shit. She'd have to stay on the door, feet clinging to the ledge at the bottom, hands white from hanging on.

"I am." Darcy frowned, and she put her hands on her hips. "You need to come out."

"You're a fine one to talk," she mumbled. She couldn't hold on much longer.

Darcy's eyes narrowed, and she yanked open the door. Kate swung into the wall with a thud, smacked her nose, and groaned.

"Where—?" Darcy peered up at her, mouth contorted. "I know dresses aren't your thing, but they are not *that* hard to put on."

"I…er…" The cameras were still rolling. Marge, Zoë, and the others were howling with laughter, that complete unhinged silent laughter. Sniggers came from the crew, side gripping, silent laughter, from Susannah who bent double. "It's a security thing. Thought I needed to be on the door."

Darcy blurted out her gorgeous laugh. "Best we lower your expectations." She put her hands on Kate's hips and eased her down. *Rip.* The front of the dress flapped forward, and out was her bra and stomach on national TV again.

"Don't think anyone is in doubt you're female now," Zoë said, gaze locked on Kate's bra. Blanche slapped her across the head while also staring at the bra. Darcy stared at the empty changing room, her face bright red.

Kate pulled up the flapping material. "Think I might need a replacement."

"Cut, move to the catwalk segment," Marge managed, tears rolling down her cheeks. "The shot is too shaky."

The cameraman lowered his large camera, shoulders shuddering. "Sorry, Marge."

Kate eased Darcy out of her way and walked back into the changing room. She closed the door. Dresses were not for the faint-hearted.

CHAPTER 23

DARCY CHEWED ON HER LIP and paced up and down the small aisle between clothing racks next to the changing rooms. She *should* go in there. She *always* helped her patient and talked them through stepping out in clothing they were unsure about, but she couldn't with Kate. She didn't know how it had looked on camera when Kate had flashed that bra, but it had to be incriminating. It *felt* it.

Zoë and Blanche chatted away to Kate's mum on one side as Mikey danced around. Susannah was next to Marge, both eying Darcy like she might dissolve into tears, and she…she could not go into a confined space with Kate.

"We're about to go live again," Marge said, nodding to the cameraman. "Are you going to help her?"

"No." Short, sharp, flustered.

Susannah raised her eyebrows. "She broke one dress, Mum. She might put this one on *when* she's taken it off the hanger."

Darcy tittered, actually tittered. Nerves. She rolled her eyes. Anyone would think Kate was giving birth to their child—what? No. Panic hunched up her shoulders, and she bit her lip. She was not thinking *that* ever again.

"And rolling." Marge's eyebrows contorted into a half-glare, half-confused expression until she looked like she had wind.

"Kate is trying again with her dress." She rolled her eyes. Slapstick and style. "For many women, dresses, skirts, they are terrifying prospects." Not many resorted to climbing doors, but she could imagine some wanted to. "These items of clothes are for the 'girly girls' as Kate calls them. As if these women are the only ones who have the right." She wagged her finger. "Why should you, dear ladies, be forced not to wear something out of intimidation?"

"Maybe we just don't want to wear them?" Kate grumbled from her changing room. "Or feel like a bloke in a dress?"

"It has very little to do with gender and more to do with confidence," she shot back.

Marge smiled like she might propose. Why? And it was rather unnerving. Even Susannah beamed at her.

"And a body shape that suits them," Kate muttered. "Zoë said I'm angular or something."

"We have been through this. You're a mix." She shot a glare at Zoë and started pacing. "Don't pay any attention to her; she designs clothes."

"Hey!" Zoë put her hands on her hips as Mikey sniggered.

Darcy shrugged. "No one is that skinny unless they are only measuring their spine."

Zoë motioned to Blanche who twirled. Yes, she *was* that skinny.

"She is not real. I mean an actual woman, not a twig with a head." She clamped her mouth shut. Did she just say that...on TV?

Susannah snorted with laughter, and was Kate sniggering? Sounded like a snigger. "Get out here, woman, or I am coming in to get you." She scowled at the door and resumed pacing. It helped a bit. Didn't clamp her mouth shut, but at least she wasn't blushing.

"Tweet question," Susannah called out. "How can women feel more confident when they are in a dress?" She rubbed the back of her neck. "There's hundreds of questions like that."

Darcy met Zoë's gaze. "Wear it like no one is looking."

Yes, Zoë had always been brave, always a guide when it came to confidence. That easy confidence that was innate. She would never have hidden in a changing room. "Wear it like no one is looking." It had been Zoë's way to support her and seduce her all at once. How many times had they whispered that to each other? A rolling screen of memories tormented her. The first time: behind the scenes at the fashion show, lined up, ready to go. Newish lovers, full of passion for each other, dressed in next to nothing under long trench coats.

"I'm..." She longed to lean in, right there, and sneak beneath Zoë's coat. Longed to forget they couldn't—shouldn't be so close. "I'm scared." She meant

them, she meant the fact that she hadn't had a period for over two months, the fact that this fashion show was a big one, the biggest they'd been in.

"Wear it like no one is looking..." Zoë whispered and winked at her, a flush of pure desire in her eyes. "Just me... Wear it for me."

Even when she'd adored Zoë, it wasn't enough. She couldn't feel comfortable. She wanted to, she wanted to be proud of the gorgeous woman who was always there for her...but she couldn't, and if she couldn't with Zoë then she *never* would. No. She blinked the memory away, eyes misting. Lonely was better than breaking someone else's heart. It was better to stay lonely, yes.

Susannah glared at Zoë, who raised her eyebrows. "How do you wear it like no one is looking in public?"

"By remembering that you have the right to wear what you like." Darcy resumed pacing, faster. She felt dizzy. "Now get out here!"

Kate shoved open the door—electric-blue evening gown, tapered at the waist to create shape and plunging from string straps to show the contours of a pert chest, out over the hips and down past the knee.

Darcy walked into the clothing rack. It clattered to the floor with a clang, and two cameramen jumped out of the way.

"Okay?" Kate hurried over and stooped to help her only showing off another lacy bra. This time in black. Darcy stumbled upright. Okay? No. Not okay. Kate's eyes were so close, blooming with colour, the electric blue pulling out touches and flecks. Why did just looking at Kate rip the calm from her? How did it feel so good just to look at her?

"If you still think you are a guy in drag, you need to take my membership away," Zoë mumbled with an elongated groan.

"And mine." Blanche let out a wistful sigh.

Darcy couldn't pull her gaze from Kate, from the gorgeous green eyes, from the smile trying to reassure *her*, from the warm hand holding her arm. She didn't care that half the sponsor's shoddy clothes were on the floor, that Mikey was cheering all by himself for some reason, that Zoë, Blanche, Susannah, and the cameras were riveted to Kate and her. Waiting. "You're beautiful."

Kate's throat flexed—showpiece necklace really would work around the long, elegant neck. Very kissable, too kissable. "I feel...awkward."

"The heels are too high for you," she whispered, her tone intimate, her body unwilling to move, to put distance between them. "You're elegant enough without them."

Kate smiled, the same smile that had seen her half-naked on top of her own dining table. "I don't feel too much like a bloke in this one."

"Because I picked it." And she'd designed it. Trust Zoë to have it made. If she didn't know any better, she'd think it was Zoë's way of guiding her all over again…just this time into Kate's arms.

Kate cocked her head.

Darcy leaned in—caught herself—back up, back up, now. She jumped backward and clattered into the second camera.

"Cut, move to sponsor segment," Marge said like she didn't want to.

Darcy turned from Kate as Mikey cheered and gave her a thumbs up. Susannah studied her, eyes narrowed.

"Break?" She squeaked. "Best we give Kate some…um…hair…make-up." She cleared her throat. "Lunch…yes…lunch." She strode off through the store, ready to find the fire escape. Kate stirred something even Zoë hadn't…something that seemed to pull at her even in front of a camera. What was she doing? Kate must see it; she must know. What if Kate felt it too? Not good, escape, yes… It was better she run.

CHAPTER 24

Kate yawned as she dragged herself to the apartment. She'd stayed behind to be introduced to hair and make-up. She didn't know why she needed to curl her eyelashes, and mascara made her itchy. She sighed. Perhaps Bennie had been right and she wasn't girly enough.

"Mum, Kate's home," Susannah chimed out, head in her tablet on the sofa.

Kate stopped. Oh, that sounded way too good.

Mikey galloped from the direction of her bedroom and waved. "We're doing jumps." He flashed a goofy grin.

Darcy galloped in behind him. How much that picture would make her fans giggle? Style Surgeon and imaginary show jumper. "Did I hit the water?"

Mikey turned over his shoulder. "Nope. Perfect."

Darcy beamed at him. The warmth curled up through Kate and squeezed at her heart. Darcy was so beautiful. Kate leaned against the door, wanting somehow to just take a picture or film it. Mikey clearly had a hero thing going with Darcy, and who could blame him?

"Kate-oh, you look sleepy." He galloped over and threw himself into her arms. "Your hair looks funny."

She nodded, and it bounced about. "They thought I needed feathers."

He frowned. "You a duck?"

Darcy chuckled and strolled over. She reached out and fluffed up Kate's hair. "Feather*ing* is when you chop two inches from the tips." She took a strand of hair and made a scissor action. "Then it brings out Kate's eyes and sculpts her cheekbones." She eased the hair back and stroked the pad of her thumb over Kate's cheek.

Because that didn't make a tickle run the length of her spine and plummet somewhere really not appropriate. "Went with perming my lashes." She widened her eyes with a scrunched-up mouth, and Mikey chuckled.

"Perm?" He leaned in and head-butted her nose.

Ow. She rubbed it and his forehead. His spatial awareness had been rubbish *before* he fell. "Yeah."

Darcy tutted and lifted her face up by the chin, peering at her like a doctor. "Wonderful job." She ran her thumb over Kate's eyebrows. "Excellent shape."

"Luigi did it." She so wanted to lean in and kiss her.

"*That's* his name!" Darcy grinned and turned over her shoulder to Susannah, eying them with some deep thought, if the crinkled brow was anything to go by.

"Why don't I take Mikey and your mum to the shop?" Susannah blurted out like Mikey had never seen a shop before.

"We have shops in Wales," Kate said with a smirk.

There was Darcy's full-bodied laugh. "Best I say nothing."

"I bet." Cheeky, huh? Kate slid her hand to Darcy's ribcage and tickled. "Oi, you'll get Sproutman on his soapbox."

Darcy howled with laughter again. Not just a wriggle away or a squirm, but a full, girly shriek of laughter while slapping her hands. Oh, that was priceless.

"Tickle?" Mikey grabbed his own ribs. "Again."

"You got it." She snuck another tickle in. Darcy shriek-laughed again and added hopping about to the slapping.

"Stop it." Darcy held her finger up, smirk on her face, challenge in her eyes.

"Yes, let's go and get some milk," Susannah said like she wasn't covering her mouth to hide her snigger.

"We *have* milk." Darcy raised an eyebrow at her. Yeah, Kate didn't need to be her mother to know Susannah was being shifty.

"Rice milk," Susannah said like she'd just thought of it. "You want to come for a walk, Mikey?"

He barked at her.

Susannah and Darcy stared at him.

"That's what my stepdad says when he's off to the pub and takes the dog." Kate ruffled his hair. "He teases Mikey with it too." Why he thought it was funny, she didn't know, but then he'd thought having an affair with a married mother of two was a good idea.

"You can't go anyway," Darcy said, her tone all mother's orders.

Susannah responded with the classic teenage scowl and slunk onto one hip. "Why?"

"There's cameras outside." Darcy furrowed her brow like she'd get snappy, then relaxed her face and smiled. "You may have guessed I'm on their spot-and-snap list at the moment."

"Aren't you always?" Kate asked, then shrugged as both McGregors scowled at her in perfect unison. "They love you."

"I love you." Mikey gazed up at Darcy, awe in his eyes.

Darcy cleared her throat. Aqua eyes misted, and she splayed her hand over her chest. "My dear Sproutman, I am very fond of you too."

"And me." Susannah bumped Darcy's hip. "Let's go tell your mum that."

Darcy put her hands on her hips. "What are you up to?"

"I think you need to break Kate in about rehab," Susannah said, but it was a lie, if the averted gaze counted for anything.

Darcy narrowed her eyes.

"Let's go." Susannah flashed a smile and galloped off. Mikey galloped after her.

Kate stared at her feet. Could tension in a room throb? Felt like it. Felt like the space between them thrummed. "Rehab?"

"Yes," Darcy mumbled, staring after Susannah and Mikey. She sighed and straightened her shoulders. "It's a segment on how to attract men."

Why would she need that? Kate rolled her eyes. "Open another button on my shirt?"

"That's incredibly shallow." Darcy eyed her. "You're worth a lot more than that." She dropped her gaze to Kate's lips. "A woman can attract a man with her intelligence *and* beauty."

"Right. Pop another button on my shirt." She winked at her. Worked for the bloke in the gym. He'd given her a whole month's membership free once.

Darcy tapped her on the nose. "No. I don't want them offering payment, just a date."

"How does that help me again?" She got the fact it was a show, but if a guy liked her, he liked her, and she still wouldn't be interested.

"Because it's part of the show." Darcy sighed at her like she was being difficult, then held her gaze, full stun-look on. "Just try?"

"My eyelashes got a perm, doesn't that count?" She batted them and fixed on Darcy's lips. The gloss shimmered in the overhead lights. Looked… delicious. "What if I—?"

Darcy kissed her. Fruity gloss-covered lips captured her own, followed by a slender hand that threaded through her hair. The other hand eased her back against the door. Okay, conversation over. She was good with that. She pulled Darcy closer.

"Are we getting milk?" Mikey asked from somewhere down the hall. "I'll get Kate-oh."

Darcy pulled away, put her fingers to her lips.

Was it her or did they kiss…a lot? Darcy wouldn't kiss her if she was having an affair with Zoë, right? Why had Darcy kissed her? She shuddered out a breath. Why did it feel so…wow? "You like the eyelashes or the button?"

Darcy pursed her lips as Mikey galloped in.

"Kate-oh." He grinned. "We're not getting milk. Snap scum outside." He booed at the window.

"Yes." Darcy's smile was flustered. "Yes, they are." She turned and booed at the window too.

Susannah strolled in and raised her eyebrows. "You heckling the curtains, Mum?"

Mikey giggled, then looked up at Kate. "You make-up messy." He tutted, paused. His eyes went blank, and he wandered off.

Susannah and Darcy looked at her. Oh shit. Lipstick again. She shoved her hand over her mouth, but Susannah raised an eyebrow and smirked. "Should tell Luigi about that." She was focused on Darcy, eyebrow raised.

"Yes. He…needs to be less sloppy," Darcy mumbled, her cheeks as flushed as her neck. She strode into the kitchen and yanked open the fridge. "Oh look, we're out of milk. I'll go get some."

Darcy strode at her, and Kate shuffled out of the way. "What about the cameras?"

"I'll…I'll jog." Darcy hurried out of the door.

Susannah flashed a cheeky smile, then glanced Kate up and down. "Seriously, if you're going to snog, you need to carry a hanky."

Kate shrugged. "I wasn't expecting it. I'm not sure why we were."

"I do." Susannah grinned. "She never snogged Marshall."

"I doubt she would have done it around you if she did." Kate cleared her throat. How did she have these conversations?

"Didn't need to. I've never seen her *that* flustered before." She glanced her up and down again, then grinned and strolled off down the hall.

"Ever?" Surely Zoë had her blushing?

Susannah stopped outside her door. "Ever."

Kate leaned against the counter with a groan and touched her fingers to the greasy remnants of lipstick. Now, why did that make her grin from ear to ear?

CHAPTER 25

HOW DIFFERENT EVERYTHING FELT AROUND Kate and her calm smile. Darcy had been doing the show for years. It was safe, rewarding, easy on her. Each segment was for a good reason, and the rehab was no different. She took her blossoming patient to somewhere public and got to work on body language. Namely, it was to attract men, which had been fine, but now she was faced with *Kate* attracting a man, and her stomach clenched like she'd had a marathon Pilates session.

Maybe she should have talked to Kate instead of kissing her? Maybe she should have asked why Kate was kissing her, why Kate looked at her that way, but it was her fault; it had to be. Kate was in a vulnerable position. She must be awed by the program or the cameras, or maybe being around Darcy and Zoë was influencing her. Yes, Kate hadn't said anything about relationships. She'd been flustered in the examination when meeting a man had been mentioned; she'd been defensive, that humour creeping up when they'd talked about the rehab…and Kate had said herself the kisses were down to nerves. Darcy drummed her nails on her thigh. Yes, it was her fault; Kate was just responding to what she wanted. Must be.

Mikey was back in school for the week, so it was just the four of them: Marge was quiet up front with the driver. Susannah was on her tablet. Kate was opposite her in a strapless dress in purple and a large showpiece necklace, her hair styled to perfection, the feathering drawing out her green eyes and strong cheekbones. Kate smiled, her eyes twinkling with a nervous energy as she dropped her gaze to Darcy's lips. It was just a reaction to nerves, to being in a strange environment. It was. Kate cocked her eyebrow as if wondering what was going through her head, and Darcy clung to her jacket like it would save her.

Marge glanced over her shoulder at Susannah. Susannah nodded, her expression resolute.

"More press?" Darcy asked, trying not to look too uneasy. John had called three times during the day, saying that Zoë and Blanche only exacerbated the gossip, because it was clear Blanche felt threatened. He wanted a clear statement. She was not giving any such quarter.

"No. I just picked the restaurant. They have been really supporting you this show," Susannah said, her smile tight. "I want to show them you pay attention to the people who love you."

Darcy smiled. "There are many out there who love me." And they had impeccable taste. "But shows of support always look good." And she needed to get John back on side.

Susannah rolled her eyes. "I knew the fake had to be lurking in there somewhere."

"We're here. Ready?" Marge pulled out her camera, then nodded to the crew outside. "And rolling."

Darcy got out behind Kate and Susannah. "Rehabilitation is the way to make your clothes work for you. It's not just what you put on but how you wear it." She flashed a quick smile in Kate's direction while keeping her gaze on the camera. If she didn't look at Kate, maybe it would be less painful? "Let's show you off."

Susannah squinted as flashes went off all around them—press had arrived. She nodded to Marge, who led them into a small restaurant.

"Ms McGregor, it's a pleasure to see you. We have our best table ready," a large woman with short dark hair said. Waistcoat? Very retro. Went with the wide-legged trousers and well-tailored shirt. Someone was a fan.

"It's a pleasure to be here…" She looked to Susannah. A name would be helpful.

"Seren," Susannah said with a charming smile. "Mum wasn't sure if you were Jemma. She keeps getting you mixed up."

Seren laughed. "We're pretty much interchangeable." She glanced at Kate, then did a double take, and cleared her throat. "And you are Ms Bonvilston. Good to see you."

Kate shook her hand with an anxious smile. "Weird that you know my surname. My boss can't even remember it."

Seren laughed. "Oh, everyone is talking about *you*." She winked, then glanced at Darcy. She led them through gaggles of wide-eyed customers to a secluded table at the back. "Jemma is working on something special." She glanced at Kate. "No gluten."

"None for me either." Darcy smiled and took a seat. "Or Susannah."

"No gluten all round it is." Seren left, and Marge and Susannah took up a table across the walkway from them. The crew took up spaces at strategic tables. They would be as discreet as they could with huge cameras.

"Why no gluten?" Kate whispered, then chewed on her lip. "Am I allowed to ask that on TV?"

Kate could ask anything she liked as long as she kept that gorgeous smile on her face. "Of course you are. I gave it up with Susannah."

Susannah nodded. "Better for her figure."

"Or a show of support?" Kate asked and grinned over at Susannah. "Couldn't imagine anyone giving up gluten for me."

Susannah glanced at Darcy, studying her, then dropped her gaze to her tablet. "Tweet question."

"We haven't done anything yet," Darcy muttered. How could Susannah think it was just about her figure? She let out a chuckle to cover the tone. Nerves. Snappy on camera was not good.

"Ivy from Berkshire says that if she gives up gluten..." Susannah snickered, then laughed. "If she gives up gluten, will Kate marry her?" She shrugged. "She's eighty-four."

Kate stared at her. "She's drooling over me? Are you sure she doesn't mean Darcy?"

Darcy leaned on her fist. How could she blame Ivy? "Do we need rehab at all? We'll just marry you off to Ivy."

Kate let out a breathy chuckle. "Ivy, you don't have to give anything up. You're fantastic as you are."

Who needed help with being on TV? Kate didn't seem nervous, but then when had she ever? It was only the kissing that showed it. And *why* had Kate kissed her? Why would a woman into gay men find that helped to calm nerves? And *why* had it felt beyond a kiss somehow?

"Well, Ivy, you'll have to wait until I'm finished with her." She tensed. Sounded proprietary. Susannah raised an eyebrow and exchanged a glance with Marge. "We need to work on body language." She fussed with her napkin. Ignore the flush; ignore Kate's twinkling eyes. "The way she carries herself may be giving off the wrong signals to Mr Right."

Susannah and Marge exchanged another glance.

Kate blinked a few times.

Why was she looking shocked? Didn't she think Darcy could find her a man? She could pull a man. "You show insecurity in…odd…ways." Pleasant ways that involved slow kisses filled with aching need. "You tighten up when men are around." Then got mouthy. At least to her, but she wasn't a man or making an approach. "And make little eye contact." With men, anyway. Not unless she was bantering with them. "So by giving you practice, you can attract a man."

Susannah held up her phone. "Ivy says forget the body language, she makes fruit cake. She can make gluten-free fruit cake."

Kate snorted with laughter. "Cheers, Ivy."

Darcy rolled her eyes. "So how do you approach someone you fancy?"

Kate sighed. "Badly, by the sound of it."

"Do you have moves?" How could any man worry about body language when Kate looked so incredible—and did even in a security uniform?

"No. I haven't needed any. I dated in my social circle." Kate stumbled over her words and stared at her hands. Heartbreak? Regret?

"And how did you know it was more than friendship?" Some previous patients bawled at this point, but Kate just shrugged.

"They came onto me," she said as she studied the tablecloth.

Not helpful. She looked around. "See this gentleman here. How would you signal that you liked him and were happy for him to come over?"

Kate eyed her, then the guy. He was rugged with designer stubble and big pec muscles. Yes, he'd look good next to her. Jerk.

"Try it." She hoped her tone stayed calmer than she felt. The man sat at a table with three other men.

Kate shook her head, a bemused smile on her face, then got up and strode over—not elegantly—and within seconds the men were laughing with her as she thumbed over her shoulder. Then two of the men started feeding each other dessert. Ah.

"Get back here," she snapped, and Kate strode back over. "When you're in a dress, you do not stride like you're in uniform." Had she listened to Zoë at all?

"Sorry." Kate plonked down into her seat. "He's not interested."

"Quite." She fixed on her. "You don't stride over; *he* has to come to you." And any man with eyes…who was attracted to women…would swan over. He'd flash a charming smile and say some bland line. Kate would blush and gaze up at him… And now she wanted to poke some imaginary suitor? Wonderful. "You catch his eye, hold it…beckon him to you with that smile." She held Kate's eyes, smiled, and dropped her head to the side, feeding her hand through her hair. "Could you doubt what I wanted?"

Kate's eyes deepened, her necklace bouncing with her breathing, and she cleared her throat.

Darcy's pulse thudded.

Marge coughed.

She flicked her gaze to the water glass and tapped Kate's warm hand. "Your turn."

"You're not a guy, though," Kate whispered with a sultry smile, her gaze on Darcy's lips.

"Just pretend I am." She swallowed the ache of it. Trust her to fall in love with a woman who would more likely enjoy a candlelit dinner with the men on the far table.

Wait—what? Had she just thought that? No, no, no. Kate glanced at Marge and Susannah. No. She hadn't just thought that. She couldn't think that. Nope, no way.

"Just make eyes at me, woman," she snapped and tapped Kate's hand again, wanting to grab it, to hold it, to run her thumb over the elegant long fingers and… Breathe. "Stop being difficult."

Kate raised an eyebrow.

"Yes. I'm bossy. Get on with it." And it hurt she had to push. Hurt that her heart was pumping so hard, that Kate was there, so close, so beautiful, yet could never be hers.

"Alright…" Kate fixed her with a smouldering gaze that held her there, then dropped to her lips—Kate licked her own. That potent gaze raked over her cleavage, then flicked back to her eyes with *that* look. The look that made her come undone.

Oh shit. Darcy shuddered out her breath. Why was Kate single? Who resisted that? She couldn't. She wanted to yank her across the table…or onto it…or… Oh dear. "Yes, well… That's great."

Kate raised an eyebrow, still gazing at her, calling to her, pulling her to lean across.

"No issues with eye contact, then," she squeaked, picked up her napkin, and flapped it around. Torture. That's what this was—torture. She looked to Susannah. Hopefully she'd scowl or tell her off for looking at Kate in such a way but, no, Susannah chewed on her lip as she stared at her tablet.

"Tweet question?" Darcy asked just to focus on something other than diving across the table.

"Er..." Susannah exchanged yet another glance with Marge.

"Out with it." Darcy scowled. She needed questions.

"Miles from Dover asks if it wouldn't be easier if Kate just focused... on you." Susannah wheezed out a breath. "He says you make a hot couple."

Oh shit, even Miles from flipping Dover could see her drooling? What would Kate's mother think? She trusted Darcy to help her daughter, and what? She was making a fool of herself. A complete fool. Panic thudded through her and she stood. "Cut."

Kate grabbed for her hand. "He's joking."

"Move to Zoë and Blanche's piece on lighting." Marge lowered the camera, studying her. "Darcy?"

"I can't... I have... I feel unwell." She hurried from the cameras and closed herself in the bathroom. She felt...unwell...yes, or maybe a better term would be lovesick. She slid down the door with a thud. Lovesick... Love.... Oh shit.

CHAPTER 26

KATE FIDDLED WITH THE TABLECLOTH, not sure what to make of Darcy hurrying off. She looked distressed. Yeah, it had been intense staring into her eyes; it had been romantic, but nothing too obvious. Why had it freaked Darcy out so much? Hadn't she been with Zoë for years? Hadn't she let Zoë kiss her in public? Like anyone watching would think Darcy would look at her.

"I should go check on her," Susannah whispered, chewing on her lip. She looked at the camera crew, who had given up on waiting for Darcy to come back and were eating the feast of delicious food Seren and Jemma had provided.

"She'll need to be back out here soon," Marge said, covering the receiver on her phone with one hand and jotting notes with the other. "John wants us back live. We have a filler running now, but we need to have a live round-up." She winced and pulled the phone away from her ear. "We need some recorded footage here too."

Susannah nodded and went to get up, only for Zoë to stroll in and take up a seat opposite Kate. "You got me instead. Darcy called me. She has a stomach bug, and she doesn't want the owners to think it's their food."

Sketchy at best. Kate fiddled with the tablecloth, twirling the strands around her finger. Zoë met her eyes and leaned in as Marge and the camera crew rushed to set up. "It's not your fault, sweetheart."

Then why did it feel that way?

Susannah glanced in the direction of the bathroom again, and Zoë reached across the gap and took her hand. "She's gone home. You're stuck with me and Blanche for the night."

"I should be there for her." Susannah's scowl was all Darcy in a temper.

Zoë squeezed her hand. "No. Trust me that it's better you just let her figure it out." She sighed and turned to Kate as Marge picked up her phone again.

"What do you mean, she's around Gregory Hampton's house?" Marge snapped, then glared at Zoë. "She is meant to be sick." She pulled the phone away. "What is going on?"

"You played her, and now you get a show. Hampton's been fishing for attention for months." Zoë sighed and held onto Susannah's hand as she tried pulling free. "So let's get this round-up filmed so I can explain to my wife why I've come running...again."

Kate rubbed at the tablecloth again, then nodded. Why had what Zoë said shot searing hot pain through her chest? Why did her defeated tone make Kate feel so...helpless? "She did this to you?"

Zoë smiled a sad smile, heartbreak in her eyes.

"And rolling," Marge said with a growl.

"So, Kate here is a lady, and I know way more about pulling the ladies," Zoë said to the camera, full, dazzling smile on display like she hadn't had that raw hurt in her eyes only seconds before. "Darcy has handed over to the expert."

Seren bustled over with the food, then stopped and blushed from ear to ear. Oh, she was definitely a Zoë Windermere fan. "I hope the gluten-free version is okay?"

Zoë flashed her a charming smile. "Honey, it's my job to keep healthy and looking good. Gluten-free is the way to go."

Susannah rolled her eyes, and for the first time, Kate understood why—fake. Hadn't they just seen Zoë chomping on donuts not long ago? The front presented, no matter the feeling inside, was completely fake.

"So, what am I doing so wrong that no man would bother looking at me?" Kate asked and thunked back into her chair. She couldn't be bothered with this, show or no show.

"Oh, honey." Zoë let out a bellowing laugh. "FYI, viewers, Darcy seems to think that good old Kate here likes guys..." She rolled her eyes. "Poor thing hasn't a clue that Kate's ex just had a guy's name."

Kate raised her eyebrows. "She does?" Hadn't kissing Darcy given her a slight clue that she might be into women?

"Yep. Best we keep that between us." Zoë winked and looked Kate up and down. "The rules are different for us; our body language is not the same, and neither is our flirting." She smiled at the camera. "So, listen up 'cause this is how to pull in the ladies."

Kate leaned her hand on her fist. She didn't want to pull any lady. All she wanted to do was run after Darcy and stop her. Gregory Hampton. She knew of him from tabloids. He was some rich business guy who looked... slimy. Yuck.

"Honey, I need your focus," Zoë muttered and tapped her on the hand. "We'll spend the evening working on your flirting skills." She winked at the camera. "Which you can catch on the next show, but here's the quick rundown of how to get ladies—"

"I can't." She rubbed her hands over her face. "I can't... I like *her*." She couldn't be fake, and she didn't care that it was on camera. The realisation swirled up, and she rubbed at her neck. "I...I can't."

Zoë flashed a warning look at her. Darcy didn't need pushing, she got that.

"I really like her..." She glanced at Susannah, who beamed at her. At least one McGregor didn't want to beat her. "Darcy hasn't done anything." Anything much, if she didn't count the kissing bit. "I think I freaked her out." She turned to the camera. "I didn't mean to, but...I...I *love* her."

"And cut, move to the credits." Marge stared at her and blew out a breath. Her phone rang. She looked down at it, then shoved it to the side.

Zoë cocked her head, her focus on Kate, then slumped her shoulders and let through a gentle smile. "So let's find you a lady who won't freak out."

"I don't want that." She didn't know what Darcy had told Zoë or why, but she couldn't lie. She couldn't be fake. "I don't even know her, and I love her."

Marge leaned on her fist. "Yes, you just told prime-time television."

Susannah got up and hurried over to Kate's chair. "Then please go and find her." She pulled out her phone. "The driver will know where." Kate stood, and Susannah slumped down and fixed on Zoë. "You can teach me instead. I don't know how to attract anyone."

Brave kid.

"We've got tweets coming in like crazy." Marge gave her a thumbs up.

The camera's red light blinked on, and Zoë pulled over her tablet. "Tweet question: Jane from Hereford is asking how to know when a woman is interested."

Susannah smiled. "She makes a lot of eye contact?"

Zoë nodded and waved at Kate. "Go." She turned to the camera. "Yes. Eye contact crosses all boundaries..."

Kate hurried from the table out into the evening air. The car was waiting. He was quick. She pulled open the passenger-side door and jumped in.

"You should sit in the back, Ms Bonvilston," the driver said with a smile.

"That's for posh people." She winked at him. "Don't suppose you know where Gregory Hampton lives?"

"Yes, but if you're looking for Ms McGregor, she's in her Kensington house." He roared them off through the traffic. "I believe she may be watching the show."

Kate lay her head back into the seat. "Oh dear... Wait, what house?"

"Her private residence. The apartment is for the show." He smiled. "Ms Windermere knows a lot about her, ma'am. Trust her to help." He zipped through an impossible gap and around the waiting traffic at a red light.

"Guess I'll have to," she mumbled and looked out at the clear, orangey glow of the sky overhead. "I only hope Darcy isn't going to punch me."

He chuckled. "She reserves that for actors, ma'am."

Her laugh came out a snort, and she smiled at him. Yeah, hopefully her elite role as a pencil security guard would win favour... Hopefully.

CHAPTER 27

DARCY POURED HERSELF A GLASS of wine. She'd panicked, completely panicked, in the bathroom. A long, sobbing phone call with Zoë had only sent her running to Gregory Hampton, who, thankfully, wasn't home—knee-jerk reaction. She was terrible for them. Now she'd had a tweet and short video from Zoë, showing she was with Susannah and teaching her all kinds of flirting tips that were completely ridiculous. Who attracted a woman by sliding her arm around the back of the chair? She frowned. Okay, it was quite sexy when Zoë did it, but then Zoë was sexy. Being attracted to her had never been an issue. She shook her head and downed the wine. Better to forget that.

Someone knocked on the door, and she poured another glass. She'd sent Gladys home for the night for peace and quiet. Yes, whoever it was could go away, especially Gregory. She felt sick enough as it was. How could being in love with someone she didn't know make her feel so…acutely? How could she and Kate ever work anyway? Regardless of the simple statement that Kate wasn't into men—her stomach swirled again—or the sweet way Kate said she liked her, all the while covering for her—her stomach clenched. Kate had said she loved her—her heart thudded—oh, how did she ignore that?

Someone knocked the door again.

She sighed and wandered to it. Maybe it was Gregory and she could put him right? She yanked open the door, ready to yell, only for Kate to be there.

"Hi."

Darcy's stomach ached…along with every single pore. "You shouldn't be here."

"No." Kate held her gaze with determination, confidence, not a trace of uncertainty.

Her heart thumped, the cold air tickled her cheeks, and desire trickled through her stomach. That look, that sultry, sexy, cheeky, irritating look. Intense, too intense. Heart pounded, making it hard to catch her breath. No, she needed, she shouldn't... It was stupid. Should send her away. Had to send her away. Had to resist...find control.

Kate's eyes twinkled. Her lips glistened in the light from the streetlamp. "I'm not leaving."

The words soaked in, breath sharp to her ears. It was torture. Kate was there, there for her. How... She needed... Her pulse pounded... She should... "I should send you away."

Heartbeat heavier, straining.

"'Should' means you won't." Kate leaned one hand on the doorjamb. "Ask me in."

Heavy, hard-pounding, heart... Needed... She needed... Oh, pure, sweet need...

"No." She went to shut the door.

Kate caught her hand and pulled her outside. The touch. That soft, warm touch. Need... Oh, how she needed...

She growled and yanked Kate to her, wrapped her arms around Kate's bare shoulders, threaded her hands into her soft, glossy hair. She sank into soft, waiting lips, her heart faster, heavier—her kiss intense. The ache in her stomach radiated out, rippled through her—deeper, more frantic.

Need. Desperate, tear-filled need.

Kate gripped her waist, slid a hand to the middle of her back, and eased closer, the kiss growing, building momentum—more, fervent. Needed more. She fed the sheer thrill pounding through her body. Too good. Kissing her was too good.

"In." She dragged Kate inside, slammed the door, and shoved her against it. When had she ever been this crazy? This desperate just to get closer? Zoë had come close...yes...but never this, never complete overload with a kiss.

Kate yanked at her shirt, slid her hands up, the feel of her fingertips tickling over her sides and up her ribcage, eased over her breasts. Building, aching need—more, needed more.

She growled and shoved herself backward, panting like she'd jogged the London Marathon.

Kate searched her eyes, her hair completely in a mess, lipstick tracking each messy kiss, each move of her lips. Her cheeks were flushed, her eyes beckoning, and her showpiece necklace rose and fell like a magnet.

"How dare you tell everyone you love me." She yanked off her shirt. Was she mad? Was she desperate? Crazed, whatever it was, it was... She couldn't take it anymore.

"I love you." Kate said it with such force her eyes sparkled. "I don't know why, I don't know how. I just do. I love you."

"Stop saying that." She yanked off her bra, dropped her trousers, and stepped out of them.

Kate smiled a half-smile, gaze running up and down her. "Why? It's making you strip."

"Yes." She turned and headed to the stairs. "Move."

"I love it when you're bossy." Kate caught her halfway up. Pulled her close. She'd undressed. Soft warm skin against her own thighs, against her buttocks, against her back. Warm hands slid over her hips, sending aching ripples through her. Sharp breath. She closed her eyes. "You get that, right?"

"Shut up and kiss me." She arched back, captured Kate's lips, and eased into a slow, rolling kiss, a kiss that teased, if Kate's whimper was anything to go by. Yes, she loved that sound.

Kate shoved her up the few remaining stairs. "I'll give you 'shut up and kiss me.'" Kate yanked her around and hoisted her up until she had to wrap her thighs around Kate's slender hips. "You thought I liked men. *How* could you think I liked men?"

"You dated someone called Bennie. Your mother did not give details." She smothered Kate's elegant cheekbones with kisses, smothered her neck. She grazed her teeth over the side of the smooth skin beneath Kate's ear.

"I love you, you hear me?" Kate slid a strong hand in her hair and eased her back, holding them inches apart. "And you are *so* not a bloke."

She laughed; she couldn't help it. It sounded half delighted, half like she was going to claw at her. She sank into Kate's lips, tugged at them, trailed her fingernails over Kate's back. "Say it again."

"Which part?" Kate gasped and stumbled to the left. "Where is your room, woman?"

"There are five. As long as it's not the one on your left, I really don't care." She half groaned, half roared as Kate raked her shorter nails over her thighs. "Say it."

"I love you." Kate rammed her into the wall, then grunted.

"That's the wall, idiot." She hauled them through the doorway, gripping the doorjamb. "Keep saying it."

"I love you," Kate whispered, throwing her onto the bed. The dim glow from the streetlight beyond the window illuminated her figure, her soft skin, her smile. "You're a bitch, but I love you." She climbed onto her, grabbed her hands, and placed them behind her head. "I love you."

She pulled free, eased Kate down, and groaned—much like Kate—as soft, strong warmth wrapped around her. "I am a bitch."

"Yes." Kate nipped at her earlobe, her neck, her collarbone. "I love you for it."

She lay back and closed her eyes with a smile. "Good. I'm sick of pretending."

CHAPTER 28

KATE ROLLED OUT OF BED, feeling like she'd been beaten. Good beaten, as in Darcy was in a whole other league from any woman she'd ever been near. Beaten as in she was aching everywhere and pretty sure she could have scars on her back. Beaten as in somehow she'd fallen asleep in the morning—and only when Darcy had let her—and beaten because Darcy hadn't slept in the same room.

Clothes were folded up on a chair for her, including a pair of boxers, but it was past noon and the house was quiet. She sighed and dressed—felt like an intruder somehow. Could she still be done for trespassing if she showed the bruises? Then again, maybe Darcy would just claim self-defence.

She wandered out onto the landing. Staring back was a huge picture of that iconic moment with Darcy and Zoë in high contrast black and white—yeah, trespassing.

"Don't look so glum," Darcy whispered from the stairs. She had a tray with toast and more orange juice. "It's there because Susannah wanted me to keep it."

She tried to shove her hands in her pockets, then frowned down at the fitted jeans. Where were the pockets?

"On the front," Darcy said with a soft smile on her face—must have been up a while. The energy that people had who loved mornings buzzed around her.

"Oh." Kate shoved her hands in the pockets. Yeah, that was not as comfortable. "You sleep alright?" Awkward much?

"I didn't sleep." Darcy smiled and took her by the hand, leading her back to bed. "I rarely sleep more than a few hours at a time."

"Then how do you have the energy to stand upright?" Why was Darcy in gym clothes? How had she needed more of a workout?

"Practice." Darcy placed the tray on the bedside table and pushed her down. "Hopefully you'll find the toast more palatable." She shoved a piece in her mouth. Kate chewed on it as Darcy sat beside her and curled one leg up under the other. "I shouldn't have invited you in…or let you stay over. You understand that?"

"This where you tell me to keep quiet, or you'll make me wear puffy pink?" She chomped on the toast. Not bad. Better than the cardboard cornflakes.

"This is where I ask you to respect that I've let you in and…you have a massive amount on me right now." She sighed and flicked back her blonde hair. "And I hope you don't get offended that I'm having this conversation with you."

"You think I'll sell out?" Offended, that was an understatement. Ouch.

"I need to hear you won't." Darcy met her eyes, gentle, resolute. "I feel as vulnerable as you. I don't know you." She hugged herself. "Kate, if you talk to anyone, I lose my career and…Susannah. I know she thinks in idealistic ways, but…" She picked at Kate's jeans. "Zoë lost a massive amount of professional friends. Personally, they don't care; publicly, she doesn't exist anymore."

"But she's doing alright." Had Darcy missed the slick look, the designing career, the billboard wife?

"No, she was asked not to attend London Fashion Week." She rubbed her palm over Kate's knee. "Several stars turned down wearing her clothes to the premieres, and…" She leaned in and kissed her. "Blanche is only on the billboard because the designer is a personal friend of mine and he stuck his neck out."

"Aren't most of the designers gay?" Was it her, or wasn't fashion pretty camp on a good day?

"The male ones." Darcy kissed her again and sat back. "They'll all accept her again, but when you break a mould, you get punished. Rumours fly around, and it takes years to claw back." She stroked her fingernail over Kate's forearm. "It probably doesn't mean a lot to you, but it's our livelihood."

She chomped more toast. Were there rumours about Zoë? Who listened to the rumours? "There's plenty of gay people on TV, in the arts."

"Any that you see working?" Darcy peered under her eyebrows. "They as successful as they were before they opened their mouth?"

"I dunno. I don't pay attention to it." She finished up her toast and placed it on the table.

"Yes, because it's just gossip about someone you don't know." Darcy sighed and pulled out her phone. She handed it over. "Read it."

Kate took it then frowned. Some young model was saying that she had a steamy affair with Zoë and how kind and gentle Zoë was. "She did?"

"No. Do you know why I know, why Blanche is less bothered about this little issue?" Darcy leaned onto one hand. The light from the snowy sky bathed her in a white, high-contrast light.

"Not sure I want to ask...?" She glanced through the doorway at the picture of the catwalk.

"Zoë is very much a product of the fashion scene. This girl is too short, has hips wider than a twig, and her teeth are not perfect." She took the phone back. "She'd rather date a man."

Okay, Zoë was really superficial. "That's...shallow."

"No, that's what she likes, what attracts her...as in to completely dismantle what career she has left, to lose that twig she enjoys the attention of..." And it sounded like Darcy was angry about it. "Plus risk her family's irritation, along with mine and Susannah's... The girl would need to be something Zoë couldn't resist."

Darcy flicked through the phone and handed it over again. "Read this one."

Kate sighed and took it. She wasn't sure if she wanted to. She liked Zoë; she didn't want to think of her looking at someone like that. She scowled. It was a story about Darcy this time. A young man, no more than twenty, saying that he was Darcy's lover and she'd lured him in and had been very sweet.

She laughed. "Oh, I know that one isn't true. I've got scars to prove it."

Darcy winked. "Yes, but if you were John, in charge of allowing the programme to go ahead, or a school inviting me in to talk about women in fashion...?" She took the phone back. "Would you want me on an advert for your product, risking that this could be true and I did this?"

"No." Oh. She took her orange juice and downed it, ready for the bits to make her gag. She didn't. It was smooth. "I wouldn't do that to you."

"But you could change your mind at any time. Do you think John would hesitate in removing me from the air if he thought for a second that we were lovers?" She smiled and stroked Kate's cheek. "I have women in my house for the show. I break you down to build you up. You're vulnerable."

"I'm not dense most of the time." She frowned and gripped the glass. "I don't think you do this with every…patient."

"Maybe you don't, but you don't control if I have a job." Darcy flicked her gaze to the doorway. "Mine depends on me being a brand. A brand people trust."

"I can't take back that I said I love you, and I won't." She handed the glass back. "You took the bits out."

"Yes. You prefer it that way." Darcy leaned in and kissed her, fleeting, teasing. "I like that you said you love me, but I cannot respond to it on camera."

"Is that a permanent decision?" And could she hack that?

"Yes. My job depends on it, and it secures a home for Susannah." Darcy sighed and got up, flexing her calves. "She comes first."

"How do I fit?" Both Zoë and Darcy protected Susannah. Susannah, like Kate, didn't understand. How could she ever understand? To her, Darcy could just do something else. She and Zoë could open a shop or something. Did they even need to work?

"The same way Zoë did for so long, although Susannah likes you a great deal, and there's no reason to hide it from her now…in private. In public, we will always be friendly, but never more. It's all I can offer." Darcy stretched out her shoulders. "But you need to figure out if you can live with it."

"Wow, I feel so cheap." She got up and strode out the door.

The picture of Zoë and Darcy looked back at her. Fit the label, Darcy's label, just like she'd fit Bennie's label and Laura's label. She headed down the stairs, somehow knowing Darcy wasn't going to follow. Not a show of if she cared or not—who knew what Darcy felt—but a statement of what was expected. If she didn't fit the label, the scissors would come out; that's what Blanche had muttered about Darcy calling her. Fit the label, be a model… No, an unthinking dummy who just did as told. She shook her head as she hurried out of the door. Cameras flashed, and she stumbled down the steps. A label.

She scowled, wiping the tears from her eyes. She'd always hated labels.

CHAPTER 29

DARCY FOCUSED ON MUNDANE TASKS: laundry, mopping, polishing, even though Gladys had done a good job. Snow had fluttered down from the late-February sky. She tried to ignore the gnawing clench in her stomach and the flutter of excitement from replayed moments. Over and over, she replayed Kate's eyes filled with hurt. She'd been honest—what more did Kate want? Did she truly expect some public announcement? Did she think that she was in a romance novel?

As she vacuumed the stairs, the evening dusk eased in until she needed to flick on the hallway light. She sighed and flicked the wires around the vacuum cleaner and stared up at the nautical barometer on the wall. Duplicitous. Her father had been two different people. He'd flitted from one home to another with no thought of the damage. She'd hated him for it, never spoke to him again for it. So then, why did it feel as if she had become him?

"Honey," Zoë said as she strode into the hallway, shaking off her coat. "You gonna make me a coffee? It's freezing out."

Susannah trudged in behind her and shook the snow out of her hair. "I'll get it." She walked over, kissed Darcy on the cheek, and looked at her like she was some kind of hero. "Is Kate in the kitchen?"

Yes, the same look Darcy had gazed up at her father with. Would Susannah come to hate her as much? "No, she went out."

Susannah nodded and waltzed off, bouncing as she went. Made a nice change from the skulking teenager.

"What did you do?" Zoë let out a long sigh and took the vacuum cleaner from her.

"What do you mean?" Why did Zoë have to pick up on everything? Wasn't it bad enough she knew her so well? Why did she have to prove that every five seconds?

"Housework." Zoë tapped the vacuum cleaner. "You only do the housework when you're stewing."

"I am not stewing." Much. "Now, why are you here? Shouldn't you be at the apartment or with that twig of yours?"

Zoë raised an eyebrow. "We're attending your book launch. If you can call someone else writing your words *your* work."

Darcy frowned. She headed to the calendar in the kitchen—some things from her mother were embedded—and chewed on her lip. "Marge wants it as part of the program."

"Yeah. So where's Kate? Need me to go offer ice?" Zoë's tone was far too teasing. Darcy tensed. Susannah raised her eyebrows. She dropped the spoon in the cups, making coffee jump up at her, and Zoë laughed. "You know, in case you socked her one?"

Susannah sniggered and seemed to discount any assumptions. "Hope you took your ring off first, or she'll get a scar like Marshall."

Darcy glared at Zoë.

Zoë studied her, then scowled. "Oh, you didn't mess it up already?"

"Excuse me?" She heard the irritation in her voice. Odd. Sounded like Zoë had hit a sore spot.

"You did, didn't you?" Zoë threw her hands in the air. "The woman goes and says she loves you to millions of viewers, and, what, you tell her you gotta be some fake face?"

"It's none of your business what I told her." She turned from Zoë and headed into the hallway. She would have to dress, find something fitting for the occasion. She needed a shower. How could she have forgotten?

"Not my business?" Zoë stormed after her and caught her elbow. "You gonna shove me out the door again too?"

"You walked out of your own accord." And her voice was getting higher. Silly to rise to baiting. Calm. "I didn't shove you anywhere."

"No?" Zoë gripped her by the arms. "Just because you don't say the words out loud doesn't mean you aren't saying it with your eyes." She flicked her hand toward the door. "What you tell her? She gotta shut up and put up?"

"Yes." Her voice had a gritty sound. She rubbed at her throat. Needed a lemon tea, yes. Would do no good to read from a book when she was hoarse.

"Are you stupid?" Zoë gripped her arms tighter like she wanted to shake the sense into her. "Someone actually loves you for the bitch you are and you send her running?"

"She doesn't know me." And that was a growl. She shrugged Zoë off and stomped to the stairs. And the temper was bubbling. "You don't know me."

"Don't I?" Zoë stomped up after her. "You gonna lie to yourself about that too? You gonna lie and say that your mom didn't take it out on you that your dad was a slimeball?" She stomped closer. "You gonna lie and say that you couldn't bear the family who took you in when your mom died, that you couldn't bear the thought of playing the same play your parents did? You gonna be a fake or a failure like them?" She stepped into her space. "You gonna lie and say that watching me and Kate walk out the door didn't rip a hole right through you?"

Smack. She slapped Zoë across the cheek.

Zoë blinked.

Susannah put her hands over her mouth at the bottom of the stairs. Wonderful. Not only was she her father, but she'd added in her mother too.

"You have no idea what you did to me, walking away," she whispered, glaring into Zoë's eyes. Blurry. Tears? That was helpful. What did crying solve? "You broke me."

Zoë's eyes glinted. "You broke me first."

"So let the girl go home when the show's done and save her the trouble of a broken heart." She turned and strode up the stairs. The best way not to be her parents was to ensure no one had to live with her scars.

CHAPTER 30

KATE WANDERED UP AND DOWN the riverbank of the murky, swirling Thames. Snow filled the air, and people hunched over, hurrying home from work or scurrying from the bus to the shop or Tube stations. It was so different to Wales. People smiled or said hello in Wales. They didn't have to know you. But in London—maybe because everything about it felt so cold—people seemed harsher, unfriendly, suspicious. The metal lampposts speared into the snowy mist and glinted in an eerie glow that cast itself over the Gothic stone architecture of Westminster to the fairground ride of the London Eye. She passed the crowds lined up to see buildings from a glass bubble, and her heart sank with a swell of loneliness. Stupid to fall in love with someone she didn't know. Stupid to think someone like Darcy could love her. What had she been thinking?

"Kate?" Some woman called out. Sounded older. She turned over her shoulder. Who did she know in London?

The woman was in her fifties, perhaps—big, thick, puffy jacket and a big beaming smile on her face. Her two friends, also ladies around the same age in matching puffy coats, waved and pulled out their phones.

"Ooh, it is you!" The woman hurried over and peered at her like she was in exhibit. Er, had they taken a wrong turn in the museum? "Can we have a picture?"

"Sure." She held out her hand. Maybe they just wanted someone to get the London Eye in the background. "You want to huddle together?"

The woman laughed. "No, we want a picture *with* you." She pulled out her phone and shoved a selfie-stick in it. "That okay?"

Surrounded by three puffer jackets, what could she say? At least it was warm. "Um…okay?" Maybe they knew Mum?

"You were so brave." One of the friends said. "You bared your heart, you did, and I hope Darcy appreciated it." She bumped Kate's shoulder with hers. "Not sure she's on your team, though."

The other friend leaned across the front of Kate and poked her friend. "She'd be lucky to have her, Bev." She grinned up at Kate. "I'm as straight as they come, and I'd have had a moment over that." She chuckled a husky chuckle. "So romantic."

The first woman nodded. "Me too. We loved the show before, but it's miles better with you in it."

They pointed up to the camera and Kate faked her best smile. Weird. That's what this conversation was: weird. It was the kind that Mum had with her mates out shopping or at whatever faddy exercise class they were into.

"You know, Wardie loved the bra," the second friend said with a titter. "I said to him, 'Luv, if my boobs weren't hitting my kneecaps, I'd stick one on for you.'"

The first friend reached across Kate and patted the other friend, howling with laughter. "Oh, my Bill goes all silent when you're on, Kate. He's got the hots for you, he has."

"Don't blame him," the first woman said, squeezing Kate's arm. "You're a looker, you are."

The three women giggled.

Oh wow. This was just getting weirder. Now she had images of large breasts drooping into a lacy bra, some man having the hots for her, and the three women heckling her about it. A flash popped again. She clamped her eyes shut. Ow. She scowled through the blue dots at some guy with a camera. He'd been following her? Yeah, she'd seen him behind her a few times.

"Did you get to talk to her?" the first woman asked, focus on her. "I heard she was sick."

The second friend frowned. "I heard she went over that Gregory what's-his-name's house. There were pictures of her."

The first friend "shh'd" her and glanced up at Kate. "Nonsense. She's better than him."

"She was better than that Marshall bloke too," the second friend shot back. "Didn't stop her holidaying with him in the Canaries, did it?"

All three looked to her like they wanted an answer, and the guy with the camera's flash popped again. Right, should she answer? What did she say? Yes, she just spent the night with her, and then Darcy had treated her like a fling? That she'd felt so...important? Special? Cherished? Then, come the morning, like some cheap tart with just a simple conversation.

"Hey, Kate!" a guy yelled out from the queue to the London Eye. "I'll marry you!"

A few people from the queue looked over, then grinned. Some just stared from the guy to Kate.

"Kate, did she tell you she loves you back?" another guy asked, walking up to her with a group of tourists with backpacks. "Does she love you?"

"Kate? Hey, that's Kate Bonvilston!" someone else yelled, and people turned to fix on her. Creeped forward toward her.

"Kate, can I have your autograph?" From the left.

"Selfie? I want a selfie." From the right.

Flash popped.

"Kate, we love Mikey. Will you tell him?" Right. Left. Front. Back. People moving at her, towards her. The three women bustled closer. Flash popped again. Crowd around her, tugging at her for attention. She stumbled backward. Wow, why were they so set on her? What did a picture with her mean? She wasn't anyone.

"Kate, you think you have a chance with her?" Flash popped again. "You think some dog-faced stalker like you will get her attention?" Flash popped more. Blue shapes. Blinding light. "Come on, Kate, smile for the camera."

She stumbled towards the road, and a car screeched to a halt. The door opened. Zoë grabbed her and yanked her inside, and the car screeched off.

"Are you trying to get mobbed?" Zoë muttered at her, checking her over. "Great, they ripped your jeans."

She righted herself. "Why were they so crazy?"

"Are you kidding? You got more hits than the national soccer team." Zoë rubbed at her shoulders. "You must be freezing."

"Huh, yeah." She was shaking, she knew that much. Crazy flipping people. "I don't get it."

"I know." Zoë met her eyes. "Look, Darcy is like a national institution. An international star. Not only that, *everyone* knows her. If they know

Gucci or Dolce and Gabbana, Calvin Klein underwear, Hilfiger, not to mention any beauty product, she's been their face. Everyone knows her face." She leaned in and tapped her on the forehead. "The show is just small fries to her."

"I get that. If they were mobbing her, I'd get that." She frowned. "Why me?"

"She's been that face, that personality, that poise, since she was sixteen. No one gets to see beyond the veneer. No one." Zoë sighed and sat back, smiling at the driver. "You, you just dismantled her in front of millions of eager viewers."

"I didn't. She's been the same." Hadn't she? Darcy was as she always was: professional, edged with bitchy, glossed over with a stunning smile.

"No. No one has ever seen that much personality from her. I can't remember when I did." Zoë smiled at her as the driver roared them through the lightening traffic. "You got through the chink."

Kate laughed. Sounded confused and shaky. "I got a spiel telling me to keep my mouth shut or I could walk."

"You got a defensive reaction to the fact she let you stay over." Zoë stared out at the passing shops, the people, the buses. "She flipped when I pressed her this afternoon."

"She did?" When did Darcy ever show more than a prickle of irritation?

"Yeah. She slapped me." Zoë wheezed out a breath. "She even managed to cry in front of me. That's something I haven't seen in a *long* time."

Darcy had cried? That hurt. That dug into her aching stomach and cramped it up. "I didn't mean to make her cry."

Zoë met her eyes. "It means she cares. She can't hide that she cares." She nodded to the crowd of people outside some building and the red string barrier. "And she needs you."

Kate rolled her eyes. "The show needs me to show up. Darcy McGregor doesn't need anything from me." So Zoë had rescued her to drag her back in to play nice. Great. "I don't want to play nice."

Zoë nodded, understanding in her eyes. "So don't." She held the door handle. "I let her get away with it. You don't have to."

"If you couldn't get through to her, what chance do I have?" She folded her arms. No, she couldn't. She couldn't be beaten by Darcy's smile, her shimmering look, her kiss, her icy barbs.

"More than you realise." Zoë smiled at her and squeezed her hand. "You know, she spent three years writing this stupid book." She glanced out at the crowd. "*I* know what it's about, but when did book launches ever look like that?"

"I can think of a few, but not nonfiction." She shrugged. She read a lot. She wasn't one for book launches, though. She downloaded books. Quicker.

"Exactly." Zoë squeezed her hand once more. "And she needs you here personally right now. Forget the show. The book is really important to her."

She'd never heard Darcy mention it. She gazed at Zoë in disbelief.

"Yeah, if she's silent about it, it means something." Zoë shoved open the door and held out her hand. "If you get out, my wife may not beat me."

Kate sighed and took her hand. Flash, flash, flash. Calls, cheers. "I really dislike attention," she muttered as Zoë led her along the carpet.

"Wave and smile, honey." Zoë flashed dazzling smiles at the cameras. "Just wave, smile, and walk on."

Kate waved, must have looked pathetic—elbow clamped to her side and a flap of her hand. Should she go for a Queen-style wave? That'd look crazy.

"You look like you're at the dentist," Zoë said with a chuckle. "Wave!" She grabbed Kate's arm and thrust it into the air. "Smile like you aren't freezing."

"I have a hole in the backside of my jeans," she muttered back. Hadn't the cameras seen enough of her underwear?

"Wear it like no one is looking," Zoë whispered and ushered her along the row of people all yelling and thrusting microphones at them. Zoë chatted and charmed. The interviewers loved her.

Kate stepped back as Zoë engaged the camera, and she snuck in through the doors. Wearing things like people weren't looking was for models. She was not a model.

Susannah spotted her and smiled, beckoning her over with a wave. Darcy stood chatting to another interviewer inside and glanced over. Her eyes filled with relief. Was it relief? Her shoulders eased downward like it was. Kate sighed and nodded, hoping Darcy couldn't see the hole in her jeans. Not a model, no, but she would grin and bear it for now.

CHAPTER 31

DARCY FIDDLED WITH THE RING on her finger. The large bookstore, one of only few remaining, was filled with celebrities, with VIPs, reviewers, a camera crew reporting for some entertainment channel, Marge and a skeleton crew for the show, Zoë, Blanche, Susannah…and Kate. Why was she here? Her tone had been quite clear that she wasn't going to put up with being discreet. Why was she acting like they hadn't argued? And *why* were her jeans missing an entire back pocket? Had Zoë abducted her?

"You ready?" her agent, Paul, asked with a smile. He'd been stunned when he'd read her manuscript—as if being beautiful meant her brain had fallen out. Zoë was sure she'd just hired a ghostwriter and lied. She rolled her eyes. Zoë would have done that. Not Darcy. It was too…exposing to have someone dig at her private thoughts.

"Darcy, are you okay?"

She shook her thoughts free and nodded. "Yes. I'm ready."

Paul strode to the podium and smiled at the audience. "Darcy's book isn't quite an autobiography. It isn't a guide or a 'how to' book. We were only allowed to put some pictures in because I promised to buy the right shaped jeans." He tugged at them, and the audience chuckled. Why, she wasn't sure. His jeans before had made him look like a slob on a tight budget. He looked like he was an agent now. "It's a compelling read; yes, Darcy can write, and it's quite the story getting to know her."

Know her? She doubted anyone who read it would remotely know her. Susannah frowned and turned to Zoë, who shrugged. As if she would tell a book anything they didn't know. She tutted, then all eyes fell on her and she shot a dazzling smile at Paul. Yes, pretend that he wasn't speaking drivel.

"So, this book, 'the frozen image' shows that Darcy McGregor is more than just a beautiful face." He motioned to her and she strode over, trying not to roll her eyes. Cliché much?

"Thanks, Paul." She took up the podium. Kate studied her like she was curious as to what the book was about. Maybe she could just give her a copy—then would Kate stop trying to pry answers from her? "Fashion has been a friend. Sometimes it's been an untruthful, unkind friend, but we always seem to make it up." She flashed a dazzling smile. The audience laughed, easily pleased. "But it provided the escape I needed and provided me with a wonderful daughter."

Susannah pursed her lips. Yes, she thought that was a show too.

"So here is the opening. I hope you agree with Paul that I can write. If you don't, please pretend you do." She smiled again, the audience laughed again, but unlike everything else she had done publicly, this made her hands tremble, her knees tremble. She took a deep breath. "There has always been a frozen image in my mind which returns to me in important moments. I was ten, sitting on the front step of the council house my mother owned. Three boys were fighting over something down the street, hurling abuse at each other. The man next door had come home drunk; he was a violent man, and his wife was trying to keep the door barred from him. My mother was on the pavement in front of me, screaming at my father because she'd discovered he had another family. It was the moment when I realised I didn't live in a cosy, happy home, and I never would again." She took a deep breath. Reading in front of an audience was easy usually, bearing parts of her that hurt was not as easy. "That image haunted me when Susannah was born. Happiness was not something I knew or expected to have, but I made the decision that she was never to see that. I never wanted her to be hurt like that. I wanted her to live far from the damage I'd left behind."

She dared to look at Susannah. She had her hands over her mouth, tears in her eyes. She hadn't wanted Susannah there at all. She didn't want her to read the book, but Zoë insisted.

"So, I focused my sights on reaching for a better life and needed to learn how to catch attention, to hold it, to harness it, and to turn it into a career." She met Zoë's eyes. "And for that, I needed a little help."

She closed the book and stepped back. Silence. Good silence? Did they think she could write, or had they fallen asleep?

"Questions?" Paul asked, a smug look on his puffy face.

Kate nodded to her as hands shot into the air, and she breathed out a sigh of relief. Must be good if Kate liked it. Kate was a reader. Confidence oozed up, and she eased into a smile. Yes. If Kate, Susannah, and Zoë liked it, that was all she cared about.

The audience had loved it. Every copy there had been sold in minutes, and there was a long line of people waiting for her to sign theirs and have a photo. Paul looked like his eyes might turn to pound signs, and she flicked her gaze over to Susannah, Kate, and Zoë loitering with Marge in the corner.

"Darcy, that was so poignant, so raw," one lady said, handing over her book. "I don't know what I was expecting, but it wasn't that." She beamed and flicked her blonde hair back. Not natural. Too much tinted moisturiser. "Marshall doesn't usually go for rough people."

Marshall? "Yes, well…perhaps he should remember that his grandfather worked on the docks before his big break." She smiled at the lady. Whoever she was, she was clueless. "He's hardly aristocracy himself."

The woman laughed. "He did?" She leaned over, thrusting her breasts forward as the camera shutter clicked. "He's a smooth talker."

"If you say so." She leaned back, hoping the woman would hurry up and move on. She produced her most polished smile and reached for the next book.

"He said you look a picture," the lady said, pausing and glancing back over her shoulder. "Said that the book should be called 'the fake image.'" She laughed again, like it was hilarious, and strode off.

Darcy shook her head and turned back to the line. Odd woman.

Kate shoved her hands in her front pockets. The unease of hearing Darcy read from the book prickled at her. She wanted to read it, yet she really didn't. It definitely wasn't going to include her relationship with Zoë, so what did it include?

"Did you know?" Susannah stared up at Zoë, hugging herself. "I didn't know. Why didn't she tell me?"

Zoë wrapped an arm around her shoulder. "Yeah, I knew. Took a lot of elocution lessons to get her talking like that." She smiled down at her. "When I met her, she had a really strong accent."

Susannah glowered over at Darcy, then stomped off. Marge lowered her camera and sighed. "Think I'll delete that bit."

Zoë nodded to her and hurried after Susannah, then Marge wandered over to Darcy, and Kate stared at the cover of the book. Darcy in front of a tall window, high contrast, white against the black details of the window panes, Darcy's long legs stretched out on the window seat. She was looking out, a pensive look on her face, pulling the focus in, right to her eyes. Not the masked look that she always produced in all the other pictures, but a raw look.

"How's the stalker doing?" some woman whispered next to her, then laughed. Kate looked her up and down. Wow, she didn't know a lot about make-up, but orange definitely wasn't good. "Did she tell you to keep your mouth shut?"

Kate looked around. No. The woman was talking to her. Great. "If you're going to try ripping my jeans, I warn you that Zoë is mean with a tape measure."

The woman leaned in, false smile—Kate coughed—and too much perfume. "Marshall said she was hot for him. Followed him around, begging for his attention. Didn't like it much when he let her down easy."

"How sad are you?" Kate shook her head and turned away.

"Oh, come on. You think she's hot for some cheap tart like you?" The woman walked around to stand in front of her. "She's heartbroken over him. Can't you see it? He knows it too."

"Honey, Marshall is nothing but some soggy-cheeked jerk who thinks he can act." Blanche strode over and slid her arm around Kate's shoulder. "And he's lucky Darcy as much as breathed on him."

Kate stared at her. Was Blanche really talking or had she just passed out?

"Marshall is a red-blooded man who is better than any…" The woman paused, then laughed, then held up the book. "He is a real man inside."

"Everyone has red blood unless they have a very bad circulatory problem," Kate mumbled. She never got that saying.

The woman looked her up and down. "What?"

Blanche blurted out her laugh.

"Blood is a mixture of plasma: water and proteins, red blood cells, white blood cells, and platelets." Kate shrugged as both Blanche and the woman stared at her. Okay, so her A Levels came out when she got nervous too. Another defensive trait: humour, kissing, and biology... Odd mix. "And the lymphatics clear the waste products."

"What are you talking about?" The woman glared at her as Blanche laughed harder.

"Everyone is made up of cells and water. Bones, muscles, tendons, ligaments, blood, etcetera..." Kate smiled at the woman. "So no one can really be better than anyone else, and everyone's insides look the same."

"What?" The woman waved the book around. She looked thrown off.

"She's a geek." Blanche kissed Kate on the lips. "But we love her."

Darcy scowled over. So she was watching, then.

"Honey, if you're gonna kiss her, it's only fair I do." Zoë strolled over and kissed her on the lips too.

Right. Well if she wasn't bright red before, she must be now. And...yes, Marge was filming it, and Darcy looked like she might smack her across the head with her book. It was hardback too. Didn't fancy that.

"Disgusting." The woman turned and stormed out.

Zoë raised her eyebrows at Blanche. "Any reason?"

Blanche winked at Darcy and smiled. "Just getting my own back." She strolled off, and Kate chuckled. Yes, she might have been, but was it her, or had Blanche defended Darcy?

CHAPTER 32

DARCY HAD LET ZOË AND Blanche take Susannah and Kate back to their house. She could tell by Susannah's scowl that it would take a while for her to snap out of her pout, and she didn't trust herself not to either slap Kate for letting anyone kiss her, or kiss her too just to remind her *who* she enjoyed kissing.

London was in the midst of its evening rush hour as she headed toward Oxford Street for the next live segment, and her driver was, once again, zipping through with expertise. "How is the baby?"

He beamed into the rear-view mirror. "She's doing really well, thanks to you."

She waved it off. The traffic backed up, and she leaned on the windowsill. It was snowing again. That meant people would be camped out in front of their TVs and watching the evening's episode. It would be the first one since Kate's declaration. She chewed on her lip. She hadn't been within feet of Kate since she'd walked out the door. "How is your wife?"

"She's trying to cope with breastfeeding." He pulled his mouth to the side. "The nurses all keep telling her she has to, but I keep telling her we can buy milk, that she doesn't *have* to do anything."

"Yes, they can bully." She tutted. She had fought off their tactics, stuck to formula, and Susannah was healthy *and* intelligent. "It should be her decision. Not everyone can do it."

"Is that in your book, Ms Darcy? Because she's reading it, and she'll listen to you." He said it with a cheerful tone, but she could hear the worry in his voice.

"It is. Chapter three, I believe." She smiled at him as he zipped around a backstreet. "If you want me to talk to her, just ask."

He smiled. "You've done so much already. We wouldn't have her if it weren't for you."

"Nonsense." She stared out at the crowd of cameras waiting at the department store.

"Never." He screeched to a halt. "You're wonderful in our eyes."

She nodded and got out of the car. Shutters, calls, flashes. She strode in through the doors and over to Marge. "Why are you looking more sour than usual?"

Marge sighed and pulled her over to the side by the elbow. "Kate wants to pull out." She glanced over at where Kate, Zoë, Blanche, and Susannah were whispering amongst themselves. "Mikey is being bullied after she said that she loves you." Marge's gaze turned hard. "Doesn't help you have ignored her."

"I didn't ignore her." But then, she wasn't telling Marge about spending the night with Kate. "Who is bullying him?"

"Kids at his school. Headteacher was trying to deal with the bullies, but one of Mikey's friends told their parents, and they got involved, and there was a fight outside the school gates." Marge pursed her lips. Her top lip was very…furry. Went with the pipe-cleaner hair. "Kate's mother has pulled him out of school for now. Mikey has no idea he was being bullied."

"Better for him." She nodded to the camera, slamming down the urge to throttle someone. "Kate can't pull out. Let's get on with it."

Marge stared at her, then scowled. "As always, you're a delight to work with." She motioned to the cameraman. He eased his camera onto his shoulder, and the red light flicked on.

"As so many of you were keen on seeing Kate turn the tables, here we are, back where we started." She strolled over to Kate. "And what have you all concocted?"

Zoë flashed a cheeky smile. "We have to do the examination first." She nodded to the changing room. They always did the examination in the apartment where there was a special changing room and the lighting was less glaring, the mirrors more accurate. The idea was to find body shape, not terrify people.

"Get in the changing room. Time for you to stand around in underwear." Kate's hard stare filled with hurt.

"No. Why don't we pull out a mirror and I will do it here?" Lighting was more flattering outside. The garish lights and funhouse mirror in the changing room would *not* do. She nodded and one of the crew scurried into the changing room with a screwdriver. "So what are your first thoughts, Kate?"

Kate turned to the camera. "You dress to hide who you are."

And she was trying to get a rise. "Or accentuate my natural form."

"No, I'd say you're hiding." Kate folded her arms. "And I'm the doctor right now."

Her laugh exhaled through her nose. "If that makes you feel better, Kate." She smiled. Yes, her tone was calm and controlled, but Kate's eyes narrowed.

"It does, Darcy," Kate snapped as the crew member carried out the mirror. Hopefully the store wouldn't mind.

Darcy unbuttoned her shirt and pulled it off. The crew let out muffled groans, and Kate's long neck flexed. Yes, she modelled underwear, among many other things. She knew exactly how to unveil herself. "As the camera can see"—she pointed to her breasts—"I am wearing a bra that not only fits but supports." She flicked the toggle between the cups. "And this marvellous little contraption allows me to have a natural feel." She tightened the string, and the crew murmured. "Or, as you will hear from my colleagues, create a more voluptuous look."

Blanche nodded. "Important when you need to create some volume."

Zoë raised an eyebrow. "You have ample volume."

Blanche smirked at her.

"By drawing your attention here," she continued, ignoring Zoë gazing at the twig. "I create a waist and emphasize my long stomach." She ran a hand over it.

Kate coughed, the crew mumbled, and Marge cocked her head. Susannah, she was peering down at her own stomach like she wondered how to do the same.

"Pilates, darling." She turned back to the camera. "All this pulls your attention away from my hips, which need careful working around."

"Your hips are fine." Kate shook her head. "Why would you need to work around them?"

She looked to Zoë. "Put on your designer hat, please."

Zoë pulled her mouth to the side. Yes, she was reluctant. She'd personally loved Darcy's hips, but this was not personal.

"Zoë?" She motioned with her finger.

Zoë sighed and headed over. "They have good shape, but it's an inch wider than balanced." She met Darcy's eyes as if somehow it was a crime to be honest. "You tend to hold water there."

"Which means?" She rolled her finger in encouragement. Why was she wandering around the obvious?

"We'd call them saddlebags." Zoë hung her head. "But they really aren't."

"No, they aren't," Kate snapped. "Load of rubbish."

"I work hard to ensure that there is maximum drainage from the muscles." She shook her head at Kate. Was she being angry or defending her? "And do the relevant exercises to counter it when I need to display them to a camera." She undid her trousers and slid them down. Several members of the crew spluttered out their breath, some wheezed, some groaned. Yes, she did love her high-leg silk underwear. "Quite often, if I am wearing a dress, I have special shorts that pull in my thighs."

"You don't need shorts. Your legs are perfect." Kate marched over and tapped them. "There's not an inch of fat on them, they're toned, not to mention I don't think cellulite has come anywhere near you."

"I use a treatment." She chuckled as Susannah folded her arms, looking ready to either tell Kate off for slapping her thigh or her for stripping down to her underwear. "I had stretchmarks from pregnancy that I also had treated." She smiled at the camera. "The only difference between me and any new mother out there is that I know the right things to use to draw your attention where it needs to be." She tapped the string on her bra again.

Kate scoffed and turned her around. "This bum is rock hard."

Zoë nodded. "If it wasn't, she wouldn't be a lot of use on a billboard."

"Yeah," Blanche said, tapping Susannah on the arm and grinning at her. "You do not want droopage when you're a fifteen-foot image."

Susannah chuckled. "I thought Photoshop could help that."

Blanche wagged her finger. "I don't need any touch-ups." She thumbed in Darcy's direction. "And neither does she." She mouthed "bitch" at her.

Darcy poked out her tongue. Yes, she was. "The line of my lingerie is designed to accentuate the curve under my buttock here and create an effect that the designer knows any man will be riveted to."

Zoë laughed. "Honey, I am no guy, and right now I want to grab your ass." She shrugged at Marge, who scowled. "What?"

"Swearing," Marge mouthed at her.

"Ass?" Zoë rolled her eyes. "The whole bit about me grabbing her... butt...was fine?"

Marge shrugged.

"I would prefer if you don't," Susannah muttered and folded her arms. "Mum is not a piece of meat."

"No, she isn't." Kate narrowed her eyes. "I vote for a pair of boxers and a sports bra."

Zoë howled with laughter. Blanche grinned like she'd enjoy every second, and Susannah nodded in approval. "Thanks, Kate. At least you respect her." She held up her phone. "Tweet comment. Susannah from Kensington says, 'put some clothes on, Mum.'" She wagged it at her.

"You call shoving me in men's clothing respect?" She raised an eyebrow and pulled up her trousers, much to the dislike of the crew, if the moans were anything to go by.

"I call covering you up and showing you that it doesn't matter what shape you are, you're a human being who deserves to be talked to not ogled." Susannah fixed on Blanche. "That goes for you too."

Kate nodded to her. "Then let's get you in some proper underwear."

"Cut and move to adverts." Marge rubbed at her neck. Her phone rang. She handed it to one of the cameramen. "Tell John I'm busy."

Kate's eyes glinted with hurt again. "You're too good for my ideas?"

Clearly, her comment on men's clothing had hit a sore spot. "I was not making a reference to you."

"Yes, you were." Kate folded her arms.

"I was not." She folded her own arms. The crew *oohed*. Hmm. Probably best to put her shirt back on. "There's no need to pout."

"I'm not pouting." Kate ripped the shirt from the floor and threw it at her. Cheeks were a little flushed there. "You think clothes change where you come from?"

Oh, that was low. Someone had read the book. "They do."

"They don't. I know plenty of people from council estates, and they are lovely." She glared and shoved the shirt around Darcy's shoulders. "They are not that bad."

"Where I lived was." She batted Kate's hands away and took the shirt.

"It produced you." Kate motioned to her like she wanted to slap her. "I'd say that gives them a head start on most places."

And she wanted to kiss her. Irritating. "You're just biased."

"Yes, I am." Kate threw her hands in the air. "Now get in there and put on boxers."

"Don't boss me around." She yanked her shirt closed.

"Why, not so much fun when it's you?" Kate grabbed her arm and dragged her to the changing room like she wanted to throw her inside. Yet desire ignited in her eyes.

"Stop looking at me like that," she snapped and ripped the door back. It slammed to the wall and dropped from the top hinge. "See what you did?"

"That's right, blame it on me." Kate shoved her at the next changing room.

"I am; you were the one swinging on it." Darcy stomped in through the door and slammed it shut in Kate's face. No way was she coming in. She leaned her head to the door. How was she going to keep it professional? How?

<hr>

Kate folded her arms as she waited outside the changing room. Darcy was infuriating. How could anyone who looked as incredible as her think she had a thing wrong with her? Who'd done that to her? Was it modelling? She hammered on the door. "Are you sleeping in there or something?"

Zoë exchanged a glance with Marge. Yeah, she was moody.

"Calm yourself, Kate," Darcy said in her unruffled tone. "I will be worth the wait."

Kate turned and glared at the doorway. Rub it in. "Just get out here." Wow, had they swapped roles. She stopped. Maybe Darcy was nervous or something? "I know you'll look wonderful."

"Don't assume I have any issues with wearing ridiculous items of clothes. I was a catwalk model." She said it with a smugness.

"You're a supermodel, and you're *still* modelling." Kate hammered on the door again. "The camera is waiting."

Darcy pulled the door back and strode out with utter confidence, all sheer charisma and female grace. Her body looked fluid, even more toned and... Oh, she made boxers look...wow.

Darcy reached out and pushed Kate's mouth closed. "Do try to find some composure."

Where from?

"As you see, the tightness of these boxer shorts pulls across my thighs, drawing attention to them even when a darker colour often fades out the area and lighter colours draw your eye." Darcy turned like she would on a catwalk and looked over her shoulder. "But, even in ill-fitting clothes, it's about confidence."

Zoë murmured her agreement. "You wear the outfit, not the other way around."

Blanche leaned on Zoë's shoulder. "I think they work for you. Pair of boy shorts would be better, but not bad."

Darcy raised an eyebrow like she was genuinely touched.

Susannah covered her eyes. "Mum, do we have to see you so naked?" She turned to Marge. "Put some clothes on her."

Darcy chuckled. "The bra flattens my bust, which is important support for running and other activities, yes." She hoisted up her breasts. "But they don't give me shape."

"They give you plenty of shape. What are you on about?" Kate moved her hands and prodded the toned, firm stomach. "Washboard." She stroked her hand over Darcy's shoulders. "Elegant." She hoisted Darcy's breast up. "Doesn't matter how you dress these, they look good." She snapped her hands away and tugged at the shorts. "And these make your legs look athletic."

"This makes me look androgynous." Darcy met her eyes, the glimmer of a pulsing desire there. "You would make a fantastic designer."

Kate frowned. Was Darcy right? She looked to Zoë, who nodded. "Sorry, honey, she's got you there."

Shit.

"You look sporty." She folded her arms. "And less like you're selling yourself."

Darcy arched her eyebrow. Yes, they both knew full well how much she liked the lingerie. Rub it in again.

"Anyway," she muttered and handed over a pair of jeans and a T-shirt. "Stick them on."

Darcy took them, flicked them off the hanger, and pulled them on like she was used to it. Yes, she must have been a dummy for a lot of designers. Baggy jeans slung low on the waist and a tight T-shirt.

"And I'm now extremely androgynous." She turned to Kate. "These jeans pull the eye to my stomach, which is flat, and has the same effect as the cleavage." She ran her fingers along the top.

Kate swallowed.

"The baggy shape does cancel out my thighs, and the side pockets create a masculine line." She smiled like she was pleased at Kate's choice. "You do shorten my legs, though, and, no doubt this goes with a flat shoe or a boot?"

Shit. She had her again.

Darcy smiled that patronising smile. "The T-shirt you've chosen is tight to my biceps and triceps, which accentuates the muscle tone there and elongates my shoulders, again androgenising my form." She tapped her chest. "The breasts make an appearance, but they aren't your focus, because they are pushed down." She pointed to her arms and her neck. "But these are."

Zoë squinted like she was trying to think, or maybe baggy jeans hurt her to look at. "You pull it off, though."

Blanche cocked her head. "You really, really do."

Zoë raised an eyebrow at her.

Blanche shrugged. "What? Like that's a surprise?"

Susannah shook her head. "I don't like it."

"And why is that?" Darcy smiled at her like she knew.

"You look as...on display as you did before. I just don't get why." She frowned and looked to Zoë.

"Because she's not attracting a guy but pulling out the traits a woman is interested in." Zoë pulled her mouth to the side. "I prefer the cleavage."

The crew murmured their obvious agreement.

"I'd rather people just looked at you because you had something nice to say," Susannah muttered, then held up her phone. "Tweet question: Sally from Hertfordshire wants to know if you feel different in those clothes."

Darcy nodded. "Yes. I feel more assertive. It makes me feel like I have a dominant presence." She fixed Kate with a charming smile. "But I feel shorter."

"You don't look it." Kate chewed her lip. She liked Darcy in the outfit as much as she liked her in the bra and pants. She looked good. She didn't care what she was in, or not in; she just wanted to kiss her.

Darcy's eyes softened like she knew it. "But it's about *feeling* too."

"What's wrong with androgynous?" she mumbled. If she didn't say something, she was going to grab her and kiss her until someone dragged her off.

"Nothing." Darcy smiled and stroked her cheek with the pad of her warm thumb. "If I feel good, if I am attracting who I wish to attract, and I have confidence, then these clothes are as sexy as lacy bras."

Oh, great. Back to lacy bras. Was she blushing again? She touched her cheeks, and Darcy chuckled.

"I'm sure, if the audience wants it enough, Zoë could explain all the rules of making androgynous look incredible." She motioned to Zoë. "She is the poster girl for it."

Zoë winked at her. "You got it."

"Then let's make Darcy androgynous." Kate folded her arms. She didn't know why she was saying it, but it felt…childish.

"If you'd like, Kate." Darcy smiled at the camera. "I'm sure Blanche will happily model for some aspects?"

Blanche nodded. "Yeah, I will. I'd love Zoë to dress me."

Zoë beamed at her. "You would?"

"Yup, honey. Gay me up." She grinned and held Darcy's gaze. Was that a wobble? Darcy was smiling, but it was that practiced smile. "Scared you can't pull it off next to me?"

Darcy narrowed her eyes. "You're on."

"Cut!" Marge grinned like she'd cheer. "What are the tweets saying, Susannah?"

Susannah stared at her phone. "The LGBTQIA…" She looked to Zoë. "Did I get that right?"

Zoë nodded. "You got it."

"Well, the entire community just woke up. It's crazy trending again. Hashtag Gay Me Up." She wheezed out a breath and looked up at Darcy. "They are loving the fact you're being so supportive."

Darcy shrugged. "Supportive? I thought you felt I was fake?" She turned and strode back into the changing room and shut the door.

"I'm not sure what you are," Susannah mumbled and stuck her phone in her pocket. "Other than messed up."

"I'd say beautiful," Kate whispered to the door and smiled over at Susannah. A picnic-blanket dinner was needed to cheer her up.

"You're biased," Darcy whispered back, but her tone wasn't snappy this time, or patronising, but a raw, cracked sound like she was holding back tears.

"Yeah, I am." She placed her hand on the door, wanting to push it open and hug Darcy more than anything else. She'd read the book. It hurt reading what she'd been through and heartened her that Darcy had used her pain to give Susannah a great home. Anyone reading the book would think she was a hero. Was she? "I love you."

Darcy shuddered out a breath. "I've no idea why."

"Because you look good in boxers." She pushed off the door and strode away before she did something she wanted to, and Darcy's blurted, breathy, bubbling laugh rang out. Sounded better each time she heard it.

CHAPTER 33

DARCY HURRIED FROM THE CAB, pulling her coat up against the sleety rain. The large house had two cars in the drive and a work van. Hopefully, they would be in. She knocked on the door and tried to squeeze under the mini-porch roof.

"Lo?" A guy with a shaved head, blue eyes, and a bodybuilder's physique looked her up and down, then raised his eyebrows. "Kate's not here."

"Is Mildred?" She glanced up at the rain. It was getting heavier.

"Yeah." He pulled open the door. "I'll call her now…" He strolled off down the hallway. Guess she'd let herself in. "Luv, Darcy's here for you."

Mildred laughed. "Pull the other one."

He strode into the kitchen as Darcy shut the door behind her. "Nah, she's really here."

Mildred poked her head out. She had the hair dye foil on, a cigarette on the go, and some kind of face cream. "I'm not really presentable."

"I see women looking far worse." She strode into the kitchen and smiled at the man who leaned against the fridge. "Are you Kate's stepdad?"

He nodded. "Yeah."

"Good." She pulled out a chair and sat next to a staring Mildred. "I would like to know what you are thinking about Kate."

Mildred sucked on her cigarette. "She's outspoken. I don't know why she put you in that position, but when she gets something in her head…" She flicked ash into a brimming ashtray. "I don't know what to say to the girl."

"I mean, I know she's a pretty kid," the stepdad said, "but she's not exactly your league, you know." He held up his hands when Mildred glared at him. "I just mean, you're famous. You holiday in exclusive places because they want you to be seen there. Kate is a security guard."

"Kate could pull in punters." Mildred sucked on her cigarette again. "She doesn't want to."

"No, exactly. She wants to dress like a bloke." He rolled his eyes and picked up a cup from the side. "She could be a pretty thing."

Darcy leaned onto the table, trying not to inhale fumes. "I love her."

Mildred nearly swallowed her cigarette, and the stepdad spat out whatever tar was in his mug.

"I have every confidence that Kate could sell just about anything with her smile." She fixed on Mildred's eyes. "I can't do that to her. She doesn't understand why, but Mikey is suffering because she was truthful. I'm guessing you will have experienced the same?"

Mildred put her cigarette out. "Nothing I can't handle."

The stepdad folded his muscled arms. "Anyone says a word to me, and I'll knock them sideways."

"What happens when it's cameras outside your door, because Kate happens to have been rash in something she says, or people throwing things over your car because they don't like that Kate is living with another woman, or someone targeting Mikey because they think it'll get them attention?" She stared at the table. Swish kitchen but the table was cheap and covered with cigarette burns. "I don't want her to miss Mikey. I'm not going to move to Cardiff."

"Why?" The stepdad wagged his mug about. "What's the issue with Cardiff?"

"It's not home to me." She smiled at him. "I'm not saying I won't visit, but I love London. I love where I live, and Susannah is happy there."

"So we can visit you too," Mildred said, pulling another cigarette out of her pack. She gave one to the stepdad, who took it and then offered the packet to Darcy.

"I don't smoke, thank you." She held up her hand. The passive smoke was going to take months to clear out of her lungs.

"Thought that's how you all kept thin," Mildred said, lighting another cigarette.

"Some do. I prefer exercise." She had always hated it. Her mother smoked. Chain-smoked, like Mildred, one big haze of tobacco and chemicals. "I offered to protect her. That we could have a relationship as long as it was discreet."

Mildred laughed. "Oh, I bet she took that well."

"Yes," she mumbled. "I hurt her, but I cannot put her, Susannah... Mikey...you...every one of Kate's friends and ex-friends...and myself through it."

"Kate deserves better," the stepdad said, then shrugged as Mildred stared at him. "Hey, I'm not stupid. The girl went through it with that idiot."

"Bennie," Mildred said as if Darcy wouldn't know.

"And Laura?" She had prised the rest of the information out of Marge. Marge hadn't been an easy witness, but the threat of a lip wax had paid off.

Mildred scowled.

"And it's Laura's children bullying Mikey?" She'd assumed it was. It would make sense.

"They are behind it, yes." Mildred sucked on her cigarette. "One of Mikey's friends told their mother, who went and said to Laura to keep a handle on her kids, and it got nasty." She sighed. "At least that's what we can tell from the gossip. You know how it is."

Darcy nodded. "Which is why I worry."

"Look, the girl's already told everyone she loves you," the stepdad said, lighting up. "So what difference will it make if you say you love her?"

"Right now, she's a contestant on a show that is charmed by some famous face." She didn't know how to explain it. The celebrity lifestyle was so insular. "In a few months, that fades, things go back to normal, and people will forget." She met Mildred's eyes. "If I tell people I love her, it changes. She's no longer just a contestant riling me up, she's a hot topic. Her picture becomes worth money, her past becomes fodder for prying eyes." She pulled out her phone and held it up. "She was mobbed on the riverbank the other day. This will happen all the time. She won't be a security guard in a pencil factory anymore; she'll be Darcy McGregor's girlfriend...partner...wife."

"But she'll be happy?" The stepdad said and sipped at his mug, cigarette inches from his eyes. "She's not happy here."

Mildred nodded. "And if you're not considering it, why you making sure we are behind her?"

Darcy frowned. "I'm actually here to ask if I can go into Mikey's school and do what I do best...then whisk him to London and keep him there until we have a break in filming." She put on her best smile. "It will keep him safe from bullies, and Kate could do with some assistance."

Mildred eyed her. "I'm not sure I believe that you're not checking we're okay with you and Kate."

Ah, the mother's tone. "You're entitled to believe what you wish to."

Mildred chuckled. "Then I'll believe you said you love her and you're too scared to jump." She glanced over at the stepdad. "Believe me, you'll jump eventually. It's best to do it before you hurt other people."

Darcy smiled. "Then will you let me take Mikey with me?"

"'Course. He'll enjoy every second of it. You'll have to pick him up from school, though. I sent him in today." She flicked her cigarette around. "It's too exhausting for me. I'll watch on the telly." She gave her a toothy grin, foils flapping as she did so. "What is it that you do best?"

"Change images." She winked and got to her feet. "And thank you."

"For what?" The stepdad eyed her.

"For not telling me I'm not good enough for her." She pushed back her shoulders. "It helps."

"No one is better than anyone else," Mildred muttered and flicked her cigarette ash. "And don't you forget it."

Darcy nodded and strode out of the house to the waiting cab. "Do I need to ask if you know where Mikey's school is?"

He grinned and shook his head. "Nah, I know the place." He shunted them into motion.

She looked out the window. Mikey was being bullied. She tapped out a tweet about the importance of embracing differences and smiled. Now to turn Mikey into the coolest kid in school.

CHAPTER 34

KATE FOLDED HER ARMS AS the crew gave up and decided on a break. Everyone was there, ready for filming, but Darcy. She fiddled with the clothes stand next to her. Some plastic thing jutted out at the top. Had Darcy just decided she wasn't going to be dressed? Was she too busy to bother turning up? Was she okay? She shoved her hands in her pockets. What if she wasn't okay? She would contact Susannah if she wasn't, right?

"Susannah, did you know about this?" Marge asked, hurrying over with her phone.

Susannah looked down at it, then shook her head. "No. She didn't say, but then she didn't tell me about the book." She rolled her eyes. "Not like she says anything to me anyway."

Zoë wandered over from muttering about a whole collection of badly shaped jumpers, or sweaters, to her. There were a lot of differences between English and American names for clothes. Why? Were they going to say a cardigan was not a cardigan, because the people of Cardigan in West Wales would be pretty irritated. Then again, did they actually make them or get named after them? Cardigan was cold sometimes. Maybe someone decided that yanking a jumper on over the head was too stressful? She picked at the stand. Maybe she needed to stop thinking so much?

"Atta girl," Zoë chimed at the phone. "She knows when to step in."

Kate frowned. Step in?

Susannah glanced over with a furtive look, like she didn't want to say. "I've never seen anyone cheered out of school before."

What were they on about? Kate picked at the stand again. Maybe Darcy had gone on a date with some gorgeous woman or was following Gregory whatever-his-name-around, but that wouldn't have made Susannah happy… and she'd mentioned school. Hmmm.

Kate pulled out her phone and flicked to Darcy's Twitter account: *Bullies, FYI, labels only useful on clothes. No knock-offs. Everyone is designer. #EmbraceDesigner.*

Okay, bit random…or had she heard about Mikey? She chewed on her lip. Oh no, her heartstrings couldn't take that kind of thrumming. Mikey was a soft spot.

She searched through the hashtag. Pictures posted by parents she knew. Darcy in front of the entire school, charming smile, Mikey at her side. Tweets like: *Darcy is amazing, what a hero; Mikey's BFF pops in, Darcy McGregor! Mikey and his sidekick take on bullies; Bullies suck, let's close them down.* Kate read through them—there were hundreds. Mikey was a hero in them. #EmbraceDesigner pumped out until it was trending. She picked at the plastic and yanked it. Darcy was… Oh shit, how did she walk away from that? She yanked the plastic again, and it came free.

The stand collapsed. Clothes slumped to the floor, and it clattered over, knocking two more clothes stands over. Oops.

"I feel your pain," Zoë called over with a chuckle. "I'd trash the lot."

Marge tutted at her. "Snob."

"It's not snobby. If you're going to pay fifty pounds for something, least it could do is be the right size." Zoë scowled at the clothes on the floor. "It's offensive."

Kate hurried to pick up the clothes. She wanted to cry. How pathetic was that? But did she want to cry because Mikey was a hero, because Darcy had stepped in, or because every time she convinced herself Darcy was scum, she went and proved she wasn't.

#FlippingConfused.

"Kate-oh!" Mikey's triumphant call ripped through her remaining resolve, and she sobbed out a breath.

She looked up in time to catch him hurling himself at her. They thunked into the pile of clothes with an *oof.*

"Hey, how come you're out of school?" She cuddled him close. Maybe she could just hold him until she stopped being a baby?

"Darcy rescue." He snuggled in with a contented sigh. "She say I hero." He chuckled. "Sproutman is cool."

She squeezed him, more tears blubbering down. "You've *always* been cool to me."

He peered up at her. "Have?"

She nodded. "Yup."

"We were missing a vital cast member," Darcy said to Marge as she stared at her. Same "what is the issue?" tone as always. "Every designer needs her sprouts."

Zoë nodded. "Missed the dude. Honey, you gonna finish up heckling your agent and get over here?" She frowned over at Blanche wandering around, phone glued to her ear.

Blanche held up her hand and carried on chattering.

Zoë rolled her eyes. "If the guy wasn't so gay, I'd be worried." She smiled at Susannah, who gazed up at Darcy like she'd launch-hug at her. "It's in there somewhere. She just can't let you see she's human."

Darcy tutted at her and met Kate's gaze. Then she frowned, concern in her eyes as she must have seen the tears. She moved forward, then stopped and sighed. "Why is Kate dismantling the store?"

Susannah glanced over, then frowned exactly like Darcy with echoed concern. "Shopping is painful?"

Darcy blurted out that laugh, then seemed to decide something with a nod and strolled over. "You don't like patterned camisoles?"

Kate sat up, Mikey nestled into her, and shrugged. "If I knew what they were, I'd say yeah?"

"They're…" Darcy waved it off. "You are quite dangerous in department stores, aren't you?"

Kate looked around her. "I think so." She pulled herself to her feet and smiled. It was just a relief that Darcy was talking to her, looking at her, smiling. "You abducting children?"

"They let him go, and I had permission," Darcy said. Mikey ducked under her outstretched hand and gave her a cuddle. Darcy raised her eyebrows like she wasn't sure what she'd done to deserve such affection. "Besides, if you are going to dress me, I need an ally." She winked down at him. "He knows how to dress."

Mikey pointed to his green T-shirt with some kind of crocodile on it, or maybe it was an alligator. She wasn't sure which was which. "Green and blue work."

"They do. It's a wonderful combination when used well." Darcy squeezed him. "Some little fashion myths need a rewrite."

He nodded. "Designer."

She beamed down at him. "Exactly."

He spotted Susannah and cheered, then launched into a stutter run at her. "Susannah-oh!"

Kate let out a long breath. Right. Not easy to ignore loving Darcy right now, was it? "Thank you."

Darcy held her gaze. "It's my job. He's my Sproutman." She winked at her, then leaned in like she wanted to kiss her. Instead, she pulled a stray camisole off her shoulder. "Best we keep you away from doors and clothing stands, hmm?"

Kate narrowed her eyes. Tease. "Maybe I caught it from you? You knocked them over first."

"Yes, well…" Darcy stroked her cheek and turned. "I've always been a trendsetter."

CHAPTER 35

An evening of fun: clothes picked out as Mikey cheered and Susannah laughed, Kate and Zoë, Blanche and Marge enjoying the cheer. Viewers loved it, tweeted, sent questions as Darcy tried on every item, showed them how to wear it, Blanche heckling from the side. The large aisle between Clothes and Kitchenware became a runway. Kate pulled lights from the household department, Zoë pulled white sheets from the linen to act as a backdrop. Marge pulled a Nikon camera from the electronic section, all on camera, all loved by every person watching.

Darcy had Mikey pose like a model, Susannah too. Flash, click, laugh. Flash, click, laugh. Kate relaxed the more Darcy let through the tips she had picked up through years of modelling; Kate gazed too long at her in different lights, smiled too warmly when she laughed, looked at her like a lover. Unconscious, yes, but clear for all to see. It took so much not to smile back, not to show how good it felt, not to pose in ways that only Kate—and Zoë—would know the significance of. She was careful to be pleasant yet not beyond professional. Careful, restrained, detached.

She lingered behind in the store and let the others go on to the apartment. She hoped that by staying away, everyone would retire for the night before she got home. So instead, she had the driver take her to Seren and Jemma's restaurant.

"Susannah was very keen to show support for us," Seren had said with her jolly smile as she led her to the kitchen after their tour of the restaurant. "We want to make it a safe place for people to enjoy a meal together without issues."

Darcy made sure to talk to the clients—definitely rainbow coloured. Would have been a better place to have come on Valentine's Day with Zoë.

"I had to leave because I was unwell, but I didn't want you to feel it was your food."

Jemma, a sinewy woman with a tall chef's hat on, beamed at her through the hatch to the steaming kitchen. "We know." She exchanged a glance with Seren. "We're just delighted that Kate was so romantic and here in our little place too."

Romantic? With whom? Best not to scowl. "I take it she liked the food?"

"She didn't get chance to eat it either, but hopefully you'll both have the chance to visit again." Jemma laughed, a twinkle in her eyes. Why did Darcy get the feeling she'd walked into a verbal trap? "Love tends to make you lose your appetite at first."

"So I hear." She rubbed at her stomach. Keep smiling. Nice polite smile.

Seren gave Jemma a pointed look and cleared her throat. "This is why we keep her in the kitchen." She beamed at Darcy. "Zoë, Susannah, Marge, and the crew were fantastic." She nodded, her cheeks flushing. "You're all welcome back anytime."

Zoë and her charm, but then, Susannah seemed to have a way with people even if she didn't think so herself.

"It's important that Kate and Zoë have places that celebrate them," she managed, sounding polished, professional and hollow all at once. "They are beautiful people."

Jemma cocked her head. "You stuck up for them both, and Mikey. We saw." She nodded and leaned through the hatch further. "You're beautiful just like them."

Seren nodded. "You're an amazing ambassador for equality." She led Darcy to the door. "We're honoured Susannah brought you here. She's a wonderful young lady."

Darcy couldn't help the huge smile that burst through. "She is. She really is."

<hr />

As she got into the car afterwards, only Susannah's words that she was a fake rolled through her mind all the journey back to the apartment and all the way to the door.

She hesitated outside it, relieved there was no sound from behind it. Perhaps everyone had gone to bed? She snuck inside and to her room. Fake?

Was she fake? Wasn't it reasonable to have a layer without a camera on it? A layer that was private? She undressed and lay on her bed, gazing up at the clouds swirling overhead. Was it fake to guard the people she loved?

A knock on the door made her sigh. She didn't want to talk to anyone.

"Darcy?" Kate whispered and walked in. "I just... Mikey was really boosted by what you did."

"I'm glad." She kept her focus on the clouds. The haze from the lights of the city gave them a pinkish-orange touch.

"You didn't have to, but I know Mum and Dad, even my stepdad, were really choked up by it." Kate sounded as if she expected to be evicted.

"Kate, my bed is open to you. You're welcome to stay or leave as you wish." A few stars peeked through the light and twinkled. Somewhere below on the street a lorry rumbled and a siren sounded. The song of a city, her city.

"Yes, but your bed has rules." Kate perched on it even so. "I'm so confused."

"Yes." She reached out and stroked Kate's bare forearm. "As I said, privately, you are welcome; publicly, I cannot do that."

Kate kissed her hand. "I don't know if I can do that." She held it to her breastbone. "It makes me ache here."

Darcy splayed out her fingers and grazed her nails over the soft skin. "I know."

"You acted like my girlfriend today, you get that, right?" She leaned over. Her face was awash with the pinkish hue reflected off the white bedsheet. "You did more than any presenter would."

"Yes. I care about Mikey." She smiled. Did Kate think she would ignore it? "I would never refuse to help where I could. Don't you see that?" She pulled Kate lower. "I just can't cross the line completely."

Kate hovered inches from her lips. "Why, when you spent the whole of this evening trying not to kiss me?"

"I don't like being gay." She brushed her lips to Kate's. She'd found the orange juice by the taste of it.

"But you're kissing another woman." Kate trailed soft kisses down her neck.

"I'm kissing *you*." She eased Kate down until she was securely wrapped around her, easing her tension, covering her worry. "You're not a label in my head."

Kate raised an eyebrow. "Think my anatomy might give it away."

Darcy sighed. "You're more than your body to me. A beautiful body, but you're... It's inside you." She held Kate inches from her mouth. "Just take me as I am."

Kate kissed up her neck again. "What does it look like I'm doing?"

"Delaying." She grazed her nails over Kate's back. "And I'm not in the mood for delays."

Kate rolled her eyes. "Are you ever romantic?" She yanked off her top. "Seriously. You make it sound like I'm filling in paperwork."

Darcy grazed her nails over Kate's stomach. "No. If paperwork gets you like this, you have a serious stationary attachment."

Kate yanked off her trousers. "You're the one who digs pencils." She fixed her with a look—half passion, half confusion. "Do you normally sleep with no clothes on?"

"No." She smiled and pulled Kate to her, tasting the orange juice on her lips, kiss by kiss. "I was expecting you."

Kate growled. "Why does that work on me?" She glared at her, passion building. "Why do I like that you knew it?"

"You like bitches, or so you tell me." She winked. Yes, Kate was a sucker, and they both knew it. "So?"

Kate sighed. And lowed her lips to Darcy's collarbone. "I love you."

Darcy let out a laugh. It sounded smug. It *felt* smug. "Now you're getting it."

CHAPTER 36

KATE BLINKED OPEN HER EYES as white light roused her. She groaned. She swore Darcy just tried out martial arts skills on her while she was too pumped with hormones to notice.

A soft chuckle in her ear made her smile.

"You're unfit?" Darcy whispered and trailed her finger over Kate's stomach. "We'll have to get that fixed."

Kate narrowed her eyes. "I do a ten-mile run three times a week. I'm amply fit." She bit Darcy's bottom lip and groaned again. Her back was in half. "But I need training of Olympic proportions for you."

Darcy pushed up, her eyes full of that aqua pop against the stark white light pouring in from the skylight. "Yes, we'll have to train you properly." She tapped her on the nose with her nail and strolled off into the bathroom like she was on the catwalk.

Kate thunked her head back to the bed. Did she like the sound of that, or did she need to bring painkillers? Or supports? Or a heart monitor? She pushed up to sitting and rubbed at her face. Yeah, she doubted her fitness-tracking band had that as an activity. Should do. The Darcy McGregor Ironwoman setting.

The shower flicked on, and someone knocked on the bedroom door. Kate stumbled off the bed. Panic pulsed through her. Where was her top? Where did she put her—

"Mum?" Susannah pushed the door ajar. Kate dived out of the line of sight and clattered off the other side of the bed with a groan. Found her top, though. "Mum, you alright?"

Darcy wandered out of the bathroom in a towel, raised her eyebrow at Kate, and smiled at Susannah. "Yes, you okay?"

Susannah frowned. "Are you? Did something drop?" She sighed. "I think we need to call Zoë. Kate's not in her room and—"

"She's just fine." Darcy pulled her lips into a wrinkled line like she was desperate to hide her smile. "She's the clumsy one causing a noise."

Kate shoved on her top and yanked herself up onto the bed, under the sheets.

Susannah's eyebrows shot up. She peered around the door, then smiled over. "Oh, that's a relief."

Darcy nodded. "I believe she's embarrassed that you've found her in here." She rolled her eyes and smiled at Susannah. "I'll be out to make breakfast. Do you know what Mikey wants?"

"Frosties," Kate said, trying not to squeak. Embarrassed? Understatement right there. She felt like her entire upper body had gone pink. "No rice milk or he'll throw it at you."

Darcy and Susannah both raised their eyebrows.

"Don't mess with the kid's food. It's not worth it." She wrinkled up her chin and shook her head. "He likes what he likes."

"I'll do it." Susannah cocked her head at Kate. "Your T-shirt is on backward."

"I know, it's digging into my windpipe." She coughed.

Susannah wrinkled up her brow. "I don't get it...but okay." She flounced off, and Mikey called out "Susannah-oh!" from down the hall.

Kate flumped back into bed.

"And you're giving me a hard time about public acknowledgement?" Darcy leaned against the door with that infuriating, knowing smile.

"The public aren't going to see me naked." Kate pulled off her T-shirt. "And *where* are my clothes?"

"In the linen basket." Darcy smiled wider. "Do you not have one of those in your house?"

"So, you just going to keep me here?" She folded her arms. "How am I supposed to get across the hall?"

"Tempting." Darcy flicked her gaze up and down her, then pulled a dressing gown from the back of the door. She threw it to her. "But in civilised society, we use a robe."

Kate got up and wrapped the fluffy dressing gown around herself. She narrowed her eyes and pressed Darcy to the door. "There is nothing about you that is civilised."

Darcy yanked her into a kiss, shoved her back, and threw her out the door. "Change. We have things to do."

Kate glared at the door, then waved to Mikey and Susannah laughing at her. She trudged to her room and threw off the robe. Bossy. That's what she was—bossy.

CHAPTER 37

THE FORTNIGHT WENT BY IN too much of a haze as every evening they were filming. Kate, Mikey, Susannah, Zoë, and Blanche had Darcy in all manner of outfits, and Zoë dragged them to shops run by people in the community, smaller shops which Darcy had enjoyed browsing around before money became no issue. Some were under new ownership, but a few still had the familiar faces, delighted faces who welcomed them in. Marge had appeased the sponsors by Mikey wearing a jacket with their name in large white letters on the back. He loved it.

Each night, they headed out for Darcy to be educated on women. Zoë had been far too enthusiastic about making Darcy do things like play pool—unnecessary waste of wood, although Mikey enjoyed potting her balls when they got close to the pocket. She also got her to try five-a-side football, or soccer as Zoë called it—Susannah's idea. She was far too talented, and Mikey had his own cheer. They watched indie films, which confused her—why the odd camera angles? Mikey had booed and thrown his popcorn at one point. She read lesbian romance books, which made her roll her eyes—she didn't do slushy rubbish—and Kate laughed at her for picking holes in the sex scenes. And, yes, they'd made her wear something rainbow coloured—that many colours in one outfit? It made little fashion sense, but at least it wasn't black.

All the while, the crew followed, Marge argued with John about family morals, and Kate seemed to struggle with their distance.

At the apartment, Kate relaxed, and Susannah and Mikey made quite the pair. Mikey had decided he was "a glut-free" and ate everything Susannah did. Susannah had researched everything she could about his brain injury and had taken to trying out techniques to show him things that would help when he couldn't speak. He'd hugged her every time she tried it. It didn't help his speech much, but it reached him, and that's what counted. She must have learned that from Zoë.

Kate had spent every night with her, as if trying to convince her to change her mind. Zoë had done the same. It just made her head swirl with that "fake" feeling until she removed herself from Kate's arms and went to the gym or did the housework. Sleep had never been something she found easy, but now it was more elusive than ever.

The apartment had never been so shiny. Gladys would be happy. She must be bored looking after the house by herself. Or maybe she wasn't and had her feet up.

They reached the segment before a break in filming, and everyone, including Blanche and her twig of a bony backside, seemed to be melancholy. They had soared in popularity, much to John's relief, even though his warning was clear: no scandal or no show. They'd navigated it, but now Kate would have to go back to Cardiff with Mikey, and Darcy couldn't just show up.

They were eating takeaway from Seren and Jemma's restaurant around the table in the apartment. Zoë and Blanche were flicking through a new ad campaign Blanche had been offered by a perfume company. Susannah was making her own Sproutwoman costume to help assist Mikey with a spider evacuation from the bath—a toy one—and Kate was curled up on the window seat, gazing at the clear night sky.

"You're quiet." Darcy handed her an ice cream and sat down, facing her.

"Yeah. I'm trying to soak it in." Kate dunked the spoon about in the bowl. "I...I've had a good time."

"Oh, don't you get melancholy. Zoë does that enough for everyone." She leaned back against the wall. Zoë poked her tongue out and went back to Blanche.

Kate met her eyes, then sighed and looked away.

"When we've finished filming, you can stay here as much as you like." She leaned over and squeezed Kate's knee. "I've told you that."

"Yes, but how do I get in here without anyone spotting me?" She fiddled with her ice cream. "How do I explain where I've been all weekend?"

"You go to the house, not here...and you use the back door, honey," Zoë said with a grunt. "FYI, it's a cheap feeling."

"You coped with it for long enough," Darcy snapped. She was sick of everyone talking to her like she cared nothing about their feelings.

"No, I didn't." Zoë smiled at Kate. "And Kate shouldn't have to put up with it."

"Kate doesn't have to do anything. The same as you didn't." She calmed her tone. Mikey did not need an argument. He was sensitive when people argued. He didn't say much, but he took a while to come out of his shell afterward. "As I said, Kate is welcome. It's up to her if she chooses to visit."

Kate met her eyes, hurt and hope shimmering in them. "Let's just talk about something else." She looked up at the sky. "Will Marge let me know when I need to do the reveal?"

Blunt and filled with hurt.

Darcy sighed and pushed off the wall, flexing her calves. "Yes."

Zoë leaned on her fist. "You're a complete..." She glanced at Mikey and mouthed "bitch" at her.

"We've covered this countless times." She leaned over and frowned at what the perfume company wanted from Blanche. "Why are they putting you in the background?"

Blanche glared up at her. "Because I have the guts to be myself."

Yes, the rainbow-community heckling was charming. "No, this girl is not even a name. She's up against one of the top male models." Which Blanche knew, but sometimes she needed to be talked to like she was a toddler. "If they don't want you up front, why not pick a top woman?"

Zoë met her eyes. "That is what I said."

"You can't accept that. If you play second fiddle, you're accepting this girl is a bigger draw than you." She folded her arms. Was Blanche even more empty-headed than she looked? "Oh, no. You do *not* share limelight."

Blanche studied her. "Why would it matter to you?"

"Why? You married Zoë Windermere. You have any idea the level that puts you at? If she rates you, however twig-like you are, that means you're top level." She flicked the advert away. "The girl plays background to you. You're the star."

Zoë nodded. "Thank you. See, you'd never catch Darcy letting another woman take her position."

"I never got that position," Blanche muttered. "I was a stand-in until Zoë spotted me."

"Yes, but she did spot you over hundreds of other models *and* she married you." Darcy shook her finger. "You may not have earned it, but you got it. Do not make Zoë look bad."

Blanche looked to Zoë and frowned. "Make you look bad?"

"You're my wife, honey. If you go taking second light, it looks like my credibility isn't worth the draw." Zoë kissed her on the cheek. "But if it makes you happy, I'll deal with it."

Blanche shook her head. "You won't." She looked to Darcy. "How do I fix it?" And she looked so much more innocent, so naïve. It was hard to grate when the girl was asking for help.

"You tell the company that you will take the lead spot, the girl takes the secondary spot, and you'll expect double the fee for the insult." She smiled at her and squeezed her shoulder. "If they don't bite, let them find someone as big as you. You'll find a more deserving product, preferably a rival one."

Zoë grinned. "And that's when the..." She glanced at Mikey who dragged Susannah, dressed in green, to the bathroom. "That's when you need the bitch to come out."

Darcy winked and strolled to the kitchen. Her phone went off, and she picked it up. "Gorgeous and intelligent, how may I help?"

"Take a look at your phone, bitch," Marshall spat in a smug tone. "The pictures show you're nothing but a fake." He hung up.

She looked down at her phone: Kate arriving at her house, Darcy pulling her in, Kate leaving her house in the morning. Oh, shit. He must have hired someone. He must have.

"What is it?" Zoë was up and striding over. "Darcy?"

"Marshall." She held out her phone and leaned on the counter, trying to calm her wobbling legs. "He's making a counterattack."

Zoë looked from her to Kate and held up her hand. "I'll get on it. We'll call the lawyers. We can stop them. Maybe." She pulled out her phone and hurried into the bedroom. Blanche hurried after her.

Kate frowned, walked over, and picked up the phone. "Shit." She closed her eyes. "Marshall followed me?"

"He wouldn't know what to do with a camera. He must have paid someone." Darcy met her eyes. "Shit, indeed."

CHAPTER 38

ZOË AND DARCY BATTLED ALL night to get the pictures stopped, but the paper had been printed and shipped to outlets. People having the "right to know" won out, and Kate couldn't do a thing to help. She just had to watch on as everyone else tried different avenues. None of it worked. They'd called Marge to tell her, she'd called John, and he'd promptly cancelled any remaining contract with them. He did agree to air the reveal, but that was it.

All the while, Darcy sat at the dining table, sketching something. Zoë hurled abuse into her phone. Blanche made hot drinks. Susannah and Mikey were thankfully unaware and asleep, and Kate… She felt like an intruder again.

Zoë rubbed at her weary eyes and took another cup from Blanche. Her smile was an exhausted one, but with what Kate knew of her, she was not going to give up yet. "Thanks, honey. Why don't you try and rest?"

Blanche frowned. "I can't rest while you're stressed out. Besides, I'm on the right time schedule for once."

Ah, California time, then. Zoë squeezed her hand, then picked up her phone again. "I'll try the editor."

Darcy held up her hand. "Leave it." She met Zoë's eyes. "It means a lot you tried, but the papers are on the stands, and the public are getting up for work. I'd rather you two get out of the crosshairs." She got up from her seat and flexed her calves. "Please take Susannah, Kate, and Mikey with you."

Zoë nodded. "You want us to pull Susannah from the country for a while?"

Darcy smiled, a tired smile. "If she'd go, I'd say yes." She met Kate's eyes. "I'm very sorry you've been drawn into this. If you want to take your family to my home on Lake Garda and stay there for a while, I will arrange everything."

And she was being talked to like a TV-show contestant. "We don't need to run anywhere. Didn't you say yourself that bullies suck? That we should embrace being unique?"

Darcy smiled. "These bullies are harder to ignore."

"Then let me say something. I'll tell them that you didn't do anything wrong." She stood up, irritation starting to bubble over. "You *didn't* do anything wrong."

"Then why do I feel like I've committed a crime?" Darcy met her eyes, cold, detached. "Why have I just lost everything I worked for?"

"Because..." She growled. "Because you are letting him win." She slammed her chair in and went to her, holding her by the shoulders. "Marshall is an idiot."

"And I damaged his career." Darcy smiled at her, but it was a polished one, a fake one. "So he's just flattened mine."

"I'm gonna knock his teeth out," Zoë snapped and slammed back her cup. "I swear I'll knock his teeth clean out of his big mouth." She strode off down the corridor, Blanche following on.

"Then I'll say I came onto you or something..." Sounded pathetic. The pictures showed it was mutual. There was no doubt it was mutual.

"Kate, you are very sweet, but you need to get Mikey away from the glare." Darcy stroked her cheek and leaned in, kissing her, soft and fleeting. "You have to protect him now. Being anywhere near me for a good while is not safe." She studied her, then sighed. "Kate, if you think those insults and jostling for pictures was bad, now every camera will want a snapshot of me, will want to get an answer from me."

"Then you need a security guard." She kissed Darcy's lips, desperate to rouse her irritation, or anything other than the defeated tone. "Let me back you up."

"No." Darcy sighed. "I don't like being gay, and you're about to see why. Protect Mikey." She turned and strolled down the hall. "The best thing you can do for me is go home."

"That's it?" Kate winced as her voice bounced off the space. Mikey and Susannah were mumbling. Zoë and Blanche must be waking them. "That's all I'm worth?"

At the door to her bedroom, Darcy turned and smiled. "It's the measure of how much you're worth. I'm protecting you." She went into her room and shut the door.

Mikey charged out of his room with a grin. "We fly early, Kate-oh!"

"Yep." She hoisted him up and cuddled him, hoping she was holding the tears back, but by the soaking her cheeks were getting, she doubted it.

"What about Mum?" Susannah muttered as Zoë led her out of her room. "I don't know what's going on."

Zoë and Blanche exchanged a glance.

Kate growled. "Marshall," she spat. She was sick of everyone tiptoeing around. "They've posted pictures. He outed her."

Susannah shook her head. "Then I'll stay with her."

Zoë glared at Kate, then ushered Susannah along the hall. "This is where I gotta step up the mom thing. I agree with Darcy; you gotta split. We're heading to the house in Hampshire. Not far." She held Susannah's gaze. "Just trust that we know what we're doing, yeah?"

Susannah held her gaze. She backed up and hurried into Darcy's room.

Zoë rolled her eyes. "This is why we zipped it." She hurried in after her.

"I feel as out of this as you do," Blanche said, dragging suitcases to the door. "They've lived with this for longer, though."

Kate cuddled Mikey, who snuggled in, already snoring in between murmurs. "Yeah, but the difference is she cares about you enough to let you help."

Blanche laughed. "You think so?" She glared back down the hall. "My dad is one of the best lawyers in the United States, he has close friendships with a lot of people over here, including judges." She turned and pulled the coats from the hook. "He'd have stopped it with one phone call from me."

Kate stared at her. "So why didn't they ask you?"

"Because Zoë felt that would be underhanded, and it would backfire on him. It's happened before. Even if they block the story here, it'll be published in another country and filter back in. Dad would get a lot of shit from it." She shrugged with a helpless sigh. "If I wasn't married to her right now, she'd send me away too."

Zoë headed out of the bedroom with a sobbing Susannah and furrowed her brow. "I heard that."

"Good," Blanche muttered. "Because I'm done playing second fiddle." She smiled at Kate, walked over, and kissed her on the cheek. "Give me your phone."

Kate handed it over, around Mikey. "Why?"

"They will cut you out." She tapped in a number and saved it. "I'm not going to. I will keep you as updated as I can."

"Honey," Zoë warned.

"If you want me to keep the ring on, you quit playing me like I'm a child." She kissed Kate on the cheek again and picked up the suitcases. "I called the driver."

Zoë blinked a few times. Hmm, wasn't expecting the backchat from her wife, huh? "I don't treat you like a child," she muttered, opening the door and shoving everyone out. Kate tried to turn, but Zoë pulled her harder. "Kate, just move."

Kate stomped out and pulled her case. "We'll call a cab and hire a car to go home."

Zoë frowned at her as she shoved everyone down the stairs. "Don't be dumb."

"Dumb?" She pivoted at the bottom. "I just got dumped and told to run back to where I came from, and I didn't miss the 'try and shut up' either." She grabbed her and Mikey's cases. "I think I've had enough of being talked to like I'm a child."

Blanche nodded. "What she said."

"And, unlike Blanche, who must love you a shitload to put up with this crap, I'm not going to." She took the cases and went to Susannah, squeezing her. "If you ever want to come see Mikey, you just call, okay? We love *you*."

Susannah hugged her back, confusion, tears, worry in her eyes. "Thank you."

Kate hugged Blanche, then glared back at Zoë. "Thanks for nothing." She pulled her phone and headed out into the still morning air. It was cool but not cold. Must mean spring was easing in. She pulled out her phone and dialled the cab number, then found a bench along the Thames to wait at. She hugged a snoring Mikey close, and her tears broke free. Yeah, she'd always been an intruder, and the intruder had just got ejected.

CHAPTER 39

THE PAPER RAN A MERCILESS story that pulled paparazzi pictures from Zoë and Darcy, from the video of Blanche's argument, and from that night Darcy had pulled Kate into the Kensington house. Susannah felt sick reading about it, especially as Marshall had been painted as some hero who had stuck up for her, telling her mum that she was wrong to lead so many people on, only to be punched.

Cameras camped outside the apartment on the Thames, the house in Kensington, and the larger home in Hampshire. Susannah was kept from the windows, from the media. Zoë and Blanche tried to keep her distracted. Kate had barricaded herself in her flat, and Mikey had headed back to school. The community had tightened around him, blocking the view to the school gates with buses. Mikey's stepdad had erected a twelve-foot fence all around the front of his house. Like Kate, her mum had remained in her own apartment without a word. Two weeks went by, and the stories were so twisted that Susannah couldn't take anymore.

"I'm not letting her give up," she snapped as she strode into the living room. Zoë and Blanche were playing some version of chess, although Blanche didn't really seem to understand the Queen could not high-kick the King. "We're fixing this."

"We can't, honey," Zoë said with a heavy sigh. "You'll only make it worse."

"Worse?" She put her hands on her hips. "Mum has been ripped to shreds by everyone. We've got models saying that she had affairs with them. They're making her sound like a...tramp!"

Blanche nodded. "That's what I keep saying."

Susannah held out her hand. "So give me my phone."

Blanche went to the dresser and pulled it out.

"Honey, please." Zoë held up her hands. "You'll just make it worse!"

Blanche handed it over and smiled down at her. "Hit him back."

Susannah took the phone and tapped out a tweet: *Disgusting how a creep targeted Mum. Bullies Suck. #EmbraceDesigner.* She hit *send.* "Like Kate said, he's a bully. They are all big bullies and I'm…I'm going to stand up for Mum *and* Kate."

Blanche high-fived her. "I have a really cool idea, if you wanna hear it?"

Zoë flicked through her own phone and read something over and over. "Embrace Designer?"

"What she tweeted for Mikey," Susannah mumbled. "I'm sick of acting like Mum committed a crime." She fixed on Zoë. "And you should be ashamed that you are hiding like a coward."

Zoë scowled.

"We counter," Blanche said, shaking her head at Zoë. "You do what you do best, Marge is itching to help, and if you're happy to help," she said, smiling at Susannah, "I know it'll work, but it's going to take dropping the fake and telling the truth."

Zoë slumped back into the sofa. "Great, we'll just dismantle what dignity we have left."

"Don't be so dramatic, honey." Blanche rolled her eyes and looked to Susannah. "If you're up for it, I got everyone on standby."

"You have?" Susannah stared up at her. "Why? Mum's been horrid to you."

Blanche winked at her. "I grew up wanting to marry her." She chuckled. "Somehow I married her instead." She thumbed at Zoë, who pursed her lips. "I got into the bigger leagues as a fourteen-year-old 'cause Darcy was working a show and the designer got creepy on me." She pulled her mouth to the side. "Darcy had a word with him. Guess she must have spotted it. Anyhow, she comes over to me and tells me that being a woman is something special, that I had to honour that no matter how glittery the carrot in front of me. I was worth more." She cleared her throat. "FYI, if I'd known Zoë was with her, even for a second suspected it, I'd have run the other way."

Susannah blew out her breath. "You didn't steal her?"

Zoë shook her head, staring in wonder at Blanche. "I may have walked out months before, but we'd… That just made it official. We'd been unhappy for a long time." She wagged her finger. "Nice to know I was the dream babe."

"I fell in love with you, not a picture." Blanche wagged her finger back. "The real, messed-up, crazy you."

Zoë cleared her throat. "I'm so going to bawl."

Susannah shook her head. "Sorry to break up your love fest, but I want to fix this." She nodded to Blanche. "Let's kick his ass."

Blanche grinned. "You got it."

Susannah and Mikey appeared on a TV show first. The tweet had made people think, and they took on the interviewers with incredible poise. Susannah talked of how amazing her two mothers were, that she was brought up believing everyone was equal. Mikey talked about how Kate was heartbroken, how Darcy was a hero, and how he wanted to give them their smiles back. Susannah told of Marshall and the real reason behind the punch. She called on the cameras that had been there to prove it. #EmbraceDesigner.

The photographers and camera crews produced photos and videos proving what Marshall did. The public stirred. Messages of support began to pour in.

Zoë and Blanche went to the magazines. Zoë talked about how hard Darcy fought to keep Susannah from the press, how their relationship suffered, of how hard it had been when she'd come out and been punished. They called on the industry to prove they were better. #EmbraceDesigner—the reaction was building. Calls came from past friends and distant colleagues moved to help. The public stirred further. Bullies sucked. The hashtag turned into embracing their own bodies, their own spirits and minds, all in support of Darcy.

Darcy's agent had left her, so Marge went to the high-street shops. She talked to each one about how Darcy had brought business back to their stores, made it fashionable to shop in person again. That she could have ignored them, but she'd embraced them. Now what could they do to help Darcy when she needed them? The stores pooled their ideas, came up with cut-outs, displays to show their support with huge posters of Darcy in her trademark pose. What better way to get PR than to use the one hashtag guaranteed to pull in customers? When else could they get Darcy's face for free in their window?

They jumped at it. The public support was building, and it was PR for free. Shops unveiled their display, the hashtag prominent, and the younger shops took a picture of Susannah and Mikey for theirs. The duo had shaken people. The hashtag filtered across all social media. The public support grew.

Zoë and Blanche went through an idea with Marge. It was ambitious, crazy perhaps. But if they pulled it off, the message would be clear. And Darcy, who had retreated, would see for herself how much she was loved.

The idea was great. It just needed a certain Welshwoman in a pencil factory to complete it...

CHAPTER 40

DARCY HAD REMOVED HERSELF FROM all outside connection. She'd been irritated at how she'd crumbled, how she'd found it hard to do anything but lie on her bed gazing out of the skylight at the blue skies. She'd kept doing Pilates, ate barely anything, and resumed lying on her bed. She'd not slept for days when Kate left, when Susannah left, but then she seemed to do nothing but sleep for a week following it.

It was an odd fusion—unbearable heartbreak that she'd let Kate go—colossal embarrassment that she'd acted so stupidly—that she'd come undone so easily, that she'd dragged Kate and her family into the mess just by association—and then agony over Susannah. She couldn't bear to call, although she'd reached for the phone countless times but couldn't go through with it. She'd spent her entire life trying not to become her mother, to curl up and give up like she had. Yet here she was. The pain felt too great. It had nothing to do with her career, or lack of it. It was about each face she loved showing disappointment at how she'd buckled.

"Mum?" Susannah's voice whispered as though she were in the room. Odd. Maybe she was hallucinating? "Mum, are you awake?"

Darcy lifted her head and blinked at the hallucination. It couldn't be Susannah. She would be in Hampshire or California. "Yes."

"Mum, you need to eat something," A seemingly flesh-and-blood Susannah sat next to her on the bed and peered down at her. "I need you to eat something for me."

A momentary flashback of her doing the same to her own mother came to her. Wonderful. "I'm no better than her." She closed her eyes. If she was hallucinating, she really *should* eat. She'd done that for herself, kept her body active. Defiance was still lingering.

"Who?" Susannah stroked her forehead. Felt real. Had she tipped into insanity too?

"My mother." May as well talk to the delusion. Maybe she could say the things she wanted to say to Susannah. "When my father left, she gave up. She never left the house, she smoked and drank and spewed anger at me. All my fault. I didn't know why, but it was."

"Mum, you're *not* going to give up." Susannah poked her in the shoulder. "You are stronger than that."

"So I appear." She sighed. Her head ached from tears. "The bit that makes me the most nauseous is that I *am* fake. Just like he was. I couldn't even tell you…" She blinked away more tears. "I couldn't tell myself."

Susannah hauled her up by the arms until she was sitting. "Mum, you did tell me, when I asked. You being scared is not the same as Granddad having another family."

She peeked open her eyes. Okay, that wasn't any thought of her own. Her stomach plummeted. "You can't be here."

"Well, I am." Susannah frowned at her, like that irritated child. "Mum, you're scaring me."

And snap.

The malaise shattered.

What was she doing? Up. Up now. She was not putting Susannah through it. "I'm sorry, baby. I'm sorry." She pulled Susannah into her and held on, squeezing her. It didn't matter what she felt or what she thought. Mother first. "Are you hungry? Do you want me to make you something?"

Susannah shoved her back and shook her head. "I want you to hear me."

Darcy got up, hurried to the bathroom, washed the tears away, turned on the shower. "I'm listening. Did Zoë keep you on the right foods? Do you need me to go out and do a shop?"

Susannah leaned against the doorjamb. "Zoë looked after me just fine, and Blanche. Zoë is just as cut up as you are." She rubbed at her forehead. "I can't even think about Kate 'cause Mikey could only say she was down."

Mikey? Darcy glanced over her shoulder, toothbrush in mouth. "When did you talk to him?"

"Blanche has planned a whole countermove." Susannah nodded, a daft, resolute smile on her face. "We've all been hitting back for you."

Darcy frowned. "Why did Zoë allow that?"

"Because I'm my mother's daughter, and when I say we're fighting for you, we're fighting." And there was the picture of herself at seventeen: resolute, floppy brown hair, set on fixing injustice. "You didn't deny a thing. You could have. You could have said anything to try and save face."

"I'm only fake to a certain point." She turned back to the sink, finished her teeth, brushed her hair. "I'd never deny I loved someone. I'd just never volunteer the information."

"Exactly. I feel like you've been protecting everyone. I feel like you're protecting yourself because of something inside." Susannah headed to her and stopped her as she went to the shower. "Mum, why do you hate being gay?"

Darcy held onto the door to the walk-in shower. She hadn't actually undressed. Hmm. "Because you have to lie. It makes you lie. No one congratulates you for being gay; you have to confess, confess to everyone you love like you've committed a crime." Best not to shower in clothes. "Or you hide, lie, like my father did."

"You're not him?" Susannah frowned up at her.

"Yes, I am. I followed him once. I wanted to see this family he'd left us for. See the children who he was supposed to love more than me." She chewed on her lip. She'd not understood why when he'd always doted on her. "He walked home from the dock. This man who he must have worked with started off at such a distance, but the closer they got to home, the closer they walked." She sighed. "He turned and spotted me and hurried away from the man so quickly, shame in his eyes." She'd assumed it was because of the second family. Only, the blazing image of his face in her mind now illuminated... Wait...wait... "*That's* why..." She put her hands over her mouth. "My father was gay." And it fell out like some jigsaw piece she'd never realised was there. "He was *gay*."

"Yes, but things were different then." Susannah sounded like she'd gained twenty years of wisdom with her tone. "You don't have to pretend you don't love Kate now."

"I can't pretend anyway." She tutted at Susannah and waved at her to stand behind the screen. "That was what floored me, you see. I ran out of fake." She slid out of her clothes and headed into the shower.

"Which is why I'm so proud you're my mum right now," Susannah whispered through the screen. "Hashtag genuine."

Darcy placed her palm to the screen as warmth poured onto her from the shower, poured through her with that fact her baby girl had done what she couldn't: reach her mother. "I'm not sorry about the show... Things may be harder..."

"So, how do you feel?" Susannah's voice was filled with that hesitation. Did she dare ask?

"Relieved." She let out a long, shuddering breath. "Like I've been let out... Finally set free."

"And Kate?" Susannah said, her tone filled with a smile.

"I do love her. You must see that." She put her face into the warm jet for the moment. "I'm just not sure I know how to do happy."

"Then good thing you've got me." Susannah tapped the glass. "I'm grinning that I've got you for my mum and Zoë... And we have Mikey." She chuckled. "He's good at finding smiles."

She laughed. Weight fell from her, sadness finally shattered from around her, and she let go of the images of her father's guilt-ridden face and her mother's lost stare. "Yes, I think he is."

CHAPTER 41

KATE TRUDGED THROUGH THE GATES of the factory. She'd stayed off work for a month—Frank's request when she broke down in tears on the phone to him—but now she just wanted to get back to doing something other than mope in her flat and avoid crazy camera-toting reporters. She shoved the main door open and switched off the alarm, only to stare at it. Huh? Had the stand-in security guard forgotten to set it? Not helpful, was it?

She headed to her office and flicked on the monitors. Why was the carpark full? She checked her watch. No, it was only eight. She slid off her coat and slumped into her chair. She'd had to run a crazy gauntlet of reporters just to get to work. She just hoped the neighbours hadn't minded her climbing through their gardens.

Susannah and the others were doing a great job of helping Darcy out. From what she could bear to watch or check online, the hashtag had gone crazy. Celebrities had gotten involved, and it had gone global. People, no matter who they were, posted pictures and comments about wanting to be themselves, about being allowed to be themselves. Marshall's family had publicly supported Darcy over him, and people were slamming him from all angles, thanks to Susannah revealing who got the pictures printed. Even the paper had been hit. They were in serious financial trouble. No one wanted to advertise in them, and no one wanted to write for them.

How had Darcy kissing her on a doorstep done that?

"Kate?" Frank tapped on her door. "Can you come to the boardroom?"

And she was getting fired, then. "Yeah."

He didn't say a thing, just led her through a silent floorplate to the boardroom. All the old codgers who owned shares had solemn looks, and

Frank took up his chair at the head. "Kate, you know how much this has affected the company?"

She nodded. "Yeah. I'll just get my stuff."

But Frank tutted and rubbed at his beard. "Oh nice, you have worked here for years and you're going to forget us?"

She folded her arms. "No, you're firing me, aren't you?"

The directors stared at her like she was stupid. Guess not, then.

Frank tapped his pencil to the table. "We're outselling every pencil company out there. You know why?"

"Because they like your lead?" What was she supposed to know? Rog was the guy for reports.

Frank bellowed out a laugh and rolled the pencil to her.

She picked it up. "What—oh." Tears clogged her throat. #EmbraceDesigner on one side. "We love Kate" on the other.

"We would really love you to be our poster girl," Frank said like he was proposing to her. "A promotion, you know? Although we really miss you fixing the photocopier."

She stared at the pencil. "Why do you want me?"

"Kate, we're a family company that has been going for over two hundred years. We made the first pencils that were used by professors and stuffy blokes. We were the first company to make a mass-market pencil." He nodded like she hadn't heard that before. "We have kept it in the family. I'm part of that family." He met her eyes with a beaming smile. "And so are you."

She opened her mouth, but some odd whimper came out. "I…" She rubbed at her throat as the board members pulled open their shirts. Mikey the Sproutman was on the front. She blurted out her tears. "You're so weird."

Frank nodded. "Yeah. What d'you say?"

"Does that mean I have to use them and not write with anything other than a pencil?" She cocked her head. She was going to frame her pencil, not use it.

"Yes, and preferably drop it into every conversation." He chuckled. "You lost your sense in London? Just pose for photos and say you like us."

"I do like your pencils." She held up her finger and flicked through her phone. She was sure she had a shot. Yes, there. She held it up and Frank walked around to look at it. "Complete inside information, but Darcy digs your pencils, mate, big time."

He cheered. "I knew it!"

"Sure you want me?" She shrugged and took the phone back. "I doubt I'm going to speak to her again."

"Yes, we want you. You fix the photocopier." He frowned and then wagged his finger. "I'm not buying it. We all watched the show." He grinned. "Told you that you'd look good in a lacy bra."

She rolled her eyes, gripped him into a hug, and walked out into the office. Every desk had a balloon with "we love Kate" on and every staff member, including Rog, had a T-shirt with Mikey the Sproutman on it.

She walked to the photocopier, yanked open the bottom, then looked back at Frank and shook her head. "Things people would do to get a machine working again, huh?"

CHAPTER 42

DARCY HUGGED HER MUG OF lemon tea. Susannah being around was a blessing. Somehow, just needing to do her usual tasks shook off the clouds and she could think. She wasn't ready to see anyone else, but Marge needed her to conclude the series.

"Mum, Marge is here," Susannah said, opening the door. "I'll make the tea."

Marge hurried in and pulled her bag off her back. "Zoë had me bring supplies." She glared at the window. "There's swarms of them."

Darcy nodded. She'd heard her neighbours complaining in the hallway. The police had been called to move them on a few times. They still came back, though; her picture was worth skirting around laws.

"I'm sorry you lost the series," she said, sounding far more composed than she felt. Marge, the crew, they depended on her. It was a regular job for them and had been for years. Now, they would have to find another show.

Marge bustled over, sat on the sofa opposite, and dropped her bag beside her. "You sound like you mean that." She shook her head. "Don't go getting all nice on me now."

She smiled. "Are you another that prefers me unlikable?"

Marge grinned. "That's the woman I know." She pulled out her clipboard. "Susannah said that you wanted to do the round-up here."

"Yes." She smiled at Susannah as she brought over two cups and a plate of biscuits. "I'm not sure if I can make the reveal in person…" She held up her hand as the pair frowned. "It should be about celebrating Kate finding herself. It should not be overshadowed by my problems."

"Mum, I think you've tortured Kate enough." Susannah thunked the cups down. "She loves you."

"She loves the thought of me." Kate would be sad, yes, for a while, but she would soon relish the freedom. It wasn't something she'd courted or even asked for. She hated attention. "I doubt she can stand the sight of me right now."

"Can you blame her?" Marge pulled the camera out and pursed her lips. "It's clear how much you care about each other, and you're cutting her out."

"Yes. I'm a bitch." She nodded to the camera. "I'd like to do this quickly before I lose my nerve…please."

Marge switched it on and nodded. "Rolling."

"A security guard who needed to find her smile." She opened as she always did, the person and their problem. "Kate Bonvilston was heartbroken, twice, and her wardrobe seemed to reflect that. I set out to revamp her style and show her who she was inside." She sipped at her cup. Hands were trembling. Hold back the tears. "Instead, this patient, and her dear super sprout of a brother, touched something in us all on the crew. I don't think I have ever seen anyone breathe such life into the people around them. It has been a show that unearthed more of me than Kate." She glanced at Susannah, who nodded. "And that wasn't quite as I'd planned." She took a deep breath. "The rumours are true. Zoë and I were once happy together. She's Susannah's mother as much as me… And…I abused my position on the show, but not intentionally."

"You didn't abuse anything," Susannah muttered, and Marge swung the camera to her. "I know you think you did, Mum, but you tried really hard not to show how you felt." She shrugged. "You can't help how you feel."

Marge swung the camera back to her.

"No, I can't. I feel tired of hiding who I am. I feel tired of ignoring the goodness and happiness that rolled onto the set in a security guard uniform and a Sproutman costume." She laughed. It was that laugh Kate always provoked from her. "My thoughts on Kate? She shines whatever clothes she wears. She is the most beautiful woman I've ever seen."

Marge peered around the camera.

Susannah hugged herself. "So why isn't she here?"

Darcy smiled at the camera. Might as well let the whole façade drop. "I'm…unpleasant." Best not to swear on camera. "I sent her away." She held up her hands. "My way of protecting myself and her. However, I can't back that up with logic."

Susannah pulled her lips to the side. "I'd say that makes you scared and human...and genuine."

She soaked in Susannah's words, focusing on the camera. "So my round-up is that style shows some levels of who you are, and beauty helps people to like you, but it is who you are beneath the skin that makes you worth more."

"Hashtag embrace designer," Susannah called out with a grin.

Had she remembered that from her visit to Mikey's school? "Yes, embrace it." She smiled into the lens. "So, Mikey, thank you for helping me find my smile... And Kate, thank you for rejuvenating me. I love you."

Marge lowered the camera, tears in her eyes. "That's the best round-up I've heard."

Darcy nodded and lifted her mug. "To a show worth watching."

CHAPTER 43

KATE WAITED OUTSIDE MIKEY'S SCHOOL with a baseball hat and a thick jacket of her stepdad's. Blanche had called them both to London ASAP. She hoped no one would recognise her. The quicker they got the reveal over with the better, but the entire time she waited for Mikey, she was riveted to the billboard opposite. It had once boasted Darcy and her thoughts on style. Now there was a monochrome picture, high key, of Susannah and Mikey laughing with that hashtag again. Even Susannah's dad and his football team—plus subs—had worn a letter on each of their shirts and made a show of it after winning a match. If Darcy had been popular before, she was everywhere now. It hurt. It hurt and heartened all at once.

"You look like a bloke," Bennie muttered from beside her.

Kate groaned. She was not in the mood for her. Not now. She turned, hoping Bennie would think she was someone else.

"I'll yell out your name if you don't face me." Her tone was blunt, cocky. She must be loving it. She was marrying Laura, and Kate had made a complete idiot of herself on TV. What better way to kick her?

She glared at her. "What do you want?"

Bennie shook her head, that smug grin on her face. "To tell you I'm sorry she is a shit like me."

Kate scowled. "You what?"

"You always pick them. Me, Laura, Darcy flipping McGregor..." She shook her head again. "When are you going to find someone who actually deserves you?"

"Why are you saying this?" She glared, then cocked her head. Bennie was being genuine, if the look in her eyes was right. She was never genuine.

"I care." She shrugged and rubbed a hand over her shaved head. "I ditched Laura. I'll always be a shit." She bumped Kate's shoulder. "But I really want Darcy to turn it around for you. I want her to make you happy." She turned and strode off into the crowd of parents waiting.

Kate stared after her and let out a long slow breath. She cared. Huh. Kate blinked away the tears. It'd do. She smiled. Yeah, it'd do.

One flight, a scrum to get through reporters in Heathrow later, and Kate stared up at the huge multi-storey poster of Darcy on the side of a skyscraper. The outskirts of London on the M4 was a maze of vivid flashing adverts, so much so she didn't know how the driver could see the road, let alone focus.

Mikey leaned over and gazed at the picture. "She beauty."

"Yeah." She swallowed the hurt. Getting her heart broken by Bennie had been enough, but she didn't have her face plastered over everything. She leaned her head to Mikey's as they passed poster after poster, billboards, and office buildings, all bearing that infuriating hashtag. Couldn't they see how much it ripped into her heart? "We love Kate" was nice, yeah, but the one person she needed to hear it from was silent.

The driver hit central London and crowds filled the streets. A police motorbike escort guided them right the way to Oxford Street.

The driver pulled over and Susannah poked her head in. "Mikey-oh!"

Mikey leapt at her and snuggled in. "Susannah-oh!"

"We need your assistance, Mr Sproutman. It's a job only you can do." She focused on him, all seriousness. "For Darcy."

He puffed up his chest. "Kay."

They hurried off and Kate rested her head against the seat in front. "Can you drive me home now? I showed up. Can you just say I looked nice and let me slink off?"

"You'd better follow Miss McGregor, ma'am." The driver chuckled. "I am on my way to pick up Ms McGregor. I'm not sure you're quite keen to see her."

She groaned. "My heart is too messed up to answer that."

"Honey, you don't need pressure marks on your forehead," Zoë chimed in, poking her head into the car, her voice full of a bustling energy. "Let's move. I got to get you dolled up."

"I'm not sure if I'm talking to you." Kate clambered out of the car. They were on the street. White marquees everywhere, people everywhere. Three women scurried past with a smile at Zoë. "Is that...?" Nah, she was seeing things. She was sure they were supermodels.

"I know." Zoë squeezed her hand and led her through the crowd of people. "I got snippy. I'm sorry. I shouldn't have said what I did."

"Forget about it." She ducked under three crew members from the show, hurrying along with some kind of scaffold. "Isn't the reveal in a local pub usually?"

Zoë ushered her into a large changing room. Mikey was being fussed over by staff. "Not when I'm the designer." She pursed her lips. "You need me to pull out my edgy side, because I can do drama queen if needed."

Kate chuckled. "No, I'll do as told...as long as I don't have to show anyone else my bra."

Zoë looked her up and down, then winked. She pulled out a tape measure. "I'll only use it on you if you argue."

Kate held up her hands. "I'll come quietly."

Zoë laughed and led her over to Blanche, who was being sprayed in different coloured paints. "Honey, I found this one trying to sneak in the back."

Blanche leaned in and kissed Kate on the cheek. "Hope you like body paint."

"Body paint—" She spluttered as the staff shot more at Blanche and three members started tugging at her clothes. Blanche wasn't wearing a whole lot. She glared at Zoë, who laughed and strolled off. Maybe her and Darcy were more alike than she'd realised?

CHAPTER 44

DARCY STARED OUT OF THE window as reporters swarmed around the car. The driver had a job not to knock anyone over as he pulled them from the underground car park.

She had decided not to go, that she couldn't face it, and then Blanche had strode in and demanded, "Are you still moping around?" and took Darcy's mug off her. "You have a show to do."

"I've decided to refrain." She curled up on the sofa. What were they going to do, fire her?

Blanche put her hands on her hips. "Oh, suck it up."

"Excuse me?" She glared up at her.

"Honey, you got found out. Everybody knows you're a lady-loving babe. Get over it." Blanche yanked her up by the arm. Strong for a twig. "I used to look up at that picture, dreaming I'd be where Kate is right now. You get that?" She scowled at her. "Every girl I ever dated swooned over you. You were a picture of strength."

"Every girl?" She wagged her finger. "Why was I a pin-up?" And Blanche had drooled over her? Oddly satisfying. Did Zoë know that?

"Because you were full of this…" Blanche flapped her arms around. "This vivacious, vibrant, sexy attitude. You took no shit. Sheer feminine strength." She let out a wistful sigh. "And you are hot." She scowled again. "So every kid who drooled over you really needs you to step up." She clicked her fingers. "Find your inner bitch."

Darcy rolled her eyes. "I'm getting a pep talk from the other woman. How nice."

Blanche pursed her lips and slunk onto one hip. "You're getting a pep talk from a kid you once helped. Now find your inner bitch."

Darcy walked over to the kitchen. She had no intention of doing anything other than curling up on her sofa.

Blanche growled, stomped over, and planted a smacker on her lips. "If you don't get your ass to the reveal, I will take your place and make you look like a cheap has-been." She nodded and raised an eyebrow. "Oh yeah. I got the girl. I got your babe. You want to lose another one? Because the next woman Kate falls for might just make her happier." She clicked her fingers again. "You want someone else making her happy?"

"No." She growled it. She couldn't stand the thought, let alone if Kate did move on.

"Then quit moping around like you're a pathetic loser and find your inner bitch." Blanche planted another smacker on her lips.

Darcy grabbed her by the scruff and kissed her back, then shoved her off. "You're too skinny to pull off my wardrobe."

Blanche grinned. "There you are."

Who would have thought that Blanche could spark her enough to make her call the driver? Darcy stared out of the car window, then frowned. Every shop, every building had her in the window. "Did I launch a product without realising?"

The driver chuckled. "Ms McGregor. I think you did something." He pulled into the side street near Oxford Street, and crowds of people filled the pavements and road. A police escort pulled alongside them.

"When did I become royalty?" Police escort? She'd been to a lot of things, but the escort was for events, not a drive to a reveal. She frowned. "And why are we going through Oxford Street? Shouldn't we be heading to the airport?"

"I think the Windermeres had an idea." He smiled at her in the rear-view mirror. "And I think everyone misses you."

She stared out. Every high-street shop had her picture and #EmbraceDesigner on it. She scowled. "I'll beat her." She slammed open the door and stomped through the waiting crowds. "I'll beat her with her own heels."

CHAPTER 45

OXFORD STREET STRETCHED JUST OVER a mile with three hundred shops lining it. Usually, it would have shoppers bustling to and fro laden with bags containing the new spring wardrobe. Now, it was filled with crowds and crowds of people. Shops draped with huge posters of Darcy, Zoë, Blanche, Mikey, Kate, and Susannah. Every shop involved in the campaign, every company, sponsored the event; in return, customers were buying from them. High-street shopping had found its feet once more. Beside the beauty of Marble Arch, people posted pictures and comments, laughed and congregated around a catwalk that split into rays, each offshoot with a platform at its head. The main runway was the longest seen for a fashion show: over a hundred yards of see-through glass suspended over the crowds below. It was dotted with lights and led back to a vast stage with a white backdrop draped from huge chrome scaffolds. Metal funnels jutted out of the top. And the stark white over the oversized doors blazed with the hashtag everyone had come to know: #EmbraceDesigner was celebrating so much more than just Darcy McGregor.

The music burst into life, and models began to pour from the doorway from every section of the LGBTQIA community, then the disabled community. Then models from every culture, every age, every size strutted out in nothing but body paint, slashed clothing, and confidence. They each turned and strode up the offshoots, taking places along the stretches, posing. The crowd cheered every one.

The crew from the show, the backroom staff to the cameramen, followed on. Their awkwardness of being *in front* of the lens was so clear to the TV cameras beaming the pictures far and wide.

Then Marge hobbled out, her hair interjected with colours, and she took up a space at the front of the stage. She took a microphone from the side and waved at the crowd. "This is our biggest ever reveal. It's a fitting tribute to the show which I've loved being part of, but now that the channel has cancelled the remaining series, we wanted to celebrate all Darcy has accomplished."

The crowd booed and heckled. Tweets, posts, grumblings about the channel flittered through the mass of faces.

"Yes, but we'd like to celebrate her, and what better way than get her to show just why she's the face you all know?" Marge rubbed at her body paint and winced as the crowd cheered. "And if you don't need therapy for seeing me in paint, then hopefully you'll enjoy more…pleasant sights." She motioned to the doorway.

The white backdrop flicked to a picture of Blanche on her billboard. The crowd whistled, and the doors opened. Blanche strode out, body painted, eyes fierce. She stopped, twirled, and the crowd cheered. Then she strode on to Marge, planted her left leg forward, and looked back over her shoulder at the panning camera. Those watching the screens down the long stretch of street let out a cheer.

She winked at the camera and wrapped her arm around Marge, taking the microphone. "As Darcy would say, 'every designer needs her sprouts.'"

The white backdrop became a picture of Mikey and Susannah. The noise from the crowd built higher. The doors opened, and Susannah led Mikey out, both in body paint and shorts and T-shirts. Mikey strutted like Zoë and Blanche had shown him, stuttered, yes, but he flicked fake hair back and pursed out his lips. Susannah giggled and followed his lead, posing all the way up to Blanche.

Susannah took the microphone. "This whole show is about finding a smile."

"Yup!" Mikey yelled out. "Smiles!"

The crowd chuckled.

"So we need someone very special for that, right, Mikey?" Susannah leaned down and gave him the microphone.

Mikey grinned at the camera, then took a breath so hard his shoulders rose. "Kate-oh!"

The cameras pointed to the white backdrop. Kate's picture filled it, and the crowd fell silent.

CHAPTER 46

KATE RUBBED AT HER HANDS, not daring to mess up the paint or her hair. Zoë was worse than Darcy when it came to being bossy. She wasn't sure how Mikey had just pulled off hitting the runway like a pro, but... Yeah, he was something special.

"Kate-oh!" he called out with his full, joyful cheer. The two ladies controlling the doors nodded to her, and they slid apart.

Shit. Shit. Shit.

A sea of faces. As in the entire street was people. Shit. The music burst into life, and she swallowed. She needed a pee. Maybe she could just nip to the toilet?

"Go." One of the ladies shoved her out of the door, and she stumbled on her heel. Oh, shit. She was only in body paint on a catwalk in front of half of flipping London. Why? Mikey waved at her and strutted about as if to show her.

She rolled her eyes. Frank would be laughing his ass off. Forget promoting pencils; she would be a comedy by herself. She stuck her shoulders back, hoping the flesh-coloured bra would hold, and went for it—probably looked like a farmer. She stopped at the LGBTQIA people and twirled. Ooh. Dizzy. Hadn't picked a spot like Zoë had taught her. Not good.

The closest model righted her and pulled her into a hug. "You got this," he whispered into her ear. He urged her on and she strode—farmer with a limp this time—to the disability team. She twirled again. Picked a point to fix on. Ooh. It worked.

The closest model pulled her into a hug. "Keep going. Just breathe."

She pushed her into motion, and Kate tried to ignore the crowd yelling and cheering. So weird. So very weird. She headed to the multicultural models, turned, twirled, and breathed out. Better.

The closest model pulled her in and pecked her on both cheeks. Then said something, but she didn't speak whatever language it was. She could say 'Hello, I like coffee' in Welsh, though, so she kissed the model back. *"Schmae. Dwi'n hoffi coffi."*

The model fanned herself.

Really? Kate shrugged. Easily pleased there.

She headed to the kids, the teens, the older models, who gave her a group hug and didn't let her twirl at all. She'd take it.

"We love you, Kate!" the kids yelled out.

The crowd yelled it back.

Kate swallowed. Scary coming from thousands of people. Really flipping scary. The models of all sizes cuddled her senseless, and the models and designers she recognised from adverts on TV all struck poses for her. She waved. That elbow in, wag-the-fingers wave. So cool.

She strode up to Mikey and hoisted him into the air. "How was that?"

He shook his head, the microphone thrust near to him. "Kate-oh... you're not supposed to hug everyone." He kissed her on the forehead. "But..." he sighed, "not bad."

She chuckled, hearing it echoed back at her by all watching.

"As we do with every reveal," Marge said, quietening down the crowd, "Darcy gives her round-up on the patient and her thoughts."

Darcy appeared on the large screen that was the backdrop. "My thoughts on Kate? She shines whatever clothes she wears. She is the most beautiful woman I've ever seen."

Kate swallowed. Darcy so needed glasses.

"My round-up is that style shows some levels of who you are, beauty helps people to like you, but it is who you are beneath the skin that makes you worth more." Darcy beamed, her full aqua-bliss eyes on show. "So, Mikey, thank you for helping me find my smile... And Kate, thank you for rejuvenating me. I love you."

Kate shut her eyes. The "I love you" echoed out and fused into a melody. The backdrop lit up with that image, Zoë and Darcy side by side on the catwalk, and the doors opened.

CHAPTER 42

DARCY WAS FUMING. SHE'D BEEN dressed—or painted—and a floor-length trench coat thrown on her. She was not in the mood to fire up the runway, and she was not in the mood to hear her own heart-bearing report blasted out to an entire street.

She stomped up the steps to the doors. She hadn't seen Zoë, but she was going to insert her heels up her—

She stopped: Zoë stood in a matching trench coat waiting for her.

"Of all the ridiculous ideas you've had, this has got to be the most..." she sighed, "sweet." She kissed Zoë on the lips. "Where did I find you?"

"Where you left me." Zoë met her eyes. "I wouldn't do this for anyone but you. Do you know how much therapy I needed for this thing?" She tugged at her trench coat. "And even more therapy for you."

"Not enough. You're still crazy." She held out her hand. "I'm scared."

Zoë smiled and gave her hand a squeeze. "Wear it like no one is looking, baby."

The doors slid open, and Darcy nodded to her. "Let's show them how it's done."

Bam.

The music burst into life, and they strode out. Lights. Cheers. More people than she'd ever seen. Stop. Turn. Challenge Zoë with her eyes. "Can you keep up?"

Zoë narrowed hers. "You're the one getting old, McGregor." She twirled, struck a pose. Sharp, skilled. Poised.

Darcy tutted, and they burst down to the next group. "Old?" She scoffed. "You're the one with a wife, Windermere." She flipped her hair back. Focused on the panning camera, snapped the eyes open, flooded the screen with her focus. Click, click, love the camera.

"Ask me that again in a few years." Zoë bent forward and flicked her head up—sharp shape, potent look. Crowd lapped it up. "Kate'll put a ring on it."

Darcy "hah'd."

They strutted down to the next group.

Snap, turn, pose.

Zoë snapped, turned, posed.

A cheer building, the crowd so loud, the music so loud.

"She going to get to drive your Ferrari, honey?" she spat at Zoë, crossed her. They twirled. Perfect timing as always. "Does she know I got to drive it?"

Zoë snapped to glare over her shoulder. Potent. Perfect model poise. "Does Kate know how often I got under your trench coat?"

Darcy growled. She crossed Zoë's path again. They'd always fought down the runway. Always pulled out that extra. She missed it. "I miss you."

Stop, turn, pose. Zoë winked at her. "Bet you do."

She strode past her. "Not as much as you miss me." She struck an arching pose. The crowd groaned, and she winked at the elderly model pursing her lips at her. "Think of it as a back stretch."

"That's right," Zoë shot at her, striding on. "You need to take care of the back at your age."

Ooh. Now she was asking for it. Stop, turn, pose. All sizes of model beaming back at her. "Do I need to check her ID?" She flashed Zoë a smug grin. "Did she make it out of nappies before you proposed?"

Zoë charged at her. They reached each other, turned, strode on to the models. "Do try not to make me look bad."

Darcy stepped her leg over Zoë's. Zoë intertwined their arms. Dual pose. Trademark. Eat that, up-and-comers. She shot a smug look at Zoë; she echoed it. "We're still the best."

"One thing we agree on," Zoë shot back.

They strode to the top of the runway, and Darcy fixed her eyes on the top of the street. No looking at Kate. No gut churning. Focus.

She and Zoë stopped back to back. That pose. She grabbed Zoë's coat. The music pounded, as did her heart, and Zoë clenched her coat.

"I love you, you intolerable ass," Darcy hissed as they stood there, crowd's gazes riveted to them, Kate, Blanche, Mikey, Susannah, Marge's gazes riveted to them. Waiting.

"Back at you, you bitch," Zoë snapped back. "Now."

Pose, grip, pull.

The coats dropped away. The crowd roared into life. The music stopped, and camera flashes rippled like a single wave of light.

Zoë kissed her on the cheek and went to Blanche.

Darcy began to move, but the crowd yelled for another pose. She struck it. More flashes, more cheers. Her knees trembling.

"Can you see why I love her?" Kate said into the microphone.

The crowd yelled out their approval.

Darcy turned to meet her eyes, gave Susannah and Mikey a squeeze on their shoulders. Kate held out the microphone to her. "It's your show," she said. "We can't do everything, you know."

She snatched the microphone off her. "I don't know what to say." She motioned to Zoë, Blanche, Marge, and hugged Susannah and Mikey. "But thank you." She shrugged and turned to the crowd. "Thank you."

They cheered.

Kate cleared her throat and strode over. She looked far too appealing in body paint. Very awkward in public. "Say it."

Darcy placed Susannah's hands over Mikey's eyes, then placed Marge's hands over Susannah's and pulled Kate to her. "I love you." She held Kate inches from her lips. "I really, really love you."

She yanked Kate into a kiss, and paint sprayed up from the stage, from the runways, from the shops. The crowd squealed, cheered, and laughed, and Darcy ran her hands through Kate's hair. #Perfect.

CHAPTER 48

CHRISTMAS WAS ONCE AGAIN IN the air, and Kate stamped her feet and slapped her hands together to try and avoid them falling off. Mikey's school had another disco. It was starting to rain, and if she kept her focus on the school, she could ignore the flipping great big billboard with her on it, advertising pencils.

"Hey, Kate," two parents called out with a cheery wave. "You're home for the weekend?"

"Yeah." She nodded. She spent her time shuttling back and forth from London to Cardiff. Darcy had bought her a Bentley, telling her that she *had* to look good travelling. Susannah had backed her up, and when two McGregors got going, there was little she could do but nod. Still, it had taken five seconds to enjoy the Bentley.

"Hey, Kate…" One of the older kids ambling out of school flashed his jacket at her. One of Darcy and Zoë's new high-street collection. "What you think?"

Looked warm. That's all that counted in her eyes. "Cool."

He grinned like she'd proposed, thumped his mates, and ran off. People did that a lot these days. Even ones that weren't in junior school.

"Kate-oh!" Mikey yelled out his happy call.

"Yeah, Kate-oh!" Susannah was with him. How'd she get here so quickly? Susannah grinned like she could read her. "Mum flew us up this morning."

Kate held open her arms, caught Mikey, then frowned down at Susannah. "She flew *you* up and let me drive three hours?"

"I think she was attempting to surprise you by picking Mikey up." Susannah chuckled and sank into a hug. "Although. She said she had something to do first."

Kate ushered them both to the Bentley and glanced up at the billboard. "Maybe getting that thing off?"

Susannah and Mikey piled into the back, breaking out into "Silent Night."

"She happens to like it." Susannah waved at three people grinning then shut the door. "Don't knock it. She's not even picked holes in how you hold a pencil."

Kate chuckled and purred the car into life. "Guess we'd better wait for her here and keep her happy, then." She tapped out a tweet: *Picking up Mikey needs for one Darcy McGregor to be on time. #FashionablyLate?*

⋯⋯⋯

Central Cardiff. A winter wonderland of ice rink and rides filled the City Hall grounds with a festive cheer. It wasn't snowing but raining – which Darcy had come to realise on visits was a common occurrence – as she darted from opening a new modelling exhibition in the National Museum out into the deluge.

She flicked through her tweets and stopped, then grinned like a complete besotted teenager. Kate knew her so well. Fashionably late indeed. If she didn't hurry up, Susannah would nag, and she seemed to nag far more. She was working hard shadowing Marge, and she was taking her A Levels. Teenagers; what could you do with them?

So much had changed. Marshall had been forced to apologise for his behaviour—worse acting than normal—and seemed to spend most of his time unemployed. Darcy couldn't imagine why. John had begged to reinstate the show after the live reveal, but oddly, she'd signed with a rival network instead. Marge had been most pleased.

Zoë and Blanche were pregnant, as they kept telling everyone. Darcy did like to remind them that only Zoë was. Where would the baby grow on a twig? Still, Susannah seemed delighted she'd have a sister. Darcy would remind her of that one day when the baby was stealing her clothes.

Mikey was, as he always was, happy, carefree, and a super-vegetable. They'd even created a toy in his honour. Mikey the Sproutman was a kid's hit. She tried not to say too much about him eating peas and carrots. She still wasn't sure about the violence issues that raised.

She stared at the line of people outside the museum waiting for a cab and pursed her lips. Why weren't there more cabs? Maybe she could text Kate and have her pick her up? She tapped her nails to her phone. No, no. She wanted to show she could navigate this city as well as her own.

She pulled her slick collar up to the rain. Kate, well, she was imperfectly wonderful. How else could she be described? She got Darcy free pencils, for a start. She'd spent every night by her side to the point Marge wanted them to have their own show. She wasn't quite sure about that. The public were crazy for Kate as it was. If they weren't careful, Kate would be too busy to see her. She was not putting up with that. Oh no. She'd captured Kate, and she was *not* going anywhere.

Darcy glared up at the rain as a mother of three muttered through the window of the remaining cab. Yes, Darcy had changed, and she hadn't changed. She had her own clothing company with Zoë, had a best-selling, critically acclaimed book—yes, literary award. The literary community had listened, but she kept much of herself hidden from the camera. She was still not the best at talking about her feelings. They knew of Kate—she grinned, not caring if her flush was on show—but they didn't know the half of it.

Mother of three was taking too long. Did she not understand the principle of catching a cab? What was so hard? All she had to do was get in, tell the driver where she was going, and pay. The rain got heavier. Kids would get soaked. They bounced around, yanking at their mother's arm. Darcy looked up at the sky. No, she hated getting soaked. She ducked into the cab and pulled a wad of money from her pocket. "Three hundred if you get to Mikey's school before Kate has to wind down the window and sign autographs."

"You're on!" The cab driver screeched the cab into life and she smiled, leaning back into the nice warm seat.

#EmbraceDesigner had moved so many, revealed the woman inside: the model, the mother, the girlfriend, the Style Surgeon. She glanced back at the stranded mother of three. And, yes, she was still a bitch...but a loved one.

She flicked out her phone and tweeted, tagging Kate in for all to see: *Kate, whether late or not, I'm worth the wait. #LoveDesigner.*

Yes, love was officially in fashion.

acknowledgements

It's exciting to start a new adventure in writing. I've been very blessed to have been inspired, helped, cheered and supported by many people on my writing journey so far. Whether mentioned below in name or not, I hope that you know your part in my own story is truly treasured.

First to you, the readers, whether you know my work well or you've just opened the book. Thank you for giving me the chance to tell you a story. I hope that it fills you with a smile and uplifts you. I'm so very honoured that you keep with me and support me whatever genre I'm throwing at you.

Thank you to everyone online, in social media or in the writing community who have touched my heart and my mind: Gena, Dani and Karen, John Taylor, Katherine Hetzel, Debi Alper and all the cloudies, the GCLS community including: the team and students at the Writing Academy, Liz McMullen, Beth and Joy; Ann, Salem and Cheryl (and Lynn.) Thank you for cheering me on. Jen, Vicky and Nikki, Cari, Tig and everyone in the UK lesfic community who make it so much fun to be around. To Carol Poyner and Ashley who in particular always let me know you're enjoying the stories. To Elisa Rolle from The Rainbow Awards for her tireless work that raises so much for charity and lifts the authors involved. In particular, thank you to Maddy who has worked so hard to see my books on the library shelves, you are truly wonderful. Thank you.

Britt, thank you for reminding me how much I love to write and to show you all the cool things I've picked up along the way. Hopefully you'll be writing acknowledgements yourself very soon!

Casey and Claudia at Bedazzled Ink for believing in me and nurturing me through so much.

Emma Darwin for being the consummate mentor always ready to cheer, challenge and chat through all things writing. Thank you for taking the time and the patience to be so in depth and for taking on the challenge of helping me improve and grow. I hope that you can see the massive difference your guidance has made.

Brie Burkeman, the more I learn of the publishing industry, the more I realise how very lucky I was to stumble onto your doorstep with a half-cooked manuscript and find someone so kind and ready to believe in me and what I could accomplish. I hope that, when you see each book of mine released, you know how much you made that possible.

Revd Sue, Mr. B, Moira, Ian, Fr. Mike and all the lovely people in the parish and beyond who remind me that light shines in so many different ways and draws me to believe I can, to help others, and to be whom I was meant to be. Love never fails.

Sue, for beta-reading, cheerleading, reminding me that someone out there likes my stories and for the honesty to point out when something isn't working. You're my trusted set of eyes, give awesome hugs, and help more than I can say.

Ian, Pat and Siân who listen, calm, and care for every inch that hurts. Thank you for taking such good care of me, for easing tense muscles and releasing them so that I can do what I love doing.

To all at Ylva, staff and authors, thank you for making me feel so welcome. Katja, for being such a kind soul and such a friendly face; Astrid and Daniela for welcoming me with a smile and *a lot* of patience; Michelle for both challenging me to pull out the best, working with me with professionalism and respect, and coming up with some absolutely stunning ideas; to Amanda for getting all the fine details and grammar spot on with an eagle eye and a highlighter. It was a pleasure to work with you. *Melanie und Dobby, danke für eure Freundschaft. Es macht wirklich Spaß, sich mit euch auszutauschen, und alles über eure Abenteuer zu lesen. Ich hoffe, ich bin besser geworden!* *wink*

Sandra, always present in my thoughts and my heart. I miss you. I see you smiling through rainbows, hope I make you smile right back. Sunflowers and leeks, who'd have thought they'd make such great friends.

My family and my mum who remind me no nut is alone. Whether in spirit or lifting spirits thank you for being you. Mum, thank you for being so confident in my writing and demanding to know why I've not got a studio tour yet in the way only mums can. For being the oracle on all things grammar, giving the best squdges, and for being baa every day.

Em and Ferb and our furry friends: thank you for looking after me, comforting me, reassuring me, pouncing me (okay, that bit is just Ferb) for chuckles, all the small stuff that gets me smiling, for being a comedy act all by yourselves, and for being a big smile, for being mini-baa and my handsome Ferbster every day.

To THS: who designed and made me with great love. Thank you for loving me. Thank you for drawing me to be whom you made me to be. Thank you for my uniqueness, my blessings, the gifts you have given me and for reminding me constantly that I am cherished. I hope this book celebrates loving one another truly and is pleasing in your sight. May you always know how I treasure and embrace my design and your love, and that I always shine as the light you wish me to be.

Jody Klaire
May 2018

about jody klaire

Jody has been everything from a serving police officer to working in kitchens before finding her home in writing. She can often be found chuckling to herself at her own jokes; being pounced by her golden retriever, Fergus; eating cake or chocolate or preferably both, and sometimes, when Fergus hasn't run off with her keyboard, she writes stuff.

CONNECT WITH JODY
Website: www.jodyklaire.com
Facebook: www.facebook.com/jodyklaireauthor
Twitter: @jodyklaire

OTHER BOOKS FROM YLVA PUBLISHING

www.ylva-publishing.com

JUST FOR SHOW
Jae

ISBN: 978-3-95533-980-7
Length: 293 pages (103,000 words)

When Claire, an overachieving psychologist with OCD tendencies, hires Lana, an impulsive, out-of-work actress for a fake relationship, she figures the worst she'll have to endure are the messes Lana leaves around. It's only for a few months anyway. And it's not as if she'll enjoy all those fake kisses and loving looks. Right?

A lesbian romance where role-playing has never been so irresistible.

WHO'D HAVE THOUGHT
G Benson

ISBN: 978-3-95533-874-9
Length: 339 pages (122,000 words)

When Hayden Pérez stumbles across an offer to marry Samantha Thomson—a cold, rude, and complicated neurosurgeon—for $200,000, what's a cash-strapped ER nurse to do? Sure, Hayden has to convince everyone around them they're madly in love, but it's only for a year, right?

What could possibly go wrong?

UP ON THE ROOF
A.L. Brooks

ISBN: 978-3-95533-988-3
Length: 245 pages (88,000 words)

When a storm wreaks havoc on bookish Lena's well-ordered world, her laid-back new neighbor, Megan, offers her a room. The trouble is they've been clashing since the day they met. How can they now live under the same roof? Making it worse is the inexplicable pull between them that seems hard to resist.

A fun, awkward, and sweet British romance about the power of opposites attracting.

JUST MY LUCK
Andrea Bramhall

ISBN: 978-3-95533-702-5
Length: 306 pages (80,500 words)

Genna Collins works a dead end job, loves her family, her girlfriend, and her friends. When she wins the biggest Euromillions jackpot on record, everything changes…and not always for the best.

What if money really can't buy you happiness?

In Fashion
© 2018 by Jody Klaire

ISBN: 978-3-96324-090-4

Also available as e-book.

Published by Ylva Publishing, legal entity of Ylva Verlag, e.Kfr.

Ylva Verlag, e.Kfr.
Owner: Astrid Ohletz
Am Kirschgarten 2
65830 Kriftel
Germany

www.ylva-publishing.com

First edition: 2018

Credits
Edited by Michelle Aguilar and Amanda Jean
Cover Design and Print Layout by Streetlight Graphics